T0354296

Once Upon A River

🍂 LEON ELWOOD CHEERS

Order this book online at www.trafford.com
or email orders@trafford.com

Most Trafford titles are also available at major online book retailers.

Printed in the United States of America.

ISBN: 978-1-4269-9617-7 (sc)
ISBN: 978-1-4269-9618-4 (e)

Trafford rev. 10/04/2011

 www.trafford.com

North America & international
toll-free: 1 888 232 4444 (USA & Canada)
phone: 250 383 6864 ♦ fax: 812 355 4082

For my wife Phyllis and our four offspring who with their untiring patience and inspiration kept me plugging to the finish line.

Acknowledgements

THOUGH THE WORK IS FICTION, the author took the liberty of using the name of his great great grandfather Aaron White for the main character. Also, the character Ralph Lane , was one of the real lost colonists.

While writing this story, I met a wonderful lady by the name of Peggy Sue Campbell. She related a story to me about a pet rooster of hers who had suddenly disappeared leaving her in a saddened state. It was then that I revealed to her that I was writing a book and intended to use a rooster in a part of it. She told me his name was Charley and asked if I would use his name. I promised that I would, so don't forget to look for Charley who was placed in capable hands.

Chapter One

IN THE FRESHLY TILLED SOIL, a glint caught the eye of young Aaron as he followed the mule and plow on its last long straight path toward the river. The year was 1796 and it was soil preparation time on a small farm along the Shalot River in southwestern North Carolina. He pulled slightly on the reins bringing Lucy, the mule, to a halt. Dropping the reins onto the plow handle, he stooped over and picked up an unusually shaped object protruding from the newly turned-up soil.

It was past supper time and Aaron knew that Hannah White, his mother, would be standing on the back porch awaiting his return from the field. The boy's father, Elisha, had passed away toward the end of last year's harvest leaving the manly chores to him. He had always helped his father, but this year Aaron knew that if he, his mom, and four smaller siblings were to survive, he was going to have to give up his leisure time and adventures so that he would not disappoint his mother.

Aaron was sixteen, a daydreamer, and sometimes when he was in one of his adventuresome moods, he would make-believe that he was in a far-off land of long-ago living and cavorting with kings and knights in huge castles or that he was a big game hunter in far-off Africa. As he gazed at the object that he had just picked up, he imagined it to be a prized arrowhead. He had been told by his Pa that Indians once lived in this very spot near the river. He said that they were very skilled at fishing and hunting. As he was examining his prized arrowhead, it began to glitter brightly. Whereupon, a strange voice shattered his reverie.

"Aaron, I am Chief Waccasaw, former sachem of a great river tribe. I come to you, my young friend, to invite you to join Waccasaw in long journey back in time."

"But my mom", Aaron began . . .

"Don't worry about your mom, Aaron, Chief Waccasaw will send Quiet Spirit to tell her to not worry about her son and not to worry about crop. Beginning now and for the rest of your journey, you will be known as Running Deer."

Aaron liked his new name and was beginning to trust his mysterious new friend. He was satisfied that "Quiet Spirit" would be able to calm his mother's fears as promised by Chief Waccasaw. The chief didn't waste any time in relating his plans to Running Deer.

"I have been waiting many moons to find you", he said to Running Deer. "I am sole remnant of my tribe and this is the reason that I have one last quest to make before I meet Great Spirit in the sky. This is why I need your help."

"I am just a young lad, Great Chief. I love adventure, I have hunted and fished with my Pa and Grandpa, but I have never been very far from home. How could I be of any help to you—a great and wise person who has become the leader of your people?"

"Do not worry, my young friend, the Great Spirit has sent you to me and nothing will harm you if you follow my instructions. You must understand that I will only be with you in spirit to guide you as you go on your journey to accomplish my wish."

"But what if I get in trouble and you are not there to help me?"

"Remember that I told you that nothing will harm you if you follow my instructions. I am going to place this amulet around your neck that you will wear at all times. When you see it light up, you will know that I have message for you."

"But what if I want to get in touch with you?"

"All you will have to do is lightly rub the amulet and begin to speak . . . I will always be there to protect you or answer any question that you may have."

"Forgive me, Great Chief, if I seem to doubt your great power, but now I feel more at ease and I am all of a sudden anxious to learn about my journey."

"Listen very carefully, Running Deer. I am going to tell you the story of my people who lived in this land many moons before the white man set foot on this soil. The first contact by a white man in these parts was made during the sixteenth century as measured by the paleface calendar. The white man was friendly at first because they did not expect to find our people in great numbers. They did not know what to expect as they came ashore from their heap big canoe. It was a strange land that they wished to explore. They knew that other adventurers from other countries had made some attempts to explore this land but had turned away. The English people wanted to see for themselves because their motive was to occupy this new land."

"It was in the same year that the Virgin Queen of England granted our land to one called Ralegh. My people do not possess land as white men do because we believe that Great Spirit in Sky, Manitou, owns all land and my people roam freely to hunt, grow crops, and survive. The following year, the paleface came in larger numbers. This group came to occupy and possess our land that was granted by their Queen to Ralegh. In trying to establish relations with us, they built cabins, planted crops, while they looked forward to the arrival of more of their people bringing needed food and supplies, because they would need the additional food until their crops could be harvested. But before help could come, Great Spirit created a storm that destroyed their great canoe. This caused all food to be lost along with their crew."

"The white explorers became homesick and fearsome and asked to be returned to their home across the water. About three years later, more whites came from same land with the intention of making permanent settlements in the new land. Out of this new colony, a fair maiden was born. My people called her White Doe. But because she was the first white child that was born in this new land, she was called Virginia in honor of the majestic Virgin Queen. When White Doe's father saw that this new colony was desperately in need of food and other supplies, he sailed big canoe across the water with a promise to be back within a year. The small band of whites that was left behind believed that they would be able to hunt in the abundant forest, fish in the plentiful river and streams, and grow abundant crops in order to sustain them for a year as they awaited the arrival of the promised help."

"When White Doe's grandfather arrived back in his homeland, he became involved in a territorial fight with other white men and was not able to keep his promise. Three years passed before he was able to return with help for his distressed countrymen. After stepping ashore to greet his people, he found that it was not to be. No paleface, including White Doe, was to be found. Many legends have been passed down over many moons attempting to explain the disappearance of the white colony, but none are true. Some very close, but others far from truth. I, Chief Waccasaw, know the truth. But it is only through your help that I can put mystery to rest. This will release heap big burden from my heart. Now, do you have any questions or concerns from what I have told you?"

"I think I have many questions and maybe some concerns, O Great Chief, but I don't know where to start."

"It is very important, Running Deer, that you understand, so you have plenty time for powwow with Waccasaw."

"Since you put it that way, my first question is this: If you know the truth, why not just tell me and send me back to my people so that I can put the mystery to rest?"

"My friend, it would not be the same if you told them a story that someone else had told you. Many tales have been passed down throughout the years about disappearance of this small band of white settlers, but it is only interesting reading material for white man. It is only a legend."

"But why do I have to go on this journey to find an answer to this "so-called" mystery?"

"There is not a simple answer to your question, Running Deer. That is why it is important that you see for yourself what might have happened at each step of the journey."

"I suppose, then, that you can anticipate my next question. When do I start this journey and where is my destination?"

"Yes, I was waiting for that question, for it is very important. I must take ample time to answer. But, first, great light in sky is about ready to vanish from heaven and bring darkness to earth. It is time to rest mind and body. You must learn a few basic things about your journey, and one most important is that you have to have a healthy body and alert mind. So the first thing that we will do is start a fire the Indian way with sticks and stones at hand. Afterwards, we will hunt for meat to cook on fire. I will show you how to use bow and spear. When our meal is over, you will take time to rest your weary bones."

As he awoke the next morning, the bright penetrating rays of the sun caused him to rub his eyes as he looked around to survey his surroundings. He felt thoroughly renewed in body and spirit and anxious to begin his journey. Before he was able to make a complete scan of the area, Chief Waccasaw appeared by his side.

"Running Deer", he said, "we have much to cover so we had better get started."

Aaron had put away all his past anxieties and fears and began to feel comfortable in his new role. "I am ready, Great Chief. As soon as you have informed me of my task and given me directions, I am ready to begin my journey."

"Very well, then, we will begin. First, I have prepared a map that you will take with you and you must keep it on your person at all times. It is very important that no one that you encounter have access to it. It is a crude map, but you will be able to follow it by using your common sense and intuition. Some folks that you meet along the way will not be friendly. And, remember, you will no longer think of yourself as Aaron. You will be known only as Running Deer which will be your name on entire journey."

Running Deer nodded and the chief began speaking in an understandable language so that there would be no misinterpretation of words between them.

"Your journey will begin at the mouth of the Chowanoke river at approximately the location of the landing of the would-be colonists from England. Your goal will be to reach the fort that was used to protect the white man from native Indian attack."

"But how will I know when I find this place?", enquired Running Deer.

"It has been many moons since this area was explored by your people and nothing will look the same. I have not yet told you of Akimko, a majestic bird that will be your guide when you feel that you are lost or in trouble. You will recognize him as a great bald eagle with piercing eyes and a huge wing span for soaring great distances. All that you are required to do is whistle twice with high pitched tone and he will be at your side. With the aid of your map and compass that I will give you and your access to Akimko, you will be able to complete your journey successfully."

"Sounds great", replied Running Deer, "can I meet this Akimko now so that I will be able to recognize him?"

"Go ahead, summon him to your side," said the chief.

Running Deer whistled twice—the way that his grandfather had taught him—with two fingers placed in his mouth. Immediately afterwards, he heard wings flapping in the distance before an imposing sight alighted on a tree branch close to his side. Chief Waccasaw was the first to speak because he knew that Running Deer would have further questions.

"You are wondering how you will be able to communicate with a bird. Akimko, he said, is not an ordinary bird because he is sent by Great Spirit to assist you on your journey. Your task will be to follow your map until you find a second map that will lead you to the end of your quest, and finally, to the solution. So, if there are no other questions, you may proceed on your journey. When you are ready you will find provisions for a day's journey, along with a hunting knife, a bow with arrows, and a spear to fish with. After that, you are on your own. Waccasaw will be awaiting the conclusion of your journey. Again, you must whistle twice with loud pitch to summon Akimko, but do not rub the amulet except for a real emergency and when you arrive at your destination".

Chapter Two

RUNNING DEER DONNED DEERSKIN CLOTHES provided by the chief and began to spread his map in the clearing so that he could determine his starting point and coordinate to begin his journey. He saw that in the beginning, the directions looked simple enough, but he wouldn't allow himself to study the map any further than he needed for the first day's travel. It was approaching fall and a slight chill could be felt as he took his first steps toward a distant, and as yet undetermined place that supposedly held the answer to an ages-old question.

Among the provisions included in his backpack was a fur-lined vest that he retrieved to wear under his deerskin outer jacket. It felt good because the bright sun of the morning had given way to a cloudy sky. He refused to think about the cold weather that he would inevitably encounter in just a few short weeks as the winter solstice drew near. The sun was high in the sky and the verdant, plush, countryside was beginning to give way to subtle shades of brown while the summer leaves were wafting toward the soil like a creation of nature that was returning to its source.

As Running Deer contemplated the vista before him, most all of his inhibitions had vanished and he was truly beginning to feel a metamorphosis of sorts from a young inexperienced lad into a capable adventurer. He wondered what his schoolmates would think of him now. He was not a subject of bullying by any means, because he was a muscular, well-built lad. But sometimes, because he was required to stay at home and take care of his chores, he was not allowed to cavort with his friends. The one fifteen minute recess at school during the fall and winter was the only opportunity for play and fellowship.

Sometimes at play, he was a loner, because the activity was too childish to suit his adventuresome moods. Also he had accepted the fact that he would never be able to live down the label of "teacher's pet". He could never understand why his peers did not show more interest in their schooling, because his Pa had instilled in him the need for a good education. This, in part, stemmed from the fact that he, himself, did not attend any school past the third grade. Still, he wanted the best for his son and wisely inspired him at a very formative age. As Running Deer pondered this, he felt confident that his acquired knowledge would pay dividends as he approached the task set before him.

Arousing from his daydream, Running Deer awoke among new surroundings. He at once reached into his vest pocket and retrieved a small compass that was part of the provisions supplied to him by the chief. He looked in the direction in which the reverse end of the needle pointed south and gazed upon huge white crested waves of the Atlantic Ocean. As the powerful waves lapped gently at the shoreline, it was as if the Great Spirit in the sky was reminding him that he had nothing to fear. As he turned his attention to the landscape that surrounded him, he was suddenly aware of a vast unfamiliar scene that was predominately wooded without any sign of anything moving—either animal or human. He thought that this might be an appropriate time to summon Akimko.

He attempted to produce one high pitched sound as described to him by the chief, but to his dismay, there were no flapping of wings. Then it entered his mind that he must have forgotten Waccasaw's instructions. So he remembered and uttered two high-pitched whistles again just as the chief had told him and immediately a large grey-breasted black bird appeared on a low tree branch near his side. Though the bird was not a golden eagle, there was something majestic about it, and Running Deer was not prepared for what happened next. He was aware that the chief had told him to rely on Akimko for needed help along his journey, but he wasn't ready for a bird that communicated with him. He also was not aware that no one else could hear the bird's voice. So, in essence, the two communicated spiritually. It didn't take him long to realize this, when after a short period of mutual introduction, he was ready to begin the first leg of his journey with his new-found friend at his beck and call.

Running Deer knew that he must be near the site that the aspiring colonists were last seen on that fateful day back in 1857. Waccasaw had instructed him that that is where he must begin. With Akimko at his side and invigorated by the crisp autumn air, he gathered his provisions, including his compass and map, bow and arrows, spear, and knife and eagerly awaited instructions from Akimko. As if by a prearranged signal the bird flew to the top of a tall pine tree and then glided back towards Running Deer with one wing stretched out to the north. As soon as it perched on a nearby log, Running Deer looked up to see smoke rising from the tree tops in the distance. It was difficult to determine how far away the smoke was, but he decided in his spirit that he must go in that direction.

As his eyes came back to earth, he looked around and there was an empty space where Akimko was perched a few moments before. He took the first step of his journey leading toward the source of the smoke. Before he had gone very far, he discovered that the forest was dense and there was no sign of a path. He determined that he would proceed as far as he could, and hopefully, there would be a clearing before long to enable him to keep sight of the smoke. He was comforted by the ability to summon Akimko for help, but he was hoping to be able to proceed on his own.

Presently, he came up on a small stream that appeared to be twenty five or thirty yards wide. The column of smoke was easily visible now, but there was a problem of getting to the other side of the stream. He decided to explore the bank of the stream, and not afraid of losing his direction, he proceeded to round a bend of the body of water. He hoped to find a narrow place so that he could cross to the other side which would save much time. As he turned the bend, to his surprise, he spotted a strangely attired person in a canoe, approaching from a distance downstream. His first instinct was to call out and hopefully this person would be friendly. On second thought, he remembered that Waccasaw had warned him that that would not always be the case, that he always should be on the alert.

As he gathered his thoughts, he was aware that the person in the canoe had also spotted him. He stepped backwards to hide himself behind a huge cypress tree and waited as the stranger came nearer. With his bow at ready, his heart quickened while this gaily attired person guided his canoe to shore less than twenty feet from his hiding place.

The stranger was the first to speak. Though he spoke in an unknown language, but friendly approach, Running Deer was able to discern his message. He informed Running Deer that a great bird had instructed him to provide a way across the stream. At once, he knew that Akimko was on the job and that this was just another example of his help.

He put his bow and arrow away and reached his hand forward in gratitude to the stranger. After this brief show of friendship, the stranger motioned for Running Deer to join him in the canoe, and as he looked up, the smoke signal was nowhere to be seen. While the canoe moved out into the water, he saw that they were heading back around the bend in the direction from which he came. Before long, he looked up above the tree tops and again the smoke was spiraling toward the sky. Then, as he turned to make conversation with his unexpected benefactor, he suddenly became aware that he was all alone again.

He was left with a canoe and a solitary oar, so he began to slice through the rippling water, first on one side and then the other. All was going well until he spotted what looked like a pair of evil eyes situated beneath two arches of prehistoric eyelids attached to the front of a long floating log. His mind began to vacillate between two distinct and weird thoughts. First, if this was truly an enormously large and hungry alligator heading in his direction, he would be facing his first test of impending danger to be overcome by his own skills and ingenuity, secondly he would have to resort to summoning help that had been made available to him. Of course, all of the bewilderment on his part could be senseless and nothing would happen. In any event, he was not taking any chances while he faced the unknown challenge.

As the gap narrowed between the canoe and the oncoming potential menace, there was no time for either to change their course. Running Deer deftly lifted his oar from the water and placed it into the bottom of the canoe while he felt for his bow and arrow. Before he could steady himself and wait for his next move, the huge alligator swam directly toward the side of the canoe with an apparent attempt to overturn it, thereby dumping his dinner into the water for easy access. The meal was not about to happen, however, because just as the huge tooth lined snout rose from the water, Running Deer's straight powerful arrow landed with a thud between those monstrous eyes. But as the leviathan struggled and recoiled from the arrow's blow, the huge tail whipped across the water to overturn the canoe. The strike from the tail threw

Running Deer several yards out and away from his canoe into deep water.

One of the first lessons that he had learned back on the farm, living near the river, was how to swim. He was reminded of the time when he and his friends were at their favorite swimming hole on the Shalot river. The tide would rise and fall in the river, and it was on a full moon in June when the tide was extraordinarily high and one of his friends was taking a dare to swim across the swollen river to the other side and back. On the way back, the boy was half-way when he suddenly experienced a cramp in one of his legs. In this situation, it was impossible to swim and he began to sink. Running Deer recalled that he didn't hesitate to swim out to rescue his friend at the risk of being drawn down the river in a very strong current. In a situation like that, he thought less of his own danger than that of his friend, so he reached him just in time to help him back to shore.

So Running Deer swam back toward the capsized canoe, while at the same time, watching for other unexpected predators. Approaching the upside-down canoe, his first thought was the condition of his meager supplies, and especially the map given to him by the Chief. His worst fear was realized when he spotted the skin-pack that held his precious provisions floating away from him and down the river. Panic began to attack him until he suddenly thought of Akimko. While he managed to stay afloat fully clothed, it was more of a task to summon for help.

The sun was moving overhead now and Running Deer knew that valuable time had been expended in the river that had looked so innocent to him at first, but had turned into an interruption that he had not counted on. He realized that fewer daylight hours remained and he was moving farther away from his goal of reaching the smoke source before nightfall. Only a few yards remained between him and the canoe now, so he forced his aching muscles to double their efforts so that he could reach out and latch onto the floating canoe. As he reached up to make connections, he looked up and saw that he was nearing an inlet to a huge body of water. He must act quicker now because it dawned on him, that in just a few minutes, he would be heading into the roiling and white-capped waters of the Atlantic Ocean.

He pulled himself up to the bottom of the upturned canoe and with all the strength that he could muster, whistled twice, and soon fluttering wings appeared as if from nowhere to settle on the surface beside him. He commanded Akimko to retrieve the floating skin-pack and oar for him. In the meantime, Running Deer moved up alongside the canoe in the water and worked to set it upright in the water, when at the same time, trying to figure out how he was going to stop his continuing progress toward an ever widening inlet and the inevitability of entering an unforgiving ocean. Even if he was successful in his attempt to set the canoe upright, the current was stronger and he questioned his physical stamina which was in a very drained state. He called on every muscle of his tired body as he fought the current and also his fear of failing. The consequence appeared overwhelming.

He managed to flip the canoe over, and just as he did, Akimko appeared and dropped the skin-pack of supplies and his oar into the boat. As he lowered the oar into the water, he was aware that he was not going to be able to change his course. In the excitement of gaining control of the canoe again, Running Deer had not noticed that the current in the river had subsided and had come almost to a halt. He suddenly realized that the tide had ebbed and that just in the nick of time, he had been spared from the uncertainty of the ocean, and he would be able to continue his journey toward his initial goal—that of exploring the site where smoke arose over the tree tops.

At first, running Deer worked the oar gently so that he could regain his sapped strength. Dusk was beginning to throw shadows across the river bank and he knew that he must soon row his canoe toward the bank to look for a suitable camping site. His day's provisions would last him through the night and he wasn't too concerned about trying his skills at hunting. With all this in mind, he made his way slowly up the river and guessed that he might have another hour before he would have to settle in for the night. As he slowly moved back up the river with the help of the reversing tide, his eyes continually scanned the river bank for a suitable landing site. Rounding a short bend, he spotted a likely site which displayed a small white patch of sand. As he drifted closer to the shore, he realized that he was approaching a clearing on the river bank that was once inhabited or used by humans.

He hoped that he would not encounter any unfriendly natives, but he began to prepare himself for any eventuality. Very quietly, he slid the canoe up on the bank, exited at the edge of the shore, and proceeded to look around the cleared area. He spotted a recently used fire pit, but could not determine how long it had been since it was used. Feeling no fear from what he had seen thus far, he decided to go ahead and set up camp for the night. As he cleared the area to prepare a comfortable spot to lie and rest his body, his mind began to retrace the events of the day and he was hoping that a better day was in store for him on the morrow. His weary body would not allow him to spend much time daydreaming, so in just a few minutes, he was dead to the world in sleep.

Sometime during his sleep, Running Deer dreamed of hunting with his grandfather. Ayers White was the sole breadwinner of a huge household. Born in the waning days of the eighteenth century, his role as hunter-gatherer came more from necessity than his joy of venture and personal pleasure. Even though he had carved out a modest homestead by the river, progress came slow in clearing the land due to the lack of tools to work with. Running Deer remembered that PaPa, as he called him, had told him that there were times when the family didn't know where the next meal would come from. So he learned early in life to be a successful hunter and fisherman.

In his dream, Running Deer went with his grandfather to hunt squirrels on a brisk fall day. After a few minutes into the woods, they came upon a tall oak which contained a rather large nest high in its branches. PaPa wanted to teach his grandson how to hunt, so he stopped about twenty five feet from the oak and told Running Deer to aim his slingshot toward the center of the nest. He did as his grandfather had instructed, and after a near perfect shot, several squirrels scattered from the nest. Before he could realize what had happened, PaPa had shot into the fleeing animals and three of them hit the ground with a thud. The squirrels were a very fine addition to the evening meal. PaPa didn't fail to congratulate him on his hunting skills. He did this by patting him on the back and promising that he would be able to shoot the real gun by next Christmas. Somehow, he knew that one day he would inherit PaPa's gun. The dream continued as the two made their way back to the house.

Before they had moved but a few steps toward the house, his grandfather tripped on a branch and settled on the woods floor. As Running Deer struggled to help PaPa up from the ground, he noticed that there was no response from him. The dream ended when he grabbed hold of the gun and began to make his way to the house for help. As he struggled to go back to sleep, his mind raced back to the time that his grandfather, who was nearing ninety years of age, was found dead on the river bank close to where his boat was pulled up nearby. The diagnosis was a heart attack, but it was said that he died of old age. Running Deer knew that his grandfather had died in peace because he was doing what he loved best. In his boat was two rabbits, a bushel or so of oysters and several striped bass. He referred to his oysters as "boys" and he would always share them with the neighbors and kin that lived nearby. An avid hunter from years of experience, his memory of his grandfather was a legacy of skill and acute marksmanship. As Running Deer relived these memories, he couldn't help but feel that their close friendship would inhabit his mind as long as he lived, that his grandfather's spirit would accompany him on his fateful journey.

The balance of the night was spent in peaceful slumber, and when he awoke, the warm sunlight which was making its way through the tree branches like garlands of sparkling gold, bathed his entire being. The first thing that entered his mind was the day's adventures before him, so he felt invigorated and up to the task. The sight of rising smoke in the near distance reentered his mind and he felt strongly that close by he would find remnants of the old fort that Chief Waccasaw had described to him. So foremost in his mind was an eagerness to move out in search of the ancient landmark. He remembered that he was farther up the river at the time that he had lost sight of the smoke, so he gathered his belongings and made his way to the river's edge to embark again on the goal that was set before him.

Another surprise confronted him at the river's edge when he discovered that his canoe was no longer there. Either he had been the victim of a theft or he had forgotten to secure the canoe in the excitement of locating this nice camping place. Not to be discouraged, his only other course of action was to make his way through the dense forest hoping to emerge somewhere closer to his intended goal. He hoped that his sense of direction would keep him from becoming lost in the wilderness. He suddenly remembered also that he would be able to summon Akimko in the event that he needed help, but he was determined to go it alone as far as he could.

The appearance of vicious animals was always a possibility, so he kept his hunting equipment at ready. The sun was higher in the morning sky now and he took his first step on this new leg of his journey. Running Deer knew that he hadn't come very far since that last meeting with Chief Waccasaw to get his final instructions. He felt, however, that he had learned some new skills after having gone through the confrontation with the monstrous reptilian and his near miss of drifting into the ocean. As he made his way through the low branches, wild grape vines, and thorns, he found the thorns to be the most painful. He looked up through the top of the trees and guessed that it was about mid-day and that he had been wandering through the thicket for about two hours. He was right on target about it being noon time because he had a slight onset of hunger pangs.

The vines had given way to a little more clearing and he began to survey the oak tree tops for the sign of a squirrel for his noon-day meal. He had never killed a squirrel with a spear, but with the animals scurrying about on the ground, he felt that he would be provided with a meal before long. Suddenly he spotted a fat squirrel and a rabbit scampering along the brushy woods floor at the same time. The squirrel disappeared in a moment among the mossy plants and leaves on the woods floor. All was not lost, however, because at about that same instant, a fat rabbit emerged from its den nearby his feet. His surprise was equally matched by the rabbit's. In its effort to escape an unknown fate, the little animal flipped over to land again on its feet to attempt a getaway. Unfortunately for it, though, the move was not quick enough to avoid a well-placed spear that was thrust by its predator.

Before long, Running Deer began to summon to memory some important skills that were taught to him by his Pa and PaPa in the art of dressing and preparing small game for cooking. Everything went well with the dressing, but he experienced some trouble with the fire. Nevertheless, after several attempts, he finally saw a glimmer of smoke and then a fire sufficient to light the small pile of branches that he had gathered. The smell of fresh meat cooking was a sweet savor for Running Deer and pretty soon his hunger pangs disappeared, for the rabbit had provided a full meal and then some. Fresh water was going to be a problem, but he felt that before much longer, he would discover inhabitants that lived near the river. So, gathering his equipment and supplies once again, he set out on what would be the most memorable part of his journey.

Making his way through the dense pine trees and wild vines once again, he attempted to follow the sun on its journey westward. His line of vision had improved significantly so he was able to make better time. After about two hours, he began to imagine that he heard faint sounds in the distance. At first, he believed the sounds were coming from either animals or birds, but as he moved closer toward the direction of the sounds, he was convinced that they were of human origin. His heart pulsing sounds reverberated in his head as he anticipated the first sight of real humans since Chief Waccasaw had issued his first instructions near the seashore. He would not allow himself to even think about loneliness for fear of being deterred from his adventurous task. He was proud of his journey thus far, but he knew that it was far from over.

The first sign of habitation was realized when the barking of a dog interrupted his psyche. The dog had picked up the scent and sounds of the approaching stranger and had obediently sounded an alarm for its owner. Cautiously, Running Deer summoned his hunting skills, became very silent, and continued to listen as the bark became louder. Fast thinking came into play as he reached over his shoulder and quietly and quickly retrieved his bow and arrow. Moments later, a small man broke through the brush ahead of him with his hands tugging on a leash. On the other end of the leash was a vicious looking pit bull. As the man restrained the animal, Running Deer made an effort to convince him that he was a friendly person who had lost his way in the woods and intended no harm. This was not an easy task because Running Deer's appearance was unlike any that the man had seen. Since there was not a problem of language, however, both of them soon realized that no harm would be done.

"Won't you join me in my humble abode?", said the man, "I suspect that you may be hungry and I want you to meet the Missus and the two younguns."

As they approached the crude log cabin, two small children came running to meet them. "Where did you find the wild man?", said one of them, "and is he going to stay with us?"

"Back in the house", said the father, "my friend and I will join you and Ma directly." Before entering the cabin, the man said "I must learn who you are so that I can fitly introduce you to the family. By the way, he said, my name is Ananias White. My great great great grandpappy was John White, what's yours?"

Running Deer could scarcely believe what he was hearing. He knew the story of Captain John White, the English sailor who had landed a small colony of immigrants at the beginning of colonization, had left them to return to England for supplies and was surprised to find them missing when he returned three years later. But could he have been this man's ancestor, he thought. And, of course, he was grimly aware that the journey he embarked upon was a mission to solve that very puzzle.

Believing it was too early to reveal the purpose of his trip at this time, Running Deer simply stated to Ananias that his adopted name was "Running Deer" and that he was making his way inland to find long lost kin folks. He felt that, in a sense, the statement was true and he was not being deceptive. After this short introduction between the two, Ananias secured the dog's leash to a tree in the yard, and they entered the cabin. It was still about three hours before supper time, but Running Deer detected the aroma of slow roasting venison coming from a kettle hanging over fire coals that were nestled at the base of an ample fireplace. Looking around the modest quarters, he was struck by the neatness of the simply furnished space. His eyes were drawn to the Missus of the house, as Ananias referred to her, who certainly deserved congratulations for being an excellent housekeeper. Before he could say anything, Ananias said—"Meet Lucinda, my wife of ten years, and these here—pointing to the children—are Judy Mae and Priscilla Jane."

The girls giggled and ran behind their mother, because this was the first time they had been introduced to a stranger. He went on to explain that the eldest, Judy Mae, was nearly nine years old and Priscilla Jane was seven. Running Deer acknowledged the introduction with a nod and before he could introduce himself to the ladies, Ananias blurted out—"and our dog's name is Walter." Running Deer diverted his eyes to look out the front window to the tree that held the dog's tether. Walter was sitting on his haunches directing his attention to the cabin's only door as if it was his job to see that a stranger was going to be welcome.

"Pleased to meet you", he said. He felt that a simple introduction would suffice because he did not want to get into a long drawn-out explanation of where he came from and especially his name change and his meeting with the chief. But somehow, he knew that before he parted with these folks, there would be a whole lot of questions to be answered. As he faced the missus of the family, and then turned toward the two girls, he said—"My name is Running Deer. I was born close by a river to the south of here and my passion is hunting and fishing." As if he anticipated the next question, he noted that he was not really an Indian, but that his Pa had given him the nickname, Running Deer, while the two of them were hunting one day. To further enforce this explanation, he went on to say that after his Pa wounded a buck, the animal ran off into the thick bushes out of sight of the two.

Convincing his Pa that he could find the deer, he ran off in pursuit and eventually caught up with it. With an arrow of his own, he brought the deer down and returned to relay the good news to his Pa. Since part of the story was true, he felt that he would be forgiven about the part for his nickname. His listeners weren't quite convinced that the story was entirely true, but all agreed that it was a good story. By this time, Running Deer had gained an audience, so he began to relate other adventurous tales that was brought to mind. Time passed quickly, it seemed, and Lucinda reminded everyone that it was supper time and ordered the two girls to set the table.

Running Deer suspected that some of the vittles that was set before him was reserved for special occasions. He could only surmise that he was among friends and was beginning to mull over in his mind as to just what he could do to repay them for their gracious hospitality. Of course, repayment was never in the minds of these humble planters. After the meal was over, the man of the house motioned for Running Deer to join him on the porch for some "man talk". His wife dutifully arose from the table with the two girls in tow as if there was no question regarding the "clean up" task ahead of them. Ananias and Running Deer seated themselves in the two rickety rocking chairs to settle down to some serious get-acquainted chatting.

At first, Running Deer was apprehensive about the ensuing conversation, so he allowed his host to break the ice.

"I have no reason to doubt your explanation of what you are doing in these parts, but somehow I sense that there is more to your story. Something tells me that you have a lot of questions that you would like to ask me, so I want you to relax and feel perfectly free to trust me. My spirit tells me that I may be able to assist you somehow."

Ananias's words were reassuring to Running Deer and he indeed felt that the two of them were destined to meet.

"When you introduced yourself", said Running Deer, "and told me who your ancestors were, it reminded me at once that you might be related to some members of an English colony that was lost near the Chowanoke several years ago. It is wishful thinking, I know, but do you think that your great great great grandfather, John White, could have been among them?"

With a half smirk and half smile Ananias replied. "I've been asked that same question many times before, but I have not been able to make that connection. The reason that I singled out the name of John is precisely because of the story of the lost colonists in which I knew from stories handed down that John White was a hero in an ill-fated attempt to colonize. So, to answer your question, I too have always been interested in this mystery."

Running Deer was elated at the revelation of his new found friend and was anxious to explore further questions. Excited as he was, he hesitated to ask specific questions about the abandoned fort site of legend which was his next immediate discovery goal. He realized, also, that the smoke arising from the tree tops on the day before was coming from the White's cabin. In continuing their dialogue, he began by asking about the crops grown there and eventually to a subject close to his heart—that of hunting.

Hours went by and as the friendship between the two grew, Running Deer thought that it was time to find out if Ananias knew about the fort site and whether he would volunteer to help him locate it. After discovering that Ananias not only knew where it was, he learned that he had been at the site on several occasions. It turned out that he had also been interested in solving the mystery concerning the final fate of the missing Englishmen. Living close to the original site, he possessed a much keener interest than most folks who depended solely on written accounts that had ended with varying conclusions but nothing definitive. Due to the responsibility of providing and caring for his family, he had been unable to explore it further.

Without giving away the whole story of how he arrived at this place at this time, Running Deer confided to Ananias that the sole reason for his journey was to solve the mystery of the lost colony once and for all.

"You've come to the right place for a start", said Ananias, "but the question remains—where do you go from here?"

At this point, Running Deer removed the map from inside his clothing. "This map only helps me to the beginning", he said, "but I have been promised other instructions on my arrival there."

Immediately upon hearing this from Running Deer, Ananias's eyebrows began to rise. Running Deer sensed his friend's consternation at the statement and attempted to explain. In an awkward manner, he began by saying "I don't know, but I have a strong feeling that once I've reached the goal of the initial part of my journey, I will be able to find a final solution to the question."

"Sounds like you've been reading one of those books, too", said Ananias, "there's absolutely nothing left there to help you."

"Trust me", said Running Deer, "I will find a way."

"Very well, if you say so", countered Ananias, "I am with you—one hundred per cent, but I warn you, you're in for a huge disappointment."

So deep was their conversation, that the change in the sky went unnoticed. A sudden streak of lightning brightly lit up the atmosphere above the tree tops and within seconds, a deafening clap of thunder followed. The two quickly arose from their chairs and went to join Lucinda and the girls inside.

"In the fall of the year these storms are plentiful and unannounced", said Ananias, "but this one looks like its gonna be a doozy."

As the girls began to latch the shutters, Running Deer couldn't help but gaze upward at the cracks in the roof and in one corner of the modest little cabin. Ananias reassured his guest that there was nothing to be afraid of. "We've been through many heavy rains and windstorms and we have always been able to weather them out."

At that moment, the sound of increased wind was heard and the tree tops began to sway menacingly. A storm of this magnitude was not in Running Deer's pre-planning list of possible hazards. His mind began to conjure up scenes of impending devastation, so much so, that he began to fear for the lives of this family that had befriended him and one that he had grown to like so much. So he began to look around desperately for the safest spot in the little cabin. His eyes immediately went to one of the two beds in a back corner. By now, the wind had turned to a deep roar and heavy rain began to pour down in a deafening deluge. He grabbed the girls by the arm and ushered them to the bed where they scampered underneath. In the meantime, Ananias was holding his wife, both of them speechless and helpless. They had weathered many storms, the last when Priscilla was a baby. After each storm, repairs and reinforcements were made where required.

Presently, Ananias heard Walter barking, so he pushed the door open and ran to untie the leash so that he could bring the dog inside. What he did not count on when he jumped off the porch was that water from the rain and rising river was almost up to the porch floor. As he hit the water, he realized that there was no more sound coming from Walter. The dog had tangled himself while trying to break loose from the leash and had drowned. The storm was not letting up and trees began to crack and fall all around him. In desperation, he reached to grab hold of the porch when a huge downed pine bough fell on him as if trying to prevent him from returning to his family.

There were no sounds as he reeled from the blow that had pushed him under the water. Inside the cabin, Running Deer sought to protect Lucinda and the children, but in his heart, he knew that time was not in their favor. He did not know the fate of Ananias and he felt that it was up to him to save the three of them and himself. As he summoned strength from within, he was reminded of the amulet that hung from his neck, that at a touch, would bring Waccasaw to his rescue. In his desperation, he rubbed the amulet lightly with the thumb and forefinger of his right hand, and while doing so, he experienced a warm feeling and also a dim glow emanated from within. In an instant, there came a stillness to the raging storm outside the cabin and the appearance of Chief Waccasaw inside. Running Deer realized that his first priority would be to calm the fears of the panic stricken survivors.

Their first reaction at seeing another person in their home was that someone had come to rescue them. Lucinda was ill-prepared for her next experience. After a brief period of calmness, she suddenly realized that her beloved Ananias was not in the room with them. She had recalled that he had left the cabin during the storm to untie Walter so that he could join them in their refuge. Before she could be properly introduced to the new stranger, she bolted from the little cabin that was miraculously saved from the onslaught of the storm. The two girls began to emerge from their hiding places under the bed. She hesitated at the porch and began to survey the desolation that had taken place around their little abode and she noticed that there were signs of receding water all around, but no sign of her beloved husband.

All at once, she began to scream at the top of her lungs, and in between screams, she called her husband's name. Realizing it was all in vain, she turned to face the remaining occupants who had joined her on the outside. It was Chief Waccasaw who spoke up at this point and calmly persuaded Lucinda to get hold of herself for the sake of her children. Seizing the opportunity, Running Deer introduced the chief as a friend whom he had met earlier and told them to not be afraid of him. He went on to explain that he was a native Indian who possessed great power. He said that he had befriended the chief in the past, who now wanted to return the favor. Although this was not strictly the case, he felt that it was not far from the truth. Running Deer then convinced Lucinda that he should confer with his friend to determine the next course of action.

The chief took Running Deer aside and confided to him that Ananias had become a victim of the rising water and had drowned before he was swept from his yard by the rushing current. The dog had become a victim of the water, also, while tied to the tree. As he was relating this tragic news to Running Deer, he was anticipating the next question from him.

"You are wondering how we are going to relate this horrible news to the family", he said, "you must remember that old friends are better comfort givers than new friends or strangers are, so listen carefully."

After Chief Waccasaw laid out a plan for him, Running Deer turned and looked at the terror stricken trio huddling together in the storm washed yard, then realized that Waccasaw had vanished. Following his confrontation with the chief, he began to piece together all the events of the day so that he could proceed using the instructions given him. His mind focused on the journey that was set forth before him, but at the same time, he knew that he had a moral responsibility to this helpless family who were still unaware of the tragic demise of the husband and father. He knew that this was a close knit family and it was going to be a very daunting task to break the news to them that Ananias would no longer be a part of their life. An uncommon inner strength would be called upon to carry out his duty, but Running Deer felt up to the task.

So Running Deer accepted his obligation head-on as he called Lucinda aside to tell her the horrible truth about Ananias. He seized the opportunity, before she began to sob, to ask her to please control her sorrow for the moment for the sake of her two girls. He convinced her that it would be far better for them if she took a little extra time to break the news. Running Deer, too, felt sadness at the loss of his new found friend. Somehow, he was looking forward to the two of them working together as he moved forward on the first phase of his journey.

Putting these thoughts behind him, Running Deer concentrated on giving comfort and aid to the Whites. The weather had made a complete turnaround since the appearance of the chief, so he was able to help harvest a meager crop that remained after the storm. Judy Mae and Priscilla Jane were beginning to accept the fact that their father was no longer with them and, indeed, they seemed to have matured beyond their years.

In the fall of the year—deer, bear, and smaller animals were plentiful—making it easier for Running Deer to keep plenty of food on the table and some in reserve. He knew, though, that cold weather was right around the corner, therefore, his attention turned to gathering wood for cooking and warmth. One day when he was searching for hardwood, he was startled by a blood curdling roar at his rear. It happened to be one of those days that he left his hunting equipment behind, so he intuitively reached behind his shoulder, only to discover that his bow and arrow were missing. As he glanced over his shoulder, the corner of his eye rested on a huge black hulk.

Afraid to turn and face the animal because of the closeness, he sprinted sideways toward an oak with the lowest limb about six feet from the ground. He was convinced now that a giant black bear was on his trail and was so close that he could almost feel its torrid breath on his neck. The hastily contrived plan was to run as fast as he could toward the oak, and with his remaining strength, vault toward the limb for protection.

In his haste to reach the tree, he tripped on a vine that sent him sprawling to the ground within a few feet of his goal. Having run out of time to change his escape route, he laid flat on the woods floor hoping to confuse his attacker, but to his dismay, discovered that his nemesis was no fool. His next sensation was a sharp excruciating pain as the animal raked a claw across his back. Instinctively, he looked up to try to ward off the next swipe that he knew was forthcoming. In the same instant, a loud shot sound permeated the air around him, followed by a loud thump as the huge black carcass fell to the ground missing him by just a few inches.

As he scrambled to his feet, his first thought was a feeling of thanksgiving that his life had been spared, and then he began to look around for the marksman that Providence had sent his way. Expecting to see a strange hunter close by, he was more than surprised to see one of the White's daughters standing in a clearing about one hundred feet away with a musket at her side. As he approached her, he discovered that it was Judy Mae, the ten year old.

When the two met, they embraced unselfconsciously with silence between them. It began to dawn on Running Deer that part of the plan to help this impoverished family to get another hold on life was already taking place. There would be no questions as to how she happened to be at the right place at the right time. It was just meant to be. Nevertheless, this young lass had saved his life and it would be his responsibility to try and repay the debt. It was encouraging to him that the children had been taught skills of self preservation by their father. As Judy Mae removed her arm from across his back, she was aware of a wet feeling there, so when she looked at her hand, there was blood on it. She then focused her attention on a very nasty wound that was inflicted by the single swipe of the bear's claw. Without hesitation, she took Running Deer by the arm and began walking at a hurried pace back toward the cabin. She knew that once they were back at the cabin, her mother could properly treat the wound. The first concern was loss of blood, so time was of the essence.

Arriving at the little cabin, they were met by Lucinda standing at the porch. It seems that she was unaware that her daughter had wandered away without her knowledge. Before she could reprimand her, Judy Mae cried—"Mother, our friend has been attacked by a huge black bear and is in need of help. Quick—please help him."

Without hesitation, Lucinda ran to meet the two. Her first concern was loss of blood, so she placed her arm around his back as he placed his arm around her neck while the two of them assisted him into the cabin. Lucinda instructed Priscilla Jane to place a clean sheet on her bed so that they could lay Running Deer face down while she attended to the gaping wound on his back. While she removed the clothes from his back she became more aware of the severity of his wound.

The girls did not have to be told what to do at this point, so they began to gather clean cloths and hot water to soak up the blood that was seeping from his back. Lucinda knew that the most important thing at this stage was to stem the blood flow so that she could concentrate on closing the wounds. This was not the first time that she had acted in an emergency situation. Her memory flashed back to the time in her early marriage when Ananias was hurt badly in a hunting accident. Unfortunately, her husband was a far piece in the woods when the accident happened, but not so far that she failed to hear his cries for help. He was on the trail of a huge buck with his gun loaded when he stumbled into a hole in the forest floor. As he went down, his finger accidentally activated the trigger which caused the gun to unload a volley of shot into his left thigh. Unable to stand up, he began to yell at the top of his voice, hoping that his wife would hear and come to his aid.

The two had been married only a year, Judy Mae less than a year old, when she heard her husband's cry for help. Securing the child in its crib, she ran hurriedly toward the sound. Possessing an innate sense of urgency, she soon closed the distance between the house and her injured husband. Once she had determined the extent of his wound, she was suddenly aware that she had nothing to work with. Ananias was losing blood at such a rate that he was becoming weaker by the second—so weak that he could not advise her on possible first aid procedures. Summoning all her strength, she began to tear strips of cloth from her own garment and proceeded to tie them tightly around his upper thigh. By this time, Ananias had lost so much blood that he began to drift in and out of consciousness, but as a result of his brave wife's actions, the bleeding slowed considerably.

Her next thought turned to a troubling question. She knew that she had to get him to their cabin in order to properly administer first aid and, hopefully, save his life. She automatically looked around her to see if there was anyone that could help. Not seeing anyone, of course, she reached under his arms and began to help him stand. Whereas, he suddenly regained consciousness and put his arm over her shoulder. The superior weight and the helplessness of her husband slowed the progress considerably, but within an hour, they arrived back at the cabin only to be met by the high-pitched sound of Judy Mae in her crib.

Lucinda's first priority was to get her husband comfortably situated so that she could begin to attend to his nasty wound.

She helped Ananias to position himself on his stomach and then proceeded to attend to the baby's needs. Then she began to remove the clothing from Ananias's back in order to assess the extent of his wound. One of the staples that they kept in their household was herb medicines gathered from the forest to be used in an event such as the one facing them now. Cleaning the wound took first attention and only then did she discover the true extent of it. The crude makeshift tourniquet cloths were slowly loosened and excruciating pain began to permeate his body. She quickly mixed the homemade pain killer and began to administer it. It wasn't long before her husband began to doze off, and within an hour, she had applied the herbal medicine and dressed the wound. All of these thoughts remained fresh in her memory as she strove to turn her attention to the emergency at hand.

As Running Deer recovered, the days became shorter and chill could be felt in the air. The December solstice was approaching and it was the time of year that frontier folks turned their thoughts to gathering provisions and firewood to sustain them through the cold days of winter. There was little chance of preserving food except canning the fruits and vegetables that was gleaned from the fall harvest. Gathering meat for food was an ongoing chore and it was in this area that Running Deer would attempt to take the place of the head of the household. Though he did not possess the acumen of Ananias, he felt that he was up to the task to help provide for the family.

After a successful hunting trip, he carried his bounty back to the cabin. Upon arriving there, he proceeded to skin and clean the rabbits and squirrels for Lucinda who had already prepared a fire under the kettle. While the preparation of the meal was underway, Running Deer sat before the fireplace to rest. As he gazed upon the crackling fire, his mind wandered to the journey ahead of him. He felt an urgent need to locate the old abandoned fort which would set the scene for the final course of his journey. Whatever he would discover there would set final plans in motion for a solution to his quest. His mind then returned back to his current responsibility that events of the last few weeks had placed in his hands. The passing of Ananias had dealt a great blow to Lucinda and the two girls, but with Running Deer's presence, there was a gradual acceptance of the fact that they would have to move on with life in their little woods clearing.

There had been little connection with others since they had cleared the small patch of farm land and had erected their meager living quarters. Ananias, himself, had been a loner having come from a family that had been decimated by raiding hostile Indians. They, too, were attempting to establish a small farm in the wilderness when the tragedy occurred. He seldom talked about it and Lucinda would only say that Ananias lived farther inland near scattered villages of the sometimes hostile Tuscarora Indians. Most of these savages had made their way north into the country to flee the emerging whites. Since the establishment of colonies that had come from overseas, more and more of the local tribes were forced out of the area. It was one of the remaining tribes that had made a surprise raid on the White compound just as they were gathering their harvest from the fields. Ananias watched as his mother, father, and six siblings were slain unmercifully by the savages. He was hidden in a small copse of trees that surrounded their home site.

So tragedy was not a stranger to Lucinda. After she met Ananias, they went through a brief courtship, married, and settled in this clearing that appeared to be a good place to farm and raise a family. They had discovered the river that ran near the place that would supply abundant fish to supplement the game from the forest around them. The river would also provide a route to a village upstream that contained a small trading post. The two day trip was made usually twice a year for the purpose of trading supplies of dressed and dried animal pelts for food staples, household needs, and wearing apparel. Lucinda had become an excellent seamstress, so she was kept busy making clothes for the family. The crude sewing machine she used was not without its occasional breakdown, however, but she treated it like it was a member of the family. She managed to obtain thread and an occasional bolt of material from the trading post.

It was that time of year again that the trip up the river was necessary. Thoughts of fear began to surface in Lucinda as she realized that things would not be the same now that her husband was not around to make the decisions and help do the routine things that made frontier living possible. As she attended to Running Deer's wounds, she began to wonder what his reaction would be, if after his wounds healed, she asked him to make the trip for her. Her fears were unnecessary because

Running Deer had already anticipated her needs, so he volunteered to prepare for the trip. As if to calm her, he assured her that he would begin preparations as soon as he felt up to the trip. He reckoned that it would be soon.

The healing of the wound progressed nicely, as a result of the excellent care by Lucinda and the girls, so within a week, he felt up to the task. He began to gather all the animal pelts that Ananias had made ready while Lucinda busied herself packing some food that he would need on the trip and also making a list of provisions for him to pick up and bring back. The next morning, at dawn, the turning leaves presented a panorama of nature's beauty, while overhead, there appeared a beautiful canopy of a cloudless blue sky. A slight chill was in the air, but as soon as the sun peeked over the treetops, Running Deer knew that a beautiful clear day was in store.

After devouring a warm breakfast prepared by Lucinda, he began stashing the pelts that had miraculously escaped damage from the storm into the canoe. When everything was loaded, Lucinda and the girls took their turn to hug Running Deer to wish him a safe journey to the trading post and back. When it was Lucinda's turn, she handed him a small tote bag containing dried venison strips and freshly baked scones. As he shoved off from the bank of the river, the three of them stood with their arms above their heads until he had rounded the first bend.

Chapter Three

His journey began in tranquility and for the first time since he had entered the lives of the White family, he looked forward to some time alone so that he could put more thought into his larger goal—that of unraveling the years-old mystery of Captain White's lost colony. In his heart, he felt that before much longer, he would be able to leave his new-found friends better equipped to survive the rigors of their wooded surroundings. Of course, he did not take lightly, the responsibility that was thrust upon him by circumstance. Running Deer remembered that Chief Waccasaw had told him that all would not be easy as he made his way, but the availability of Akimko, his winged friend at ready, and the amulet that hung from his neck, gave him assurance that immediate help was at his beck and call.

He had scheduled the trading post trip to coincide with the incoming tide so it would take little effort to guide the canoe on its course even with the additional weight. It was a clear cloudless day and the serenity of the surroundings became an ideal setting for quiet and unencumbered thought. He felt that the old fort site was within easy reach, and perhaps there would be someone that he would meet at the trading post who could help him reach this important milepost on his journey. His instinct prodded him to be wary of all strangers, though, so he made a decision to not be impatient.

As he moved along on the river, in a reverie-like state, time passed quickly without him noticing the sun in its waning minutes as it traversed the sky toward its destination on the horizon. Thoughts then turned to scanning each bank of the river for a clearing in which to pull his canoe over and set up camp for the night. Looking from one side to the other, it was very evident that this section of the river was wild and uninviting. Not to be easily discouraged, he continued his journey around bend after bend until the river opened into a much wider body of water. He made the decision to hug the nearer bank on his right to continue looking for a safe place to stop for the night.

Shortly after entering the wider stream, he spotted an ample clearing. On closer examination, he also saw two canoes at the river's edge. His first impulse was to keep moving until he could find another clearing, but seeing no evidence of other campers, he guided his precious cargo onto the bank several feet from the others. Ever present in his mind was his responsibility to closely guard his cargo. Then he spotted an opening several yards from the clearing in which to hide his boat. After securing his line, he carefully made his way back to the site.

Only the sound of evening birds and the rushing of the water could be heard as he moved through the thick vines and low tree branches. The sun had begun to set and the only remnant of daylight could be seen as a shimmer upon the water as it appeared as sparkles through the bushes and vines growing along the bank. The tree canopy overhead had already blotted the light from the setting sun.

Running Deer reached the small potential campsite in ample time to gather branches for a fire and to return to the boat for food. He opened the deerskin tote bag and retrieved a couple of scones and a strip of dried venison that Lucinda had prepared for him. He then made his way back to the campsite where he put his fire making skills to work by igniting the dry hardwood branches. Pretty soon the flames were devouring the oxygen from the cool autumn air allowing Running Deer to shed the chill from his body while preparing a pallet on which to sleep. He ate the venison and scones and then settled back on the pallet to think about the remaining part of his journey to the trading post.

Before long, complete darkness had engulfed him, so he placed a few more branches on the smoldering coals so that he would be able to sleep more comfortably on his makeshift bed. Minutes later, he entered a deep sleep that was soon interrupted by the intrusion of a strange dream sometime during the night. The dream was segmented and difficult to understand. Running Deer was not a superstitious person, but there was something about his dream that allowed him to recall parts of the instructions that Chief Waccasaw had laid out for him prior to sending him off on his mysterious journey. The part that was replayed to him in his dream was the Chief's warning that everyone he met would not be friendly. As if his dream had appeared as a warning, he was abruptly awakened by the sound of cracking twigs.

He sat up quickly and surveyed the site as he reached for his hunting knife that he was careful to keep on his person. In the dim light that was provided by the dying embers, he was unable to see an intruder, but he knew that he must remain alert to protect himself and his boat load of valuable pelts. So to check on the hidden canoe, he stealthily made his way through the pitch black woods. Though earlier in the night, the last quarter of the moon shed a dim light on the campsite, now all was in darkness because the lunar orbit had made its way westward through its star strewn path. As Running Deer attempted to retrace his path back toward his canoe, he heard the distinct splash of an oar entering the water. His instinct told him that his worst fear was happening. He knew that he didn't have enough time to reach the boat to try to prevent the theft of his cargo.

As if by second nature, he thought of the two canoes that were pulled up on the shore at the entrance to the campsite. He first assumed that the boats were left at the site by hunters who would return later to retrieve them or that the owners used the site for a landing and traversed the forest by foot to their home somewhere in the area, but Running Deer knew that his number one concern at the moment was to get to the river and hopefully prevent a possible theft of the pelts plus his provisions for the trip. When it was apparent that he could not make it to his canoe in time, he carefully made his way back to the campsite and then with a hope that the two canoes were in place, he headed toward the river. There he could use one of the canoes to follow the sound of his boat as the thief made off with it. Intuitively, he figured that the scoundrel was headed for the trading post to sell the pelts before he could be discovered.

Running Deer guessed that another day's rowing would put them into the vicinity of the trading post and he knew that if the thief or thieves arrived there before he did, it would be futile to try and save the precious cargo. Upon reaching the river's edge, he discovered that there was only one canoe there which verified the presence of more than one thief. Fortunately, an oar was left in the boat, so Running Deer pushed it offshore and into the river to begin pursuit of the unknown interlopers. He surmised that although the thieves had a head start on him, he had the advantage of a lighter craft which would allow him to lessen the distance between them. However, the tide was nearing the flood stage and would soon reverse its course and head back toward the ocean. He felt that he was up to the task of bucking the tide, and he knew that it would be equally as hard for them.

Rowing with all his strength and at the same time listening for the splash of oars in the water, he was able to move up the river about half an hour before the river's current began to slow, thus his progress began to slow down also. At the beginning of a tide change, it takes a while for a rower to really be affected by its strength, so Running Deer was able to continue in the pursuit at a good pace for another half hour. A dull grey light began to permeate the blackness of night on the eastern horizon behind him. Another natural occurrence that would be favorable to him in order to offset his inability to move quickly. Soon the early morning dawn would reveal the previously hidden landscape.

He knew that, eventually, he would be able to close the gap between himself and the thieves, but he was beginning to realize that he was outnumbered, and in addition to having to row against the current which was very tiring, he knew that he had to work on a plan to outsmart them. After rowing a half hour or so, he entered a bend in the river where he could pull over to the bank and rest a few minutes to restore his energy. The sun was peeking over the tree tops now making it possible to scan his surroundings better. The absconders were still nowhere in sight so he knew that he was up against experienced river rats.

According to his calculations, he was only a few hours from the trading post and it was highly unlikely that he would be able to close in on them before they arrived there. He took an opportunity to once again look at his map, so he reached into his vest and retrieved the map that was carefully folded in its leather container.

When he centered in on the old fort, he noticed that the head of a river was shown and nearby was the remains of an old Indian village. He concluded that this could be the site of the trading post and that he had been traveling on the same river. If the drawing was accurate, and he had no reason to believe otherwise, he might be able to calculate the distance and direction from where he currently was. The map clearly showed a deep bend in the river which he believed to be the one that he had just gone through. He began seriously to estimate the distance to the trading post going by the time that was given him by Lucinda, and that had been established by the many trips that had been made by her and the family.

Running Deer also began to reason that there should be some old Indian trails as he came closer to the trading post site. He also noticed, that on closer examination, the map showed more bends in the river—five to be exact—so he began to devise a different route to the trading post. Only, his plan this time, did not include the river. He figured that if he could go overland, he would arrive ahead of the thieves and surprise them. First, he had to scout around the surroundings to see if he was correct in his assumption. He carefully placed the map back in its case and placed it underneath his clothing.

He was rested now, after the brief respite, so he reached into his clothing for his compass and began to calculate his location. He was careful to mark trees with his knife in case he might not be able to penetrate the forest and have to return to the boat. This was not a reasonable choice for Running Deer, however, but this time he would act on the side of prudence. Too much was riding on his decision and he must not waste any precious time in his effort to arrive at the trading post ahead of the thieves. He dared not entertain the thought that he might fail, because his success meant so much for the widow Lucinda and the girls. He couldn't help but believe, also, that the chance meeting with the White family was an integral part of the journey that was meant to be.

With compass in hand, Running Deer began his pioneering trek through the unknown forest. There were no landmarks to guide him, not even smoke above the tree tops, that he had used earlier. In fact, it was impossible to see the tree tops except to look straight up. Judging from the directions as shown on the map, he should stay on a southwesterly course in order to come out of the forest near the trading post. The two important and unknown factors was how far he had to go, and of course, how long it would take him to get there.

The sun was beginning to peep through the branches to introduce a modicum of light to the formerly pitch black surroundings. The sky was without clouds on this day and it allowed the sun to radiate in all its brilliance. Running Deer thought that the whole universe was his today and that no surprises should await him as he headed out. The path, indeed, was fairly penetrable for the first hour. A situation that was caused, no doubt, from its close proximity to the river. However, as the compass began to lead him away from that area, he found himself entangled in thorny vines that slowed him down tremendously. His first thought was to stay a little off course and then compensate later so as to keep within his time limitations. He knew that if he stayed on his present course, that precious time would be devoured before he would be able to penetrate the thick vines. His concern was without merit, however, because the sunlight from the top of the trees revealed a path that appeared to have been recently used.

He finished cutting through the entanglement, checked his compass again, and saw that the newly discovered path was closely in line with his bearing. Confidence began to creep back into his psyche, so with renewed gusto, he proceeded on his course taking care not to stray. An hour and a half later—still able to stay on the path—Running Deer concluded that this indeed was an old well-traveled pathway that was used by the river Indians. Who knows how long—maybe earlier travelers would have had the answer to his question.

Returning to the present, he began to try and visualize at what point in the river that the thieves were in relation to where he was on the land. Of course, he had no way to know for sure, so he sat down on a log, retrieved his map, and began to try to calculate. Gauging from his walking speed, he figured that he had covered approximately five miles. Since half of the journey was completed at his first rest stop on the river, he surmised that by using his straight course advantage, he must be within five to ten miles of the trading post.

Glancing at his map again, he figured that the canoe travelers must be at the third long bend in the river or about twelve miles from the trading post. Of course, he gave them the benefit of the doubt because of having to buck the outgoing tide. Before long, he thought, the tide would be rising again on its second daily journey to the head of the river. This would give the advantage again to the boaters who had been fighting the tide. With this in mind, Running Deer knew that he must step up his efforts to arrive at the trading post first. It was absolutely essential that he recover his canoe before the thieves had had a chance to dispose of the pelts.

As he made his way along the path, urgency compelled him to earnestly devise plans on how to surprise his unknown prey. Even though, if all went well and he arrived in time to confront them at the landing, he knew that he must have alternate plans if that did not happen. First and foremost, he was almost certain that he would be outnumbered. While he was deep in thought, he imagined that he had heard the distant splash of an oar. So coming to a halt, and being careful not to rattle any bushes, he turned toward the direction of the imagined sound. There it was again and it seemed to be getting closer. It was no longer his imagination, so he stepped off of the path and began to make his way toward the sound. Taking care not to give himself away, he moved with stealth toward the now distinct sound of paddle against canoe.

By this time, thick vines and underbrush was giving way to marsh elders and soft marshland. He then realized that his calculations had paid off to show that the old path had followed nearby the river. When he gazed out upon the river, he saw not only one, but several boats plying in both directions. He had not counted on this happening, but it occurred to him that a flurry of activity meant one thing—that the trading post was nearby. Discouraging as this was, he thought, he must continue to use vigilance in accosting the thieves. His first thought was to make his way quickly back to the path so that he could resume his way toward the trading post.

Just as Running Deer turned his head to re-enter the forest, out of the corner of an eye he spotted something familiar. Within a few feet of where he was standing, there were two scrubby characters that were rowing a canoe with his canoe in tow. Before they knew what had happened he retrieved his knife from its scabbard and with one quick slice he cut the anchor rope to free his canoe from theirs. This action by Running Deer happened so quickly that the thieves were at a loss as to how to respond. At any rate, they decided that their best bet would be to turn their canoe around and head back down the river. After all, they knew that folks in these parts didn't take too kindly to thieves of their ilk. Since they were caught red-handed, they were not sure that they would not be tracked down.

Of course, Running Deer had no intention of wasting precious time on the dastards. He was elated to have his canoe and cargo back and his thoughts now centered on the task ahead of him. He stepped into the canoe and, luckily, Lucinda had provided him with an extra oar for contingencies. In this case, without the oar, he would not be able to make it to the trading post before nightfall. Moving along with the tide now, he was approaching the last bend in the river before arriving at the trading post. He was very proud of himself for having been able to connect his map with landmarks. The balance of the trip went without event and just before the sun sank behind the trees, he was able to secure his craft to the trading post dock and make his way toward the facility.

The pelts were tied in such a manner that with ease he lifted them and slung them over his shoulders. There was more than one building at the post but he soon made his way to a line that included three other individuals with pelts on their back. The walk to the building looked to be a distance of a thousand or so feet and to get there, one had to negotiate a small grade. The well worn path was neatly maintained, however, because he thought that many feet had trod toward this very important facility. As he carefully made his way the last few yards to the building, he began to think that it was possible that some of the first English settlers could have walked the same ground that he was walking as they attempted to settle this land. First things first, he thought the task at hand was to negotiate for a good price so that he would be able to return with good news for the Whites.

New at this, he decided that it would be best to unload the pelts and then watch as some of the others went through the process before him. The trading post was busy this time of year making it difficult to concentrate on the conversations taking place up ahead at the counter. So he weaved his way through the exuberant bunch to within a few feet of the counter where he was able to view and to hear the conversation between the trader and the buyer.

"I am aware of your situation", argued the man behind the counter, "but there has been an over abundance of hides this fall and because of this my buyer will lower his price to me."

He was a skinny, obviously malnourished fellow who had the appearance of someone who was very hungry and also very astute in his business dealings with the abundantly fed trader standing before him. It was apparent that he was not going to back off on his offer, so the portly gentleman shoved his bounty across the counter with reluctance and an audible grunt.

Viewing the scene before him, Running Deer's first thought was that he must do all that he could in order to fetch the best price for the widow and her daughters. It was going to be very tough going for them now since the husband and father was no longer around to care for them. So he felt an extraordinary sense of responsibility and he vowed to himself that he wouldn't let them down. Although the buyer exhibited an air of compassion for his story, Running Deer detected a hint of shrewdness about the man that led him to guess that he was a smart negotiator. If I am correct, he thought, there is a chance that I can do a better job at trading than the poor trader that preceded me.

With an obvious air of confidence, Running Deer carefully placed the bundle of pelts upon the counter and greeted the proprietor as cordially as he knew how. He had noticed that the trader before him had confronted the buyer with a less than enthusiastic attitude, which in itself, would have opened the way for a less than honest person to take advantage of him. Nonetheless, Running Deer felt up to the task of trading now and he must do his best. In order to seize the lead in negotiating, he addressed the man thusly: "My name is Running Deer and this is my first opportunity to trade with you. I am very impressed with your accommodations here and look forward to doing business with you. I am impressed by your extensive stock and I feel certain that I will be able to buy all of my needs from your shelves. If all goes well with our transaction here today I am sure that on my next trip to the area, I most certainly will be coming back."

Before he allowed the proprietor to reply, he hurried on to say, "my pelts are skillfully processed and carefully selected for this trip. Lesser quality furs are left out of the mix and used for other purposes at home. I am sure that you will agree that they are top quality." Extending his right hand, he said, "by the way, I don't believe I got your name."

"The name is Lane", the man said, "Ralph Lane. And I am old enough to know when I have met a desperate blowhard. People in these parts are careful not to take to strangers too quickly and you are no exception."

Slightly deflated by Lane's appraisal, Running Deer's mind flashed back to the time that his Uncle Henry chastised him for taking eggs from underneath a hen so that he could trade them for candy at the local store. In that case, he tried to convince his uncle that his mother needed the eggs to bake a pie and that he would be the first to get a slice. Uncle Henry didn't buy his story and, of course, it was too late to put the eggs back under the hen, so he as a lad of seven, accepted the chastising.

Before Running Deer could respond, the trader continued. "However, I suspect that we are going to get along well". Ralph Lane realized that the man that he had just met was an astute trader. Little did he know that his appraisal could not be further from the truth. In his effort to try and repay the Whites for their kindness, he with very little effort, had struck a chord with this wilderness entrepreneur that would prove to be profitable for Lucinda and her daughters, and as an unexpected bonus, valuable knowledge for himself.

The man trusted Running Deer's appraisal of his pelts, so he proceeded to count them so that he could make a proper compensation. With the trading behind, Running Deer thanked him, and not wanting to waste time, he retrieved Lucinda's list from its safe place underneath his garment and made his way toward the dry goods section of the store. The store was well constructed with no visible cracks in the wall or high arched ceiling. On close examination, he observed that the mostly-goods stacked floor was well worn from long use. He wondered how long the trading post had been at this location and also he had more than a passing interest in the layout of the land which surrounded it. But first things first, he had chores to take care of. Anxious to get started, he knew that after calculating the next morning's receding tide, he would begin his return trip back down the river.

Almost all of the items on Lucinda's list were available, so after gathering and paying for them, he wrapped them securely and then turned to exit the store when he was hailed by Ralph. "Before you leave, may I have a minute with you?", he said.

"Certainly", Running Deer responded, "I'll be happy to speak with you. As a matter of fact, I wanted to ask you some questions, but I didn't want to take you away from your busy chores." Lane laughed at this and replied that he was a busy man, but never too busy to converse with a new friend. Running Deer was pleased at such an attitude and noted that the situation was a rarity among most wilderness folks.

"It was not difficult for me to see that you are a stranger to these parts", said the man. "This is a busy place, but most of the traders are familiar faces that I see throughout the year. I was impressed by your astuteness at trading, so I am curious as to what you are doing on the Chowanoke river."

The question took Running Deer by surprise—not having so much to do with Ralph Lane's curiosity—but his own realization that he was not aware that this river was actually a tributary of the stream shown on his map which should lead him to the old fort. Before answering, he thought that he should not give the appearance that he didn't know where he was. So with a careful choice of words, he responded that he was an explorer who was interested in rivers and streams that were not well known. That this was his first trip inland in the Carolinas. Having said this, Running Deer was hoping that his answer would not compromise his acquired relationship with the Whites nor their security. He felt that he should be careful not to disclose their situation. The recent run-in with the two river thieves led him to believe that there might be danger ahead for them if the word got out that the man of the house was no longer there.

Having settled in his mind that the less said, the better, he hoped that his reply was sufficient. Turns out, much more was on the mind of Ralph Lane. "I noticed that you bought some homemaking goods and supplies", he said, "you must have a wife and children back home."

This was not a question that was anticipated by Running Deer so he began to realize that the trader was beginning to be more inquisitive than he expected. At this point he knew that he had to switch tactics in order not to appear untruthful. "I have friends who live nearby", he said, "so I agreed to make the trip for them. As soon as I deliver their supplies, I plan to make my way further upstream in search of an old Indian fort."

"You're not speaking of the old colonial fort, are you?", Lane said.

"As a matter of fact, I am", said Running Deer. Would you happen to know how to get there?"

"As a matter of fact, I do sir, but after all these years, I can assure you that there isn't much to see. The site has grown over with huge pines and wild grape vines leaving a spot that is no different than the adjoining forest."

Having heard this revelation from the trader, Running Deer responded by enquiring if there was anything left to identify the site. Lane said "It has been several years since I have been there, and it might be difficult to locate now after all these years. It is a pity that someone hasn't kept the old fort clear of growth for historical purposes", he added.

"Surely there is something at the site that will help to identify it", said Running Deer.

Ralph Lane scratched his head and looked up as if he was scanning the sky for an answer, and said "matter-of-fact, I remember there was a huge gum tree there that had strange scars on its trunk that resembled English letters."

Before continuing the conversation, Running Deer's mind experienced a flashback to Chief Waccasaw's story of the lost colony. He remembered that the one and only clue left by the fated colony was the inscription "CROATOAN" that was cut into the bark of a tree. Could it be, he thought, that the carved letters had somehow survived over two hundred years and would possibly be a real clue in solving the mystery.

"That's interesting", said Running Deer, "would it be possible for you to take some time off from your busy schedule and accompany me to the site?"

"I think that it could be arranged", he offered, "but first, I would like to know why you are interested in the old site and what is in it for me?"

The question was not unexpected since Ralph was a trader at heart, but Running Deer needed some time to reply. Calling his sales abilities into play, he tried to give a satisfactory answer by asking a question. After all, the trader had commended him for his astuteness. "You must have associates here at the trading post that you can trust. Wouldn't it be nice to get away for a few days from your business? I have to deliver the supplies which would take a couple of days and then in two more days, I could be back to join you. By that time, you could get things in order here at the trading post so that you could leave affairs to your associates", he continued. Running Deer knew that he was pushing his luck, but he decided that he had nothing to lose by the offer.

"Well, this is not the busiest time of year for me", said Lane, "so maybe I can arrange to go with you. But first, you haven't answered my question. Why all of this interest in a centuries old outpost?"

Running Deer saw that he was not going to be able to evade a reasonable response to Lane's question. Truth is, he thought, I am not going to be able to give a satisfactory answer without compromising part of my secret instructions. So without further hesitation, he explained that an ancestor of his, according to legend, had been a member of the exploring party that had erected the fort. That it had been a lifelong ambition of his to visit the old historic place.

The answer was sufficient for Ralph Lane and without divulging his own interest in the fort, simply replied "sounds good enough for me—I'll be ready when you get back."

The trader constructed a makeshift, yet comfortable, pallet in a corner of the trading post, and after a check on his canoe to make sure his transportation was still in place, Running Deer awarded himself with a refreshing bath. His stomach reminded him that the few strips of beef gherkin was insufficient, but he knew that in two days, he would more than satisfy his hunger at Lucinda's table. Ralph had told him that he would open the next morning early enough to allow him to catch the receding tide.

The slowly sinking orange orb that was the evening sun made its way toward the dark and shiny surface of the Chowanoke river, while fluttering wings of busy osprey, pelicans, and sundry river dwellers settled into their ample quarters among the old cypress trunks. The noise and clamor of daytime activity slowly gave way to night sounds. For the first time in three days, Running Deer was ready to rest his weary bones. He was looking forward to a restful night and anticipation of his trip back down the river. He didn't dwell on the run-in with the thieves—rather he preferred to put that behind him while he looked forward to his trip to the old fort with his new buddy, Ralph Lane.

Sleep came quickly for Running Deer and for the first time in a long while, his deep sleep was not interrupted by a dream. As a result, he awoke the following morning as the bright ray of sunshine teased his eyes into opening. The savory smell of percolating coffee permeated his nostrils as he greeted the new morning. The surrounding woods seemed to go out of their way to greet him back with its accompaniment of chirping birds and the a cappella voices of the grass and tree creatures. He looked forward to the trip with almost joyful anticipation.

Presently, Ralph appeared at his side to invite him to breakfast. Running Deer did not have to be urged to join in. He knew that his next breakfast was two days away. The trader had prepared light scrambled eggs, sumptuous smoked ham, and coarse hominy grits. He thought that if nothing else happened to remind him of his mom's cooking,

Ralph's breakfast had to be the one. He denied himself the pleasure of reminiscing about his home too often, but some experiences could not be ignored. While the two of them enjoyed the meal, there was some time for conversation. As a starter, Ralph anticipated the question of his family, so he began by saying that there was a Mrs. Lane, but that she had been massacred in the nearby woods by an unknown character and that he had always suspected that the culprit was an Indian scout or warrior from a not too distant village.

Running Deer suspected that he was hesitant to talk about the event, so he did not press him for details. But, it was Ralph that wanted to talk with someone about it. It was if the horrid details had been bottled up too long within him. Running Deer was willing to listen, so the trader continued with the sordid tale of the murder. The tide reversal had not occurred yet, so there was not an urgent worry about Running Deer missing his departure time. Ralph figured that another thirty minutes could be used for telling his story to a new friend.

"My loving wife's name was Sarah Evangeline. I called her Sarah. Sarah went into the woods to gather huckleberries. It was a beautiful fall afternoon. My favorite dessert was huckleberry cobbler, so I didn't object much to her going alone, since she had done it many times before, and besides, she wasn't going very far and should be back in a short while. A neighbor happened to find her body as the sun was beginning to set. I was beginning to worry about her because she had been gone longer than usual and I was getting ready to close the trading post early to go and look for her. I had a strange feeling that something had happened, so I wasn't completely surprised by the announcement. My hunter friend spared me the details about Sarah's condition, so I hurriedly secured the post and followed my friend back to the scene. I was not prepared for the brutal scene that I encountered. Her lovely hair and scalp was missing from her head and her eyes were still open in horror."

Ralph fought back tears from the memory so much that it spared Running Deer the details of the mutilation of her body. He went on to say that Sarah had given him a son early on in their marriage, but the dreaded scarlet fever had taken him from them before his second year was out.

"So you see", added Ralph, "I have an ulterior motive in willing to accompany you on this journey. There is an inner feeling that tells me that your quest involves the local Indian tribes that were war-like and were prominent in these parts. I have never had time to research the subject, but I spent considerable time at my old grandfather's feet listening to tales that sounded too realistic to be made up. Its about time for the tide to change, so you'd better prepare to begin your journey downstream. May the Lord up above be with you on a safe trip. I shall be awaiting your return and I look forward to our forthcoming adventure together."

Running Deer was confident that the return trip to Lucinda's cabin would take less time because his cargo was much lighter. He was also confident that Lucinda would be pleased at the price that her furs had fetched at the trading post. And almost as a bonus, he was able to acquire almost all of the goods on her list. Dawn was beginning to break as he shoved off from the shore and the sounds of the night once again gave way to myriad bird sounds. All was still quiet around the trading post, but he knew it wouldn't be long before a cacophony of human voices would fill the still air when trading started. Thoughts of his long journey ahead returned momentarily to his inner psyche, but it wasn't long before he was floating peacefully down the river.

By the end of the day Running Deer had come abreast of the camping site of his first night on the way to the trading post. Curiosity prompted him to visually recheck the site for any sign of the thieves that almost got away with his canoe and cargo. The absence of canoes at the shore led him to believe that they had moved their base of operation. He had hoped that he would be farther along at this time of day, but the tide had ebbed a few hours back making it more difficult to make headway against the incoming current. So he decided to head his canoe to the shore and set up camp once again. The sun was nudging the tree tops and there was a slight chill in the air.

It wasn't long before he had a nice fire going. He wouldn't be cooking anything, for Ralph was more than generous to supply him with plenty of bread and beef gherkin that he would need for the journey. A pottery jug filled with fresh water would complete his need for victuals. Before long, stars appeared in the darkening sky, but there was no moon up yet. A makeshift pallet was set out on the ground, and after making himself comfortable, he closed his eyes in anticipation of a restful night of sleep. However, his restful slumber was interrupted in the middle of the night with a nightmare in which he was approached by a gang of wild Indians in a deep forest. One of the warriors moved near him, a hatchet raised as if to remove his scalp. In the next moment, the savage fell at his feet with an arrow in his back. He looked around and observed that another redskin held a bow.

There was a difference in the appearance of the bow wielding warrior and the attacker. Instead of the dark hair and complexion like the other Indians, he had a fair complexion and sandy hair. Although he wore the skins of an Indian, it was evident that his parents were not of the Indian race. As if the warrior had anticipated Running Deer's curiosity, he began to explain that he had come from an English exploration colony that for many years was assumed lost. He went on to explain that, as a young child, he had been captured by a friendly Indian tribe and that he had grown up among them and had accepted their ways.

Before Running Deer could reply, he awoke abruptly from a deep sleep. It wasn't long before he was sleeping soundly with no more interruptions. He awoke the next morning feeling rested and ready for the last leg of the trip. The sun was up but had not shown its glow above the tree tops. Fall was in the air bringing a slight chill, but Running Deer figured that as soon as the sun began to spread its warming rays on the river, it couldn't help but be a pleasant day. Anxiety began gnawing at him and he could hardly wait to get back to the White's cabin to deliver their supplies. He was also anxious about their safety. The tide was flowing with him now and he estimated in about eight hours or so, he would be nearing the cabin.

As he floated down the river with very little work on his part and gentle waves lapping at the side of the canoe, he had ample time for thinking. The first thought that re-entered his mind was the nightmare that had troubled him in his sleep. He was not a superstitious person, but he couldn't help but mull the scene over in his mind. The more he thought about it, it made him wonder if there was a key in his dream that would help him solve the mystery of the lost colony. He brushed it aside, however, and went on to other thoughts as he slowly moved closer to the end of his immediate journey.

The bright sun was now higher in the mid-day sky, the crisp morning air had warmed considerably while Running Deer came out of a bend to face a long straight stretch of water. The river was becoming wider, so he moved the canoe into the middle of the channel. As he looked into the distance, he noticed a pair of craft making their way toward him. After the experience with the two thieves, he decided that it would be best to be prepared in case of a vengeful attack, so he laid his knife and bow and arrow close by his side for easy retrieval if necessary. Without slowing his canoe, he continued straight ahead to gradually close the gap.

As the two canoes moved nearer, Running Deer was able to make out the form of the two men. In a moment, he thought he recognized the two as the ones who attempted to steal his canoe and cargo. His worst fear was materializing. As the canoes moved closer, they began to separate and this was not good news for Running Deer because he knew that this was not an ordinary act of courtesy. In fact, there was an ages old tactic of the military to divide and conquer, or in this case to divert the attention of the prey and then move in from both sides. His mind was racing at top speed in order to figure out his next move. His first appraisal of the two as sneaky cowards from the first encounter, was beginning to change.

Being outnumbered was one thing, but surrendering himself and his cargo without a fight was not a viable option. His ever ready constant companion Akimko came to mind, so he waited until the two were within a few yards, then gave two high pitched whistles to summon the huge bird. Almost instantly, Akimko swooped down on one of the canoes catching its occupant off guard. Caught in complete surprise, he threw his hands up to protect himself, and as a result, both he and his oars flew off into the river to join the out going current on its way downstream. His accomplice, observing what had happened to his friend, quickly changed courses and headed for the river bank on his side of the river, but Akimko had other plans. As Running Deer watched in amusement, his winged protector made another fly-over that caused the other thief to lose balance and join his partner on their boatless journey.

The great bird disappeared as quickly as it had arrived leaving Running Deer with a feeling of relief as he continued to guide his canoe down the middle of the river to complete the last few hours of his journey. The sun was still giving off its warmth and light but was beginning to dim a little as it headed towards its seat in the west. Running Deer figured that there would be another three hours daylight and he would be very near the widow White's landing by sundown, interruptions notwithstanding. This will be a good time, he thought, to eat a snack. He did not want to greet Lucinda and the girls in an impoverished state. So the next three hours was spent in anticipation of joining his hosts to share his story of all the events of the past few days.

Running Deer decided to not spend much of his time contemplating the planned trip with Ralph Lane. Feeling somewhat tired from the activities of the last three days, all he wanted to do was relax, enjoy the company of Lucinda and the girls, and catch up on some well deserved sleep. While the tide was still going in his direction, only the occasional lap of his oar in the water could be heard as he corrected his mid-stream position. When the river became narrow at times, the evening sounds coming from the forest became louder. The woods inhabitants could be seen scampering about—either running from a predator or stalking prey. This activity brought closely to mind his love for hunting. He hoped that he would be able to whet his skills before he began his quest again to look for the old fort.

The sun's glimmer on the river was dimming now and the shaded areas on the bank had already darkened further. His focus stayed on the place where he would recognize the White's landing, because he was beginning to spot familiar landmarks. As his eyes followed the landscape along the river, he suddenly recognized the huge cypress that marked the landing. He guessed that in another ten minutes he would be heading his canoe toward the bank and into this welcome site. A good thing, he thought, because the current was beginning to slow and soon he would have to buck the tide.

The sun was finally beginning to set and on this evening, there would be no moonlight. As had happened so many times before, Judy Mae and Priscilla Jane had come to the landing to await and greet their father on his return from the trading post. This time it was Running Deer that they greeted with warm hugs. Their help in carrying the supplies to the cabin was a bonus for him also. The three loaded up and began their short trek to the cabin where they were greeted by a grateful Lucinda who had already prepared a scrumptious meal of baked rabbit and fresh garden greens. Shortly after they began to enjoy their meal, the girls began to question Running Deer about his trip to the trading post. They suspected that, it being his first trip, he must have some interesting tales to share with them.

He began first by relating the story of the two rapscallions that he encountered while he was only half way to the trading post. His story solicited "ahs" from the two when he told of the sneaky theft of his loaded canoe as he was settling in for a night's rest. But this soon turned to giggles when he described how he finally outwitted them. Next it was adult talk as Lucinda expressed her gratitude to him for acquiring the needed supplies which were so important to them. In a month or so, cold weather would descend on them to leave previews of coming attractions for the long winter ahead. She didn't want to appear too concerned about their welfare so she didn't pursue the subject any longer.

Running Deer assured her that he would see to it that she would have plenty of firewood to keep them warm and he would help her replenish the pantry. The harvest was practically in and the girls would help with the canning chores. Their fruit trees were very productive this year which guaranteed them ample jams, jellies, and preserves. As the trio ended the meal, Running Deer announced that he would like to freshen up a bit and with their permission, he would like to discover again what a real bed felt like. This brought smiles from all of them and the girls assured him that they had already anticipated his wishes by preparing his bed in advance and announced that Judy Mae had helped her mother make a new quilt for it.

After gathering his bed clothes, he proceeded to the outside rear of the cabin where he would avail himself of the crude makeshift water supply and a much needed bath. Ananias was not slack when it came to providing the necessities for his family. One of his inventions in which he took great pride was a trough hewn from poplar that was positioned near the eaves of the cabin's roof where it was allowed to catch rain water. As needed, the water flowed from the lower end of the trough through a perforated wooden plate onto the bather. While he enjoyed his bath, his mind wandered to the memory of Ananias and he thought what a shame that his life had been taken at so young an age. He counted it a blessing that he had known this man and felt that it was not merely a chance meeting that brought them together. He was sure that meeting the family was meant to be and that his future quest for knowledge would be greatly influenced by it.

Invigorated by his bath, Running Deer donned his bedclothes, said goodnight to Lucinda and the girls, and excused himself to bed.

Sleep came easily without tossing and turning, and before long he was in a deep slumber. On this night, there had not been any time for tomorrow's planning, he just wanted to rest his body, relieve his mind of the task at hand, and let tomorrow take care of itself.

Charlie, Lucinda's reliable red rooster, must have sensed that Running Deer needed all the sleep he could get. On this new morning, he forewent his usual trio of cock-adoodle-doos until the sun was threading its way through the surrounding trees. Fits of dreams appeared intermittently, but they did not deter him from a peaceful slumber. He felt genuinely rested and was appreciative of the fact that providence had placed him in the hands of these gracious hostesses at this point in time. As the pleasant odor of fresh ground coffee brewing permeated his nostrils, that thought was further enhanced. As soon as Lucinda was aware that he was awake, she announced that breakfast would soon be ready.

Glad to have fresh supplies from the trading post, Lucinda was able to prepare a grand meal. Her few hens had been exceptionally productive, so she was able to serve a scrumptious omelet for everyone. Running Deer had fleeting thoughts of remaining in this tranquil atmosphere, but he knew that soon he would have to reluctantly move on and leave his friends behind. For the moment, though, he would not let anything interfere with his quietude.

Conversation drifted from one to the other, where at some point, Running Deer related more of his experiences to the trading post and back. He was careful to not mention the Akimko incident because he knew that his friends would not understand, and further, it might compromise some elements of his journey. Following the meal, he excused himself and made his way to the river where he would spend some time to calculate tide times and some time to try and forecast the weather for the two days ahead. He had already decided to spend the rest of the day at the cabin where he would make plans for his upcoming journey back to the trading post and his rendezvous with the trader Ralph Lane.

Along with his plans for the trip, he began to mull over the situation regarding the welfare of the widow and her young daughters. He still felt a sense of responsibility toward them. He dismissed any thoughts of emotional attachment, but he had been in their midst long enough to realize how closely they were attached to Ananias. Even though living in the wilderness had instilled in them a pioneer spirit, there were some things that they would have to learn to do that was formerly handled by him. There was no thought on Running Deer's part that he would ever return to these parts, because he felt that it was time to continue his journey—first to the old fort and then with the help of his map—to the end of his quest wherever it would take him. So, he decided to spend the rest of his time with the family speaking words of encouragement, and perhaps a few tips on hunting.

The surrounding forest was abundant with small game and wild turkeys and there was always a quick meal from the river. Time passed much too quickly and before long, light from the sun had slipped away from overhead and was beginning to make its way to the western horizon. He would spend this time to hunt rabbits and squirrels to supplement their winter food supply. Lucinda and Judy Mae were adept at skinning the animals and preserving the meat. Priscilla Jane was only beginning to learn. After a successful hunt, including a good size wild turkey, he thought it was time to begin packing his supplies for an early morning departure back up the river.

He had calculated that the tide would begin to rise about daybreak and it would be to his advantage to launch out on time. Before ebb tide, he probably will have reached the half-way point. He did not anticipate any more trouble from the river thieves because of the incident two days before. Priscilla Jane had snared a nice sized rabbit on the evening of the day before, so Lucinda was beginning to prepare the charcoals for a delectable rabbit roast. It is the least she could do, she thought, for a truly decent human being whom she and her two daughters had come to think of as a surrogate father. She promised herself that she would not shed any tears when he went away, but she knew that knowing him would leave a lasting impression on the family.

Following the evening's repast and fellowshipping, Running Deer announced that he would spend the balance of the evening before bedtime to carefully pack his supplies and personal belongings to prepare for his early morning departure. As she had done before, Lucinda provided a package of dried meat and scones for him to take along. This was an extra treat that he had come to expect. Fresh water was drawn from their ever-flowing artesian well to store in his leak proof beaver skin container. There were other supplies offered, but Running Deer declined because he wished to keep the canoe load at a reasonable level. He did not want excessive personal goods to slow his progress on the river.

After the packing was accomplished, it was finally time for another good night's rest. He excused himself for bed knowing that there would be time for goodbyes when they awakened at dawn. Expecting to drift off quickly, he was disappointed a little, because for the first full hour he was restless. Although his eyes were closed, his mind wandered beyond the trip back to the trading post to scenes of strange new places that he would encounter on his extended journey. In one such scene, a dark skinned man with English dress wielded a weapon in one hand while the other hand was extended as if to welcome him. After this, he remembered no more and the balance of the night was spent in peaceful slumber.

Chapter Four

CHARLIE WAS PROMPTLY ON TIME the next morning and all four occupants seemed to have arisen at the same time as a result. All preparation had been made, so breakfast was dispensed with in a hurry. In keeping with his pre-arranged time schedule, he gave his individual goodbyes, gave a blessing on the house as his grandmother Safronia used to do, and then turned his back and walked toward the boat landing. Before he got half way to the river, he turned and saw the mother and her two daughters following him. They weren't about to let him shove off without a proper send-off from the shore. Hugs were again in order and Running Deer, more than ever, began to feel an attachment to the little family that he had grown to admire and like. At the same time, he was being careful to not become emotionally attached. He knew that he must keep focused on his goal.

The first shimmer of the dawn's light played tag with the Chowanoke river as Running Deer shoved off from the bank at low tide. There was an ebb in the tide while marsh leaves and floating branches were slowly taking their place in the stream as if responding to a signal. He made his way to the middle of the stream and did not look back toward the landing. He valued his time with the Whites, but he knew that he must set his sights on the unknown. Somehow, in his spirit, he felt that things would go well for them. Nevertheless, he wished that sometime in the future, they and he would meet again.

The rising sun was hidden from view, but the view from his vantage point in the river reminded him that there was a beautiful sunrise behind the treetops that would eventually make its way overhead. He hoped for continued fair weather with an uneventful journey back to the trading post. After about two hours on the river, the speed of the current was beginning to peak while the sun was peeking over the treetops and aligning itself with the river. He noticed that there was a decidedly autumn look in the trees on each side of the river. Colors were beginning to appear that were not there on his previous trip. He had noticed the color change in autumns past, but on this occasion, they were more beautiful than he remembered.

While he marveled at the beauty of the trees, he was unaware of a contrast in the sunny sky until a loud peal of thunder jarred him out of his reverie. Always cognizant of a quick change in weather, he knew that he must begin to seek shelter at once to move out of the danger of a lightning producing thunderstorm. He scanned the banks from side to side in order to locate a clearing that would at least be safer than remaining on the river. The growth was very thick on both sides, and by this time, the thunder claps were coming more frequently and he knew that he must make a decision before the lightning came. So he headed his canoe toward the right bank, hoping that he would find safety.

Large drops of rain began to fall as he made his way toward a narrow opening in a copse of trees on the bank. The clouds had opened now and the raindrops had turned into small hail pellets. Fearing for his safety, and the safety of his craft and cargo, he doubled his oar strokes to shorten the time of reaching the bank. The extra effort paid off for him as he now quickly pulled his canoe on the shore, and with more effort, into the safety of the bushes. After tying the boat securely, he began to look for some kind of shelter in the wooded surroundings. By this time, there was less time between lightning bolts and the accompanying peal of thunder, so he knew that he was in for a harsh weather event.

The hail was growing now and in the size of large marbles. He looked the area over and at first did not see a suitable place for shelter. He found himself holding his skimpy vest over his head trying to protect himself from the pounding of the hail which was beginning to cut his face. As he continued to scan the area, he noticed a downed tree, uprooted by a previous windstorm, was probably being used by the forest inhabitants for the same purpose. Since there were no inhabitants now, he ducked under the huge natural haven to wait out the storm.

Out of the direct pounding of the hail, Running Deer began to assess his situation so that he could calculate what the unexpected weather intrusion would do to alter his schedule. He was consoled somewhat by recalling the phrase from his memory that "the best laid plans of mice and men go oft astray" or something like that. He also remembered that Chief Waccasaw had told him that his journey would not be without divers problems and some disappointments. Having satisfied himself that he would be under the nature provided shelter for an indefinite period, he began to explore the cramped space to see if he could stretch his legs and make the best of his situation. He surmised that the huge tree was very old and had weathered many a storm in its lifetime.

The sky was very dark now leaving very little light inside the tree trunk. He began to carefully move his knife on the floor and overhead, and to his delight, found that the floor of the cramped space was dry and remarkably free from grass, leaves, woods growth, or litter of any sort, so he proceeded to fold his vest in the form of a pillow. Just as he laid his head on his makeshift pillow, a yelping fox went past him and out into the forest. Very few things in his life had caused his heart to jump as if leaving his body like the cornered fox. Expecting more of the same, he braced himself for an onslaught while brandishing his knife in a circular motion. Apparently, though, the den had housed only one occupant and after a few minutes, he was ready to resume his nap.

The end of the storm was no where in sight, so after an hour or so of listening to the thunder, lightning, and clattering hail, he dozed off. It was near the end of the first day now and he could expect to spend the rest of the night in the cramped quarters. The noise from the storm had not abated yet, so it was a while before any serious sleeping could occur. He arose early the next morning greeted by the ear-splitting sound of the frogs from the surrounding trees that seemed to be in harmony with other forest sounds. The day looked very promising like a calm after the storm while the sun rays pierced through the tree branches like hide-and-seek between darkness and light.

Running Deer was acutely aware of the stiffness of his body after sleeping all night in a semi-cramped position. From experience, though, he knew that he would be as good as new following a few stretching exercises. From habit, he had grown to depend on these exercises to remain nimble and alert. He also needed to walk while he pieced his plans back together for the final day of his return to the trading post.

As he moved around the area, his eye caught an unusually large cypress approximately fifty yards away. The size and height of the tree aroused his curiosity somewhat, so he slowly made his way through the vines and undergrowth toward it. He thought how fortunate he was to have a knife that was capable of cutting away the thick growth that covered the forest floor. More daylight was penetrating the area and he was able to get a closer look at the gigantic tree. Amazingly, at a ten or fifteen feet circumference surrounding the tree, there was no growth. The sun was above the tree tops now and seemed to focus its penetrating rays directly on the sight.

When he reached the area around the tree, he began to move around it while looking up toward the top. When he moved around to the opposite side, his gaze came upon some very strange looking marks on the trunk approximately six or seven feet from the base. At first he considered it to be an optical illusion, but after clearing his eyes and narrowing his focus, he made out a letter that was carved into the bark. Moving around further, a second less discernible letter appeared. He was not yet sure what the letters were, so he thought that he should move further away from the tree to get a better look. Clearing his way from the tree, he suddenly remembered that the only clue left by the missing colony of Englishmen was a carving on a tree. His heart began to pound in his chest at the possibility of finding this important clue at this juncture of his journey.

Able to get a better look now, the second letter appeared to be a "R". As he re-examined the first letter, the sun's ray had exposed the letter "C". On the way back to his canoe, he made careful notes of his find and then tucked it into the folder with the map. He had momentarily forgotten about the current's direction but soon discovered that he would be bucking the tide for about two hours. He did not look forward to this, but he knew that he must continue on his way back to the trading post. Without an event except the stiffening of his arm muscle, he had made some progress before the ebbing of the tide and the reversal of the current flow.

It was a welcome occurrence for him, and he was able to rest his arms for a while as he drifted with the current. But now, he thought, I must exert all my strength in order to reach the trading post by nightfall.

The bright sun, overhead now, was merciless as it beat down upon his little craft. His fresh water supply was dwindling, but he refused to slack off from his constant rowing. While making steady progress with the current flow, he had lost track of time. He was made strikingly aware of this as he watched the dimming orb of the sun become larger as it began to sink below the tree tops while he was negotiating a bend in the river. He recognized the bend from his previous trip as one that had preceded the longest straight run of the stream.

He now began to realize that he would not be able to reach his destination by nightfall. Nevertheless, he counted on a fair sky and the rising of a half moon to light the way for him. The one part of his calculations that was in his favor was that the rising tide would continue for another two or three hours. Dusk was hurriedly approaching and he was becoming more anxious to see the dim lights of the trading post that his friend, Ralph, would probably leave burning for him. The closer he came to the end of his two-day journey, the more his mind would flash ahead to the events planned for the days ahead. Since Ralph had promised to accompany him to the old fort site, he had decided that the time was not yet right to divulge his findings of the previous night. After all, he didn't want anything to interfere with his ultimate goal. Running Deer, in his own mind, had determined that the carvings were connected to the disappearance of the colonists. Indeed, it had become folly for generations to make inconclusive assessments concerning them on assumptions alone.

As he mulled these things over in his mind, he suddenly realized that his craft had slowed almost to a halt. The tide had reached flood stage and within minutes would be making its return to its source. Fortunately, though, he rounded a short bend and he spotted the anticipated blinking lights of the trading post. By the light of the early rising moon and the blinking lantern lights as a guide, he rowed against the tide toward his goal. It was difficult to determine the distance, but he predicted that it would take another hour to reach.

He was nearly on the mark as he headed his canoe in toward the post and up to the dock. His over-worked muscles were aching as he tied up and began making preparations to unload his belongings. The chore would be simpler this time because the craft was not loaded with pelts. While in the midst of unloading, he was interrupted by a hearty—"Hello there, is that you, Running Deer?" Ralph was anxious to see his new friend and had stayed up to await his arrival. In his hand he carried a large lantern that would make the task at hand much easier for Running Deer.

"I was concerned about you when you failed to arrive earlier", Ralph said, "but I assumed that you had run into some weather."

"Ran into some weather", replied Running Deer, "is putting it very mildly. Last evening, I ran into one of the worst hail storms that I had ever experienced. I was very fortunate to find shelter."

Running Deer thought of the hurricane that took the life of his friend a few weeks back but he did not wish to dwell on that unfortunate event that left in its wake a widow and two fatherless children. He chose to feel that in time the little frontier family would overcome the grief and go on to live their lives in prosperity and safety. The over-riding task at hand, with Ralph Lane at his side, was to prepare for the next leg of his journey. He could not afford to become deterred from the quest that was set out before him, but his intuition told him that he could trust his partner, Ralph.

After securing his craft, Running Deer gathered his belongings, and with the help of Ralph, made their way up the short incline to the trading post. Little was said on the way, but he was sure that would change quickly after they had settled down. Ralph was the one to break the ice as he gently slapped his friend on the shoulder and with a typical guffaw accompanied by anticipated questioning, said "I don't know where to start, but first, how are the widow and her two girls?"

"Just fine", replied Running Deer, "they were very appreciative of your hospitality toward me."

"I'm much obliged for them kind words", he said, "I never want it to be said that Ralph Lane was anything but considerate toward friends."

After patting himself on the back, Ralph questioned Running Deer further about the hail storm that he had encountered down the river.

"You're not going to believe this", said Running Deer, "I had uninvited company join me in my shelter while I was waiting out the storm. As a matter of fact, I unknowingly joined him."

"Tell me more", said Ralph, who was waiting patiently in anticipation of a few laughs before the two would settle down for a good night's rest. Running Deer went on to tell Ralph about the fox that nearly "scared the daylights" out of him as he scampered by him yelping at the top of his voice. The hanging tinware in the cabin seemed to shake as Ralph roared with laughter.

Since the trip was uneventful with the exception of the hail storm and the fox tale, both men agreed that it was time to retire and get some much needed rest. They knew that tomorrow would be spent in making plans for their much-anticipated journey to the old abandoned fort site.

"Come on in to my private quarters", said Ralph, "I have already prepared a more comfortable bed than you had on your first visit." Upon entering a detached building behind the trading post, Running Deer was awestruck by its elaborate interior. He first noticed the neatly placed stuffed trophy animals staring at him from all four walls. There was ample room for two partitioned bedrooms and a sizeable area with cooking utensils hanging over a food preparation table. Adjacent to the table in the center of the room was a fireplace with a chimney protruding through the roof.

On the floor was bear skins, looking almost alive, that reached almost wall to wall, but what impressed Running Deer the most was how neatly the interior was arranged with nothing seemingly out of place. Just as he began to compliment Ralph on his housekeeping talent, his friend blurted out—"In honor of my dear departed wife, I have gone to great length to preserve our living quarters just as she left it. It's the least I could do. I know you are exhausted, please help yourself to my meager bath facilities and then you may retire to the guest room." In Running Deer's mind, all of this plush treatment was overkill, but who was he to complain.

The only other conversation between the two was a mutual "good night" and a "see you after daybreak in the morning". After lying down, Running Deer knew that he would have no problem with falling asleep, but he had to get used to the silence. As he turned over for the second time, he was already half asleep. While in a deep slumber, he was awakened by Ralph's intermittent snoring. Luckily for him, Ralph must have changed positions because the next thing he knew, Ralph's rooster, "Big Red", was giving a wake-up call. Big Red must have been more than an alarm clock, because Ralph was reaching into the pantry to pull out a hand full of brown hen eggs.

Without asking any questions, a fire was started in the cooking area and he proceeded to prepare a hearty breakfast of ham and eggs for both of them. There was no shortage of staples in Ralph's kitchen which was made evident by the nearly full sack of hominy grits and a ground meal in abundance that was used for corn pone and assorted breads. Ralph kept a half dozen pigs in a sty that was situated a good distance behind the living quarters. Each winter, he explained to Running Deer, was hog killing time. In a small smoke house nearby, hung two or three smoked hams, plus ample shelving filled with other cuts of salted pork meat.

After a short visit to the smoke house, Ralph returned with two huge slabs of ham. It wasn't long before the cooking ham filled the inside of the cabin with a delicious smell that brought back childhood memories to Running Deer. Dawn had not broken yet, but in his mind, he anticipated a great day for the journey at hand. A robust breakfast for starters could not hurt. Very little serious conversation ensued as the two of them devoured their breakfast.

After breakfast, the clean-up was shared and Running Deer expressed his appreciation for the hospitality and food. "No need to thank me", said Ralph, "nothing is too good for a friend."

With those mutual expressions behind them, they retired to the modest but comfortable living area at the front of the cabin. Running Deer noticed that Ralph had already placed on the table what appeared to be a crude map. The two sat at the table opposite each other where Ralph began by saying "I have laid out plans for our first day and I want to show you what we'll more than likely encounter as we move along the trail. Also, we want to be sure to take what provisions we'll be needing to sustain us if hunting is scarce. We must be prepared to protect ourselves in case of an attack by wild animals or unfriendly Indians." Even though Running Deer had been through both of these situations, he wasn't about to discount the warnings and knowledge of an experienced woodsman.

Running Deer nodded to affirm Ralph's concern, but he decided against letting him in on the help of the ever-present Akimko. After packing their back-pack and seeing to it that their knives, arrows, and spears would be accessible at all times, the two of them set out in the general direction of the fort. This leg of the journey would be by foot because Ralph figured that to stay on the river would be taking them too far off course, and besides, the trip over land should be exciting and they should reach their destination in a few days. Running Deer thought how industrious of Ralph to undergrowth such a wide area around the perimeter of the trading post and living quarters. When they had been walking about half an hour, they had not encountered any significant vines and undergrowth. He was satisfied that Ralph had trod this path many times before, so there shouldn't be a problem with continuing in the right direction and he said so.

"You're right, my friend. I have walked this trail many times in the past, but since the passing of my wife, I have never wandered far from the trading post. I am sure that we will run into some very wild growth that has occurred since then." As the two plodded along with Ralph randomly checking his bearings, the new growth began to obscure the pathway. The slashing noise created by their knives caused chaos among the animals along the forest floor. A fat rabbit was disturbed from its vegetative repast and went scurrying across the vision of Running Deer who adeptly reached over his shoulder and extracted an arrow. With the dexterity of an expert marksman, he bagged the unlucky visitor for dinner.

After stuffing the rabbit in his pack, the two continued on their way. Familiar marks along the path were grown over now making it more difficult for Ralph to navigate. However, good judgment and a better than average sense of direction carried the two to a more recognizable part of the old path. The undergrowth was less dense now and progress was easier. Approximately two hours had passed and the sun was beginning to clear the tree tops making it easier to travel.

A clearing came into view just ahead as the two men were making good progress along the old path. Ralph remarked that he had not seen the clearing on any previous trek. The cleared out area was adjacent to the path, so Ralph and Running Deer decided to get a closer look. As they moved closer, they spotted a small lean-to shack tucked into one corner. Cautiously approaching, they circled around to detect a possible sign of life. Seeing nor hearing none, they decided to enter the crude building for further inspection.

There was no sign that the building had been occupied, at least recently, but tucked in a corner that was better sheltered from the elements, sat a makeshift bed which indicated that someone had spent some time there in the recent past. All evidence of fires for cooking was outside the shack. Stepping back outside, they noticed that the sun was beginning to settle behind the treetops indicating that dusk was not far off. Since it was evident to them that they were not intruding on anyone, it was an easy decision to cut their day a little short and take advantage of the shelter.

There was still daylight and enough time to review the progress that they had made and time to talk about the remainder of the trip. While they began to know each other better, Ralph volunteered to talk about his ancestors. It became clear to Running Deer that Ralph might be more helpful to his cause than he had initially thought. Ralph's grandfather had been very insightful to pass along much information about the family that had been handed down through his parents and grandparents. As it turned out, Ralph's passion for more knowledge of his ancestors was not unlike that of Running Deer's quest for knowledge of the lost Englishmen.

When Ralph revealed that he learned from his grandfather that he was a direct descendant of Ralph Lane, the controversial ex-military man who was left in charge of the ill fated colony, Running Deer wasted no time in asking more probing questions about his family's past.

"Is this family history written down somewhere and in your possession or is it mostly legendary?"

Ralph replied that all of the information written down and in his possession covered only four generations, but there were bits of information still in his memory that had been handed down through his ancestors.

"As a matter of fact", he said, "my grandmother possessed a very sharp mind until the day that she passed away at the age of 103. I remember sitting at her knees on the porch as she rocked away and told stories about the Indians—or natives—as she called them. There were tales of not so friendly ones stealing corn from their field and snatching poultry from the coops and pigs from their sty. There were friendly ones, too, she said. The friendly ones were more talkative and claimed to be Croatans.

As she remembered, the natives were mostly dark skinned, but there were those who had intermarried and had produced a mixed breed. All of this was very interesting to Running Deer, so he interrupted by asking Ralph if during all the conversations or story telling by his grandmother, had he heard any mention of a colony of Englishmen that had disappeared while their leaders had gone back to England for supplies.

"Oh yes, the lost colony", he answered, "My grandfather mentioned the colony once or twice. It was always considered a mystery, but in his opinion, they were massacred by the natives. His father, my great grandfather, had offered a different story. Old Jepthah Lane had said that a small number of the colony had managed to elude the onslaught by the natives by skillfully hiding out and later making their way in a southerly direction from the outpost. He went on to say that the five members of the group who had managed to escape, stopped briefly on their way through the forest to leave a clue for possible rescuers. My great grandfather did not mention the location.

By this time, Running Deer could feel his heart pounding and he waited anxiously for Ralph to continue his story. In his mind, he could envision the handful of Englishmen walking up to the trees and selecting one to carve out some message that would help possible rescuers. They probably thought that it was a very slim chance that it would help, but it was the very least that they could do given their situation and the possibility that they were being hunted at that very moment. Still withholding the news of his discovery of the carved initials that he had found, Running Deer waited anxiously for Ralph to resume his story.

"My great grandfather", Ralph said, "told of a tree that was nearby the fort on which the word "CROATOAN" had been carved. He said that he hadn't seen the tree himself, but his pappy recalled seeing the tree when he was a very young lad."

At this point, Running Deer could contain his exhilaration no longer. He was very anxious to continue on their journey to the old historic site. He felt sure that there were many more stories that Ralph could relate about his ancestors, but he considered it best that they continue on their way. Sleep finally overcame them and the next thing they knew, dawn was breaking on another beautiful day. Gathering their possessions, they were ready to tackle the forest head on.

Traces of an old path continued to guide the two as they made their way northward. At times their progress was slowed while they hacked their way through unyielding vines and very thick undergrowth. The age-old loblolly pines stood tall like sentries of the past. In a low lying savanna, there was evidence of recent lightning fires, but accompanying rain had prevented the fire from spreading throughout the forest. Interspersed with the pines, cypress and assorted hardwoods abounded. This is a virgin forest, thought Running Deer, where wildlife is plentiful. Before the thought left his mind, a deep threatening growl reverberated through the thicket.

"Stay perfectly still", warned Ralph, "there is an adult bobcat crouched on the lower limb of that huge oak tree. If we make a move, he might pounce."

"We can't take any chances", agreed Running Deer, "but one of us will have to prepare for the kill."

Before Ralph could reply, the cat hit the ground with lightning speed and made his way toward Ralph who was closer to the tree. Making use of his hunting skills, Running Deer reached for an arrow at the same instant that Ralph retrieved a trusted Bowie knife from his belt. At the moment that the bobcat opened his jaws to attack Ralph, an arrow sang through the air and stopped the animal before it could do damage to his friend.

"Thanks", said Ralph, "I owe you one."

"I hope its not very soon", Ralph replied.

Instead of skinning the animal for its pelt as would have been Ralph's custom, they let it be. The vultures of the forest would soon take care of the remains. Slowly, they continued on their way without distraction until they noticed that the sun would soon be setting. They immediately began to look for a small clearing in which to set up camp. They weren't too concerned about hunting food yet because they had packed enough for a few days.

After hacking away for another half hour, taking care to mark their path as they went, a small opening appeared in the undergrowth beside the old path. Neither of the men realized how tired they were until they stopped to lay their gear on the grassy carpet. It was impossible to know how far they had come or how much farther they would have to go.

"After we rest a spell", said Ralph, "we'll take a look at our map and try to estimate where we are."

"Sounds okay by me", offered Running Deer, "I've been keeping an eye on the sky for any change of weather, but so far the sky has provided us with beautiful small cumulus clouds. I haven't seen a single dark rain scud. This looks like a great place to spend the night, so break out the map and let's see if we are on track."

With the diminished light from the sky, Ralph was able to spread his map out on the grass where the two of them tried to determine their progress. With the absence of a landmark, it was difficult to do, so they estimated the miles traveled considering time lost clearing the way. Just before the sun set, they reckoned their direction to be on target because of its relation to the western sky. Their next order of business was to prepare a campfire to help with a simple meal of warm lentil soup and also to provide light to lay out their plans for the morrow.

"Assuming that Mother Nature continues to smile on us", noted Ralph, "I estimate that another day and a half should put us in the vicinity of the fort. Autumn has always been very unpredictable as far as storms and heavy rain are concerned, but hopefully we can reach our goal before that occurs."

This being the first trip for Running Deer, there was little to add except "those are my exact sentiments". He was remembering his involvement at the White's place when the hurricane blew in and took his friend's life and also his escapade following a hailstorm along the river bank where he and a fox shared the same shelter. Ralph suggested an early start for the next morning, so after a few minutes of friendly banter, the fire was reduced to a few embers and the two settled down for a much needed night's rest.

Their sleep was not without interruption, however, because of the sounds of night prowling residents that were not aware of the two visitors. It seemed that all manners of animals were conversing with their counterparts and cavorting through the brush as if it were open daylight. Nevertheless, the intermittent naps served to renew their vigor, and a half hour before the crack of dawn, Ralph started a small fire on which to brew his favorite coffee. A past trading client had secured a sack of native coffee beans while on the island of Barbados that eventually wound up at the trading post. While experimenting on a blend, he had mixed some beans that had made their way from China with the Barbados beans to come up with a favorite.

"I always said that the start of any day is no better than the coffee you drink, so help yourself, my friend. We're gonna have a great day." Running Deer could not help but envy his friend's enthusiasm, so after shortbread and salted pork—along with two cups of Ralph's favorite blend—they embarked into the unfamiliar.

The new day appeared optimistic because there was hardly a cloud on a palette of Carolina blue. The temperature at this time of morning was invigorating which led to motivate the two as they continued on their journey. Running Deer had thought that following the river would have been the easiest route, but he was not about to question Ralph's knowledge of the area. His instinct about a connection from Ralph's past told him that the chance meeting of the two was meant to be. As he pondered these things, conversation was kept to a minimum while they hacked their way through the dense forest.

The bright orange colored sun was rising above the tree tops now and would soon be bathing the forest with plenty of light and a source of warmth. There was plenty of shade for occasional rest stops, so the morning went amazingly fast. A stream of fresh water was a welcome sight for them as they located a site nearby to pause and have a bite to eat. In a rare moment of quietness, the trained ear of Running Deer detected a slight murmur that reminded him of the sound of a river. Standing up, he walked out a few feet in different directions to try to determine the source of the sound. When he informed Ralph of this, his friend was quick to dismiss the idea by saying that there was not a river within miles.

"Your ears are playing cruel tricks on you", said he, "let's continue on our way while we are making progress."

Even so, Running Deer made a notation on his map, and for good measure, hacked a sizable mark on a huge oak tree nearby. Portions of what appeared to be an old path appeared in front of them now and the briar infested undergrowth gave way to somewhat easier progress. The next hour seemed to pass quickly and probably more progress had been made than the previous part of the day.

Ralph looked at the sky and announced that there would be about two more hours of sunlight so they should continue in the same direction as long as they could see their way. "By the way", he announced, "while you were following a sound, I got us a nice sized rabbit for supper."

Much progress was made in the next hour before dusk began to enclose them. They selected a site that provided ample clearance for a campfire and then proceeded to gather dry branches for fuel. It was a welcome change from the constant hacking, and in a very short time, enough dry sticks were gathered by the two to keep a fire going sufficient to roast the rabbit, make some coffee, and provide enough light to make notations on their maps. The dying embers would provide some warmth for the approaching fall temperature.

As Running Deer scrounged around the area, his eye caught the sight of an unusual object protruding from the ground that was partially covered by the sandy soil. Without mentioning the find to Ralph, he proceeded to move nearer to get a closer look. After discovering it to be a bleached bone, he immediately dismissed the thought that it came from an animal. After closer examination, he surmised it to be a human leg bone. It was not a likely place to find a human bone, he thought, so he summoned Ralph over to take a look. After some discussion, they decided to re-visit the site at first light the next morning.

A fire was started and the dry hardwood branches began to crackle while the flames lit the small camping area. A makeshift spit was fashioned by Ralph while Running Deer honed his skills at rabbit skinning. His Pa had shown him the fundamentals but he remembered that he was told that he would get better with time and practice. This is the time, he thought, to get some of that practice, because he wasn't about to ask his partner for help. The chore went smoothly except the gutting but it was handed over to Ralph in a timely manner for roasting over the fire.

While Ralph rotated the spit, Running Deer busied himself with the coffee. Warm bread would be nice, he thought, so he reached into his duffel and retrieved a handful of scones. Wrapping them in bay leaves, he placed them near the fire to capture some warmth from the glowing embers. Juices from the roasting rabbit were spattering on the coals now and the aroma brought hunger pangs that he didn't know were there. There was just something about cooking outside that appealed to Running Deer, especially because it brought back memories of his Pa allowing him to accompany him on hunting trips where they would spend the night. His Ma called it daydreaming but it was very real to him.

In a very short time, the rabbit was done and Ralph did the honors of cutting the meat into portions. Even though it was a large rabbit, there was little left save the bones. They cleaned up a bit, stoked the fire, and proceeded to lay out their maps. Ralph did much more noting on his map, but Running Deer was careful not to alter his map that was given to him by Chief Waccasaw. To the best of his calculation, however, he made note of parallels that he found along the way. There was still an innate feeling that he was on the right course, and with the help of Ralph and continued good weather, they would reach their goal in a few days. How many days? It was impossible to know. It would all depend on the density of the old trail, Ralph's memory, and of course, the weather.

"I can see that you are holding up rather well", noted Ralph, "I really admire your strength and determination." As yet, Running Deer had not revealed the whole story behind the reason for his quest. One day, he thought, I might let him in on some of the secrets pertaining to the journey. But for now, we'll just remain good friends. So, after re-packing their gear, placing it over their shoulder and back, only two last chores remained. In order to mark their path, they slash marked two of the larger trees at the campsite. This would be especially crucial for a return trip if needed and possibly for future exploring. After a limited discussion about the human bone, Running Deer reminded Ralph that they had agreed to return to the site of the bone discovery on the previous evening.

"That's right", said Ralph, "We're probably wasting our time, but we'll take a closer look."

With better light now, it was possible to see that a partially deteriorated grave marker was lying mostly uncovered near the exposed bone. Years of wind and rain had taken its toll on the remains, but it was still apparent that this was an old gravesite. On closer inspection and after removing the soil from the marker, a name had been crudely inscribed on the hardwood surface. The name was not clear enough to make out, but the year 1588 was clearly discernible.

After this discovery, Running Deer's heart leapt within him, and with much exuberance, he shared his enthusiasm with Ralph. With a crude makeshift shovel, they re-interred the bone, and after gathering a few nearby stones, they re-positioned the ancient marker over the site. Running Deer retrieved his map once again and made careful notations concerning the find. It was another of those gut feelings that this was a crucial find.

Dawn was breaking now and bright rays from the early morning sun was beginning to infiltrate the brush around them which led to a slight course correction brought on by the true eastern direction of the rising sun. In the beginning, they were faced by dense brush intermingled with wild grapevines. The vines, in a way, were a welcome sight because there were clusters of black grapes hanging from some of the vines. Wild fruit had been strikingly absent from their diet on their journey so far, so much that their bodies were beginning to crave this very necessary nutrient. Back at the trading post, apple and pear trees were in abundance as well as other assorted fruit. But, so far on this leg of the journey, they hadn't even seen a huckleberry bush.

More light being available now, they continued to hack their way northward. There were more animal sightings now including a family of white-tailed deer. It was a good sign that more scrumptious meals would be available for the hunting.

"Keep your bow and arrow at the ready", noted Ralph, "the sooner that we bag supper, the better."

The doe and her fawns disappeared quickly, but their hunting instincts told them that there would be more. Moving slowly ahead, Running Deer suddenly announced to Ralph that he thought that he heard running water. Ralph agreed but neither of them could detect the direction from which the sound was coming. Thanks to many hours on the river, Running Deer had gained an ear for river sounds.

"Let's change our course ninety degrees northwest", he said, "I believe there is a river or waterfall less than an hour away. As we approach, the sound will get louder or will become more distant. If my reasoning is off, then we can re-correct our direction and continue in the direction that we are going."

At first Ralph did not want to take a chance, but he too possessed an adventurous mind, so while the sun was now visible over the tree tops, they made their way toward an unknown siren sound.

As they moved closer to the source of the sound, the undergrowth became increasingly more dense. Had it not been for a decidedly louder noise from the unknown source, they would have changed their mind and would have continued on their previous course. The work was hard and the progress slow as they continued toward the sound. There was less time between breaks now and their thirst was taking a toll on their vigor. Their fresh water was running fearfully low creating a concern for their well-being.

It was during one of these breaks that a grey heron alighted in a tree top near them.

"There must be water nearby", said Running Deer, "because these wading birds do not wander too far from a feeding source."

"I agree", said Ralph in response, "I can't imagine why my map did not show a river or lake in this vicinity."

Heartened by the prospect of fresh water nearby, Ralph and Running Deer doubled their efforts in hacking their way toward the now louder rippling sound. Ralph was the first to spot a moss-covered wheel creaking and dumping water into a gleaming basin of water that made its way to an undetermined spill. As they approached the old mill, they determined that it had been abandoned in an earlier time, but was built sufficiently sturdy to withstand the test of time.

The pair of grinding stones were lying together, but the ramshackle remains of the supporting timbers had long since disintegrated. But still, they thought it a mystery as to why the old wheel was still turning as the rushing water commanded.

The discovery of fresh water was the highlight of this day so it didn't take long for them to sate their thirst and refill their containers. They were anxious to explore the area further now, so they unloaded their packs from their shoulders and proceeded to take a closer look around the unexpected discovery. Clearing their ways through the years of twisted growth, it was apparent to them that no human had visited this spot in a very long time. The discovery of the old mill was more important to Running Deer than it was for Ralph.

For reasons that he would not divulge he expressed elation at the find but chose to let it go at that. Careful notations were made on his map because he felt that the mill would play an important role in his quest for knowledge. Like two exuberant school boys, Running Deer and Ralph continued to search for the source of the running water. Expecting to find a wider stream or river soon, the two were disappointed. They followed a small stream with more ease than the approach to the mill.

Presently the stream widened while the sun had moved from its overhead position to make its way toward the western horizon. After about two hours of following the stream, there was still no sight of the source. The trip thus far seemed much longer because of the occasional thick undergrowth that appeared in their way. Since they were determined to locate the stream's source, they made a decision to stay the course.

Rabbits and water mammals began to appear and this was good news for them. They knew that before long now the sun would set and they would have to seek out a campsite in which to spend the night. An adult rabbit was surprised by the approaching hackers and became an easy target of Ralph's arrow. In order to prepare the animal for the evening's meal, a decision was made to clear off a suitable spot for the fire. There would be time to locate dry ground for their sleeping space.

Running Deer said "you skin this one because I want to observe a master at work." He remembered the last one that he dressed and was not completely at ease for the chore.

"No problem", replied Ralph, "I can do this with my eyes closed." So he dressed the small animal while Running Deer prepared the fire. There was ample dry branches around the area, but the fire site had to be sufficiently cleared to prevent a spreading fire. There was no evidence of a former forest fire in the area and he certainly didn't want to be the first to start one. A sample was taken of the contents of the stream and it was apparent that the clear rippling water was not polluted. In his mind, he could smell fresh coffee brewing.

He returned to the site and discovered that Ralph had already started a fire and had begun to roast the rabbit. "Now it is your turn", he said, while he turned over the cooking chores to Running Deer. In the meanwhile, Ralph proceeded to brew the coffee and warm some bread which was becoming a dwindling commodity. Tonight, he thought, we should take stock of our supplies and attempt to get a bearing on our location.

After filling their stomachs with roasted rabbit, it was time to stoke up the fire for a lengthy session with their maps. At this point, it was hard to determine whether their detour by the millstream had cost them important time or whether it had been an important distraction on their journey. Only time would tell, but they hoped that they would locate the water source soon. The heartening part of the equation was that it was decided that there being an old mill in the area, there should be signs of other activity nearby. They both agreed that if life existed nearby or if there was evidence of past activity, that the old palisade might not be far away.

Ralph updated their route on his map and finally made an estimate of their location. It was estimated that they had covered approximately fifteen miles since they left the trading post five days ago. Had it not been for the detour off the intended route, he figured that they should have been within another day or two from their goal. The discovery of the old mill, however, was an interesting distraction which added to the excitement of their adventure. After all, he thought, we are re-discovering a very old place of habitation that has not been seen by man in quite a while.

How long, at this point, is hard to determine. He remembered that his grandfather had told him that maize had been a chief crop of the natives, but it wasn't 'til after the English colonists had settled the area that a method was devised to grind the grain into a finer material so that they could make bread from it. All of this stirred up questions in Ralph's mind as to when the old mill was erected for this purpose. He wondered if the new inhabitants had shown the natives this remarkable device. There must have been some interaction, he surmised, because he had heard that some natives were friendly with the new arrivals while others chose to be wary.

As his mind dwelled on these thoughts, his reverie was interrupted by a shout from Running Deer. By the light of the near-full moon, he had been looking around himself, while taking care not to stray too far from the campsite. "I have discovered a strange elevated spot near the stream that I think bears a closer look."

"Save it for tomorrow", said Ralph, "we should concentrate on a good night's sleep so we can get an early start in the morning."

Day six dawned without fanfare but it promised to be one of beauty. There was not a cloud in the sky and their surroundings seemed to be noisier than the day before. Occasionally a white heron was spotted near the stream, smaller birds twittering among the tree tops, with random grunts and growls from animals on the floor of the forest. After a refreshing night's sleep, they felt up to the task of the day.

The first thing on their agenda, after cleaning up the site, was to examine the unusual mound that Running Deer had discovered the evening before. They returned to the site and after clearing away some of the encroaching vines from around it, found it to be a rather large elongated dirt mound which was symmetrical in arrangement. From this, they deduced that it was man-made.

"So", Ralph noted, "this has to be an old Indian burial mound. If we were to clear the area, we would probably find more evidence of a village." His grandfather had told him of such arrangements in the area but had not mentioned any specific location, so perhaps this old village site had not been visited by anyone in many years.

They made a decision to make note of the mound and continue to follow the small stream. Their guess was that, before the end of the day, they would find the source of the stream. During the next hour, the stream became wider. They were still unable to hear rushing water which might have indicated that a river was nearby, but instead a gurgling sound erupted from around a bend in the stream. After testing the depth of the water, they found that they could cross over to the other side to make their way toward a louder sound.

They forded the stream without a problem and began to follow the edge hoping to locate its source. There was no sign of an old path, so they methodically hacked their way through the vines and undergrowth until they came to a clearing along the perimeter of the stream. This provided a much needed break for them because the sun was bearing down from overhead creating a thirst for fresh water. An opportunity became theirs to survey the surroundings. The gurgling water sound was louder now causing them to focus toward its direction.

Following a few minutes rest, they continued on their way up the stream until Ralph suddenly jumped backwards and let out a loud yell. Running deer stopped in his tracks, suspecting that his friend had run into trouble. When Ralph had regained his composure, he announced that he had just missed stepping on the biggest moccasin that he had ever seen. The commotion apparently scared the snake as bad as it had scared Ralph, because Running Deer caught sight of it hightailing from the scene as it slithered off into the forest. There wasn't any doubt that Ralph would pay closer attention to his footsteps.

This being the first encounter with a snake, the two were in agreement that they would probably be seeing more of them in the area. Watching out for snakes could cause them to lose time as they moved along. As they continued around a sharp bend, they found that the stream was wider and there was an increase in activity among the birds and frogs. The stream now had come to an end culminating in a larger round body of water which they discovered was created by an underground aquifer that made its way to the surface at the center.

It was impossible to determine the age of the bubbly source of water, but both Ralph and Running Deer agreed that it was discovered by an earlier group of people who took advantage of the water power to operate the old grist mill. For the most part, the water was perfectly clear all the way to the bottom giving an illusion of being shallow. As if both had thought about it at the same time, it was agreed that it was an excellent time to take a bath. Jokingly, they said that they didn't need a bath, but they didn't want their scent to drive the animals away.

Chapter Five

AFTER THEY PICKED A SUITABLE clearing on the bank, they removed their clothes and dove into the clean, clear water. At first contact, the water was chilly, but their bodies soon became acclimated to it. The depth was a surprise but both were excellent swimmers. As they swam out into the body of water, they were not cognizant of a visitor who had appeared near the bank soon after they were several yards away from it. The intruder would have been unnoticed had it not been for a cracking sound created when he moved toward the edge of the water.

The first to get a view of the person was Running Deer who was closer to the bank. It appeared to be a man, slightly built, sparsely clothed, and very hairy. His first thought concerned the safety of their clothing, hunting weapons, and most of all, their valuable maps and notes. They were in a very precarious position, so they could only hope that this person was not up to mischief. At first, the stranger moved out of their sight making it difficult to see what he was up to. Then, as if by cue, he was seen holding their clothes above his head as if to say "I have your belongings and there is nothing that you can do about it."

Presently, he began to run away from the bank and into the forest. While this was occurring, Ralph and Running Deer was swimming as fast as they could back toward the hill. This was a highly unexpected event which, no doubt, would cause more lost time. But, foremost on their mind, was to catch this intruder and retrieve their clothing and other belongings. As they neared the edge of the water where they had entered, they scrambled to get back on the hill to give chase to the thief. No thought was given to their nakedness until they were out of the water. There was no time to gather branches and leaves for a cover because the intruder was making off with their belongings, so they kept their eyes on the parting of the branches and struck out together in that direction.

It was evident in a short time that the thief was familiar with his surroundings and would be difficult to apprehend. At this point, Running Deer gave out a whistle that created a startled look on his partners face. Without giving out his secret, Running Deer was summoning his helper in need, Akimko. Within seconds, a surprised native was stopped in his tracks and was made to drop everything he had stolen on the forest floor. There was no sight of Akimko, but the flutter of wings was heard as Running Deer's assigned guardian disappeared into the forest.

Standing before them was a fearful sprite of a man with a hairy face and long black beard. His eyes displayed that fear and were as blue as the cloudless sky overhead. After discerning that he was not going to make an attempt to bolt from them, they proceeded to don their clothing. While not entirely unexpected, the appearance of the man offered an opportunity to learn more about the area they were in and possibly a chance to pin down their location. After all, had it not been for the discovery of the ancient mill, they might have been proceeding on their own to an unknown destination.

So it was time to attempt to communicate with the stranger to try and find some answers to their questions. All the while, Ralph was still puzzled as to why the thief suddenly ended his getaway. The first to speak was Ralph, who after sizing the stranger up for possible hidden weapons, asked if he could speak English. Having not yet recovered from the sudden visit by Akimko, the man remained silent. In his own mind, Running Deer had already decided that this person was not a native Indian. The skin color and blue eyes had told him that.

After a second query by Ralph, the man blurted out "yes, yes, I speak English."

"Well then", continued Ralph, "what is your name and where do you come from?"

"My name is Japheth and I live alone in a log cabin due west of here on the bank of the big Chowanoke river."

After deciding that he was not going to cause any more harm, Running Deer and Ralph invited him to share an evening meal with them. It was apparent that Japheth hadn't eaten much in quite a while.

Also, they decided that if they were lucky, they would gain more knowledge of the area that they were in.

The surrounding trees were beginning to cast a long shadow now and the heat from the sun was beginning to diminish. There was still time left to dispatch a rabbit or squirrel from the nearby thicket, so Ralph imposed upon Running Deer to keep company with Japheth while he hunted for their meal. Without complaint, Running Deer agreed so Ralph headed out into the forest, while Running Deer and Japheth proceeded to gather dry branches for the campfire so that everything would be ready when Ralph returned.

The clearing by the water was an excellent spot to spend the night so provisions were made for their beds. As stealthy as Ralph was, his movement through the bushes caught the ear of a young doe as she watered nearby. He heard the commotion as the deer jumped from the watering hole and began to sprint away into the woods. As she turned to determine the direction in which to run, Ralph got off an arrow into its direction, but the agile animal was destined to live another day. Undeterred by his failure to drop the deer, he reloaded and continued to watch closely for other potential game.

The ensuing noise had routed a male rabbit from its burrow. Before the fattened animal had gotten over the surprise visit, a stone-tipped arrow had found its mark. In the meantime, back at the campsite, Running Deer and Japheth had prepared a suitable fire-spit and were beginning to become more acquainted. At first, the two were leery of each other, but Running Deer was determined to break the ice because he wanted to know more about this person. Who knows, he thought, this man might be part of the unknown equation that will help him in his quest.

Just as Japheth was about to explain about the family that he had come from, Ralph walked out of the forest with news of a successful hunt. Before he could assign the dressing chore, Japheth said "Let me clean it. It's the least I can do to pay for my food."

There was no argument from either of the other two, so the dressing chore was handled by their unintended guest. Then it was Running Deer's turn to do his share so he placed the dressed rabbit on the makeshift spit for roasting. Bread was retrieved from their pack and warmed over the coals. There was enough for all of them, so another night would be spent with full stomachs. There was more to be learned from Japheth, so the fire was stoked with more branches and the three gathered around the light of the fire as the sun settled behind the tree tops.

The first to speak was Ralph because curiosity was about to consume him. He asked Japheth—"Are you familiar with these parts, or are you lost?" It was obvious that this person was not on a game hunt because he did not possess hunting equipment.

"I am familiar with the woods here", he said "many is the time that I have roamed hereabouts, but this is the first time that I have contacted other humans."

It was time for Running Deer to satisfy his curiosity, so he enquired—"Do you have a family, and if so, where are they?"

Before Japheth could reply, Ralph intoned, "do you have a habit of stealing wherever you go?"

There was a hint of shame as Japheth attempted to reply to Ralph's question. "I came from a very poor family and I possess very few worldly goods. The only education I have is a self-taught ability to read some books that my English forefathers passed down to me. I came from honest and hard-working folks, and to tell you the truth, if it hadn't been for that huge bird that appeared out of the blue, I probably would have returned your belongings anyway."

Running Deer smiled, but Ralph enquired—"What bird?"

"Oh, you didn't see that raptor with a monstrous wing-span swoop down and scare the daylights out of me?"

Ralph had not, and he said so. "Now you are into fancy tales, what else did those books teach you?"

Anyway, Japheth apologized for his act and continued to answer more questions as they were asked by Ralph and Running Deer. It was revealed that Japheth had a log cabin nearby where he lived with his long-widowed mother. His father had been killed in a tragic accident near the homestead some forty years before. Hewing out a living had been tough for his father and it was during the end of a harvest season when he was attempting to clear additional land for more crops. The wind had shifted to cause a huge decaying loblolly pine to fall on and pin him.

"I was a young lad", he explained, "and was unable to rescue my father. Besides the broken bones, there was a huge loss of blood. My mother was young at the time—about thirty—and was suddenly confronted with the task of raising six children."

Ralph interjected—"What happened to your siblings?"

"I aint got no siblings", he said, "two brothers were scalped by a marauding band of savages and two sisters were kidnapped and taken to live with the Indians. I aint seen hide nor hair of them since. My oldest sister passed away three years back. Old Doc Conley did not arrive in time to save her. I spect she had consumption."

This talk of family aroused the curiosity of Running Deer and he interrupted the conversation to ask Japheth—"What do you know of your ancestors and how long have they been living in these parts?"

"I knowed my granddaddy when I was just a lad", he responded, "he would sit the five of us down before the fireplace and tell us stories about his parents and grandparents. My youngest brother, Ned, had not been born yet. His stories were fascinating to us, but we didn't know what part of them were true. He was a great story teller."

"I can understand your curiosity about storytelling at that age", said Running Deer, "because I can also remember my own grandfather relating stories from his past."

At this point, Running Deer was hankering to get to the point of his questioning and blurted out—"How long has your family been living in these parts and where did they migrate from?"

Japheth had a straightforward answer for the first question and stated right out—"My grandpa told me that his grandpa came to the Chowanoke area just a few years after the English colony disappeared around 1595. He used to tell us about the colony of settlers that disappeared, but he never offered to say what he thought happened to them."

Running Deer was anxious for Japheth to get on with his story, so he probed him further. "I see by your facial features that you might have English blood in you—what with your blue eyes and Roman nose. Did your grandpa allow that your ancestors were English?"

"He did say that", replied Japheth, "and he said that his grandmother was mixed blood—part Croatoan and part English. My ma always said that my high cheek bones were characteristic of the Indians. I would love to be able to tell you more about my family, but I realize that it is getting late and there is a chill in the air."

"Never mind the late hour", said Running Deer, "your story is interesting, so lets gather some more branches. We'll stoke the fire and we can hear more of your story."

Although Ralph was taking all of this in, he interrupted the conversation and said—"I think your story is very interesting, but I am interested in the old mill". So he asked Japheth if he knew any history of the mill, and if so, how long it had been since it was in working order.

"My memory is somewhat faded", he replied, "but I do remember going with my grandpappy on a few occasions to take corn to the mill to have ground. Its been a long time ago. There was a path from our cabin which was well trod and the journey to the mill took most of a day. I remember skipping along ahead and yelling back to him to hurry up. Of course, he was getting along in years and could not walk very fast on account of his aching bones. Anyway, on a short fall day, it was close to sunset when we arrived at the mill. There was no time left to do any grinding, so we would clear a place to spend the night. We were always ready to drink the cool clear water from the stream, so it was a welcome sight for us. The original operator of the mill, an old half-breed named Buck Thorne, had passed away several years prior and each user of the mill was expected to grind his own corn. The old mill was well constructed and had been built by an Englishman who had happened upon the underground source of water. It is said that the Indians had given it the name of Lost Water because of its unknown source."

"A remarkable story", added Ralph. "So when your grandpappy passed away, there was no more activity at the mill and it went into decay."

"That's right", answered Japheth, "there were very few other users and they have long since died. Development has been slow on this part of the river and there has been no interest among the settlers to revive it."

Afraid that he would forget one question that he wanted to pose to Japheth, Running Deer spoke up. "You said that your grandfather's grandmother was part English and part Indian. Do you know anything at all of her parents?"

"I do not", declared Japheth, "but I always wondered where the English side came in. Since this would have been about the time of the exploring English, I have often thought that one or the other could have been an English settler."

"Sounds interesting", continued Running Deer. "Now I am going to ask you a more personal question. Do you have a theory as to the fate of the so-called lost colony?"

"I, like you", replied Japheth, "have heard many different stories about that, but none have contained any proof. My personal thinking is that they were not killed by savages, but I have nothing more than that. It is possible that the colonists were near starvation and out of necessity went to live with the friendlier tribes and later intermarried. It has always been a desire of mine to learn the truth."

"What difference does it make?", asked Ralph, "most of the Indians have dispersed and more English settlers have arrived at Jamestown in Virginia. Migration has begun in our direction and pretty soon the white men with their fancy tools will clear out the forest around us to grow their crops and build their cabins made of logs. It is no longer a secret that a sticky substance can be taken from the loblollies that can be turned into a caulking material to better seal logs and the hull of their boats. A small missing colony of Englishmen is just a tiny part of history."

Running Deer wanted to chastise his friend for belittling his quest of history, but then he knew it would be better to play along with the conversation in order not to divulge his real business at hand. Ralph had been a true friend and skillful guide so he wanted to keep the relationship viable. His only reply to Ralph's statement was—"You're probably right—I only wanted to get better acquainted with our visitor."

Time had been forgotten during their conversation and without dissent, the three of them made ready for bed. The fall air was prevalent this night, but with their fur covering, it was tolerable. A slight wind blew in from the west but the dense forest was an ample shelter. It would have been a different scene if there had been any rainfall.

Sometime during the night, Running Deer had a dream that was later followed by a revelation of sorts. The dream had to do with his grandpa and a hunting trip. The two of them had bundled up and headed toward the river, where they stepped into a small boat and began to paddle downstream. His grandpa's dog, Jacob, was following along on the bank just like he had done many times before. Grandpa always said Jacob was looking after him more than attending to his hunting chores.

On this occasion, the dog suddenly darted away from the bank and headed into the deep woods. Grandpa said "he's after something" and he immediately headed the boat for the shore. He told me to grab the anchor rope and get ready to jump out. As he grabbed for his gun, he tripped on the seat causing the gun to go off prematurely. The loud blast of the gun apparently awakened Running Deer causing him to sit up and survey his surroundings. The first thing he was aware of was that it was still night, so he looked around for his companions. He noticed that Japheth was nowhere to be seen but Ralph was snoring away.

Curious, he thought, that Japheth would have left the campsite, but he had just as suddenly appeared on the scene when they met him. Nevertheless, Running Deer quietly arose, donned his animal skin vest, and proceeded to look around for Japheth. There was no evidence of anything being taken until he suddenly thought to check his map. Shuffling through his back-pack, he was unable to find it. His first inclination was to dart into the forest and try to find this man who was up to his old tricks.

Momentarily, a question came to his mind. Why would Japheth be interested in his map? He wouldn't dwell on that answer long, though, because it entered his mind that there was only one way to recover it. Stepping slightly into the thicket away from Ralph, he whistled for his feathered friend, Akimko, whereby the plans of Japheth were abruptly halted. No time was wasted in consummating the arrest. He was already half a mile away from the site when Running Deer heard the fluttering of wings that led him to the half-breed who could not believe how soon he had forgotten about that first encounter with the bird.

Running Deer did not have to ask Japheth for the map because he gladly shoved it toward him.

"I am truly sorry", Japheth blurted out, "please forgive me for being a common thief."

"You are forgiven", replied Running Deer, "but I am curious. What were you planning to do with the map?"

Japheth turned his head slightly as though he was hesitant to answer the question. But then, as if he no longer wanted to keep a secret to himself, he looked his questioner straight in the eyes and came clean.

"I must tell you", he said, "I am on the same quest as you are but I have never been able to locate the site of the old fort that protected the missing colonists. I have long suspected that I am a descendant of one of those people. For years I have had a burning desire to locate the source and have a better chance of finding the answer. I never had much schooling, but Pa always said I was smart."

"So you figured your chances would be better if you had my map", interrupted Running Deer.

"That is true", he said, "and I figured that I could work better alone since I am already familiar with these here woods."

Suddenly Running Deer thought about Ralph back at the campsite, and figured that he had better get back there. His better judgment told him that he probably should make a deal with Japheth and invite him to join them on the balance of the journey. So he extended a hand to Japheth and asked if he would like to join them on their quest.

Japheth's eyes lit up and he said "sure, I'd be obliged to."

After the handshake, Running Deer could not help but set forth a final condition that Japheth would not attempt to run away or steal anything from them. Japheth turned his face to the sky and broke out in raucous laughter. Running Deer joined him because he knew that any other attempt to steal would be taken care of by Akimko. He suspected that Japheth would not be willing to chance it again.

After a second handshake, the two made their way back to the campsite. Dawn had not yet broken, so they carefully navigated the bramble and vines in the predominately loblolly thicket. The distance was not far, so they arrived back at the site shortly to find Ralph still snoring away. The sound of the snoring had indeed served as a beacon for the last fifty or so yards. They decided to join him for a little more shut-eye.

When the three awakened, not a word was mentioned to Ralph about the night's activities. The first thing on the agenda was a hot cup of coffee brewed from Ralph's special blend. There were lingering coals still on the campfire, so it was just a matter of stoking it with additional branches. Warmed gherkin and scones were passed around until all were fed sufficient to begin a new day.

Since the events of the last two days had been unplanned, it was time—Ralph thought—to do some serious planning. After all, their supplies were getting short, and that in itself might be a good reason for concern. In the past he had relied heavily on his hunting acumen for a journey such as this, but he worried that with age he might have lost some of his skills. He had determined in his mind, though, that he would not mention these thoughts to his traveling companions. He felt obligated to Running Deer since it was he, himself, who had suggested the trip together. He continued to have misgivings about Japheth but did not waver in his allegiance to Running Deer.

He stretched his crude map on a stump and began to calculate their location given their detour from the old mill. He figured by setting his compass on a more northeasterly course, that after a days journey, they should be back on the original trail. Running Deer's calculations were in synch with Ralph's and they didn't bother to include Japheth in the decision. This was a mistake on their part because if they had followed their reckoning, they would have been several critical miles off course at the end of a day's journey.

Japheth said "I hate to put your knowledge to question, but if you follow the route that you are proposing, you will head directly towards a bend in the river and I am aware that you will have to cross it. It will be much better for all of us if we cross at the ferry."

Ralph interjected that he did not think that they would have to cross the Chowanoke, but he gave his map a closer inspection. Upon looking at it again, he located the ferry crossing that Japheth had referred to. Running Deer then unfolded his map which he knew would settle the question once and for all.

Without giving away the source for his map, Running Deer nodded and said "Japheth, you are right, we need to set our course in a northwesterly direction."

Japheth was pleased that Running Deer was in agreement and he hoped that Ralph would be also. Ralph said "it looks like its two to one, so I am not about to set off on a course by myself." He also warned that the longer trail would certainly diminish their supplies. "I suspect", he said, "that we had better start hunting for food even if it slows us down."

"Well then, its settled", noted Running Deer.

After this, all three began cleaning the campsite in order to get an early start on what appeared to be a good day for moving into the unknown wilderness. They made sure their hunting tools were easily accessible so they would not pass up an opportunity for a fresh game meal. The location of the millstream was carefully noted by Running Deer as he mulled over in his mind those landmarks that might prove to be useful in his quest.

Making sure that there were no cinders left at the fire site, and nothing was left behind, the trio plunged into day seven of Running Deer and Ralph's quest. Their new companion was pleased to be accompanying them. All three had bathed in the pond on the previous eve making the closeness more bearable. It would have been more desirable for a clothes change, but they had to settle for a partial cleaning of their attire. A few basic rules were discussed to acquaint Japheth with their method of travel. First, he was told that they were to stay in earshot of each other, and second, they were to keep on the lookout and notify each other of lurking dangers.

"I've always been a loner", Japheth responded, "but I appreciate your way of doing things. You will have no trouble from me—I am anxious for our success."

With that behind, they looked straight ahead into a dense undergrowth which would become their first obstacle. Knives at the ready, they began hacking their way into the unknown. After about three hours, they could look back and almost see their point of departure in the distance. Fall was coming on but the bright overhead sun was causing them to be thirsty due to heavy perspiration. Their fresh water supply was diminishing and causing some concern.

Japheth summoned Running Deer and Ralph for a conference. The three of them joined together, sitting on a huge fallen tree trunk, relishing the break from constant hacking.

Japheth said "according to instinct but mostly from my memory of an old landmark, we should change courses slightly and head toward that yonder tall loblolly."

At first Ralph thought that the hot sun was playing tricks on Japheth's brain, but Running Deer interrupted to say "I see it, I see it—and by the size of it, it must be an ancient landmark."

Ralph retorted "its not that far off course, so let's go for it."

It was hard to determine how far away the tree was, but one thing was in their favor. The undergrowth was not as thick in that direction, so maybe they would not have to toil as hard as they moved slowly toward it. After two hours into the new direction, they calculated the distance covered to be about one mile. The sun was beginning to swing over toward the horizon and it appeared to be setting in the same direction of their travel.

Presently, a faint sound was heard in the distance that could not be connected to a forest animal. They stopped in their tracks and zoomed into the source of the sound. The more they listened, the more it sounded like children playing. At this particular location, they had lost sight of the tall tree, but at other times, there had been sufficient clearing to make it out. In a few minutes, they sighted it again and it appeared to be in the same direction as the source of the sound.

Japheth volunteered to serve as scout and it was agreed that they should cease their hacking and hold back until they receive news from him. It was a welcome break for Ralph and Running Deer. They would take advantage of this time to re-assess their situation.

Ralph was the first to speak. "You know, friend, I might be wrong, but I have a feeling that we should have let Japheth go on his way. I smell nothing but trouble."

Running Deer thought long before he responded. "I realize that you cannot trust everyone you meet and I agree that we have to be cautious, but let's give him the benefit of the doubt. He may turn out to be a valuable asset."

Ralph agreed to go along with Running Deer's suggestion, and after about thirty minutes, Japheth returned with news of his finding. "There is a village", he said, "but it is hard to estimate the number of inhabitants. I saw one elderly person in the process of feeding a lone animal near a crude shed. On one side of the living quarters, there was a clearing that supposedly is a field for growing food products."

"We should decide", interrupted Running Deer, "whether we should explore further or go quietly on our way."

Ralph, the inquisitive one, suggested that they investigate further for the possibility of a source of food. Running Deer, the practical one, but not one to pass up a possible clue for discovery, agreed and said "lets go for it."

Outnumbered, Japheth reluctantly agreed, also. After all, he was familiar with the good and the bad that he had experienced while roaming about the forest. Maybe this could be a new experience.

Moving closer together, the three pioneers began to move out with Japheth in lead. As they moved closer toward the cabin that Japheth had described, it became apparent that more people were in residence.

The sound of playing children resumed and another person seemed to be in the process of gathering dry branches for a fire. Suddenly from their rear, there appeared a presence without warning. They turned and were facing the business end of a dangerous spear-like hunting tool that was wielded by a half-naked man.

Caught by surprise, the men raised their arms to await the next move of the strange adversary. He mumbled some instructions which was not understood. With a nod and a move by the other hand, he motioned for them to keep walking towards the crude cabin. They were reluctant to discuss among themselves the question of attempting to elude this strange man, so they continued to follow his instructions.

A well-worn path led to a compound of scattered sheds, a stable, several pig sties, and eventually to a small building that appeared to be living quarters. If there were other adults on the premises, they were purposely hiding. Four young children ranging in age from two to eight or nine could be seen peeking around the corner of the main structure. Running Deer secretly wished that there were more light, but the sun had begun to sink lower than the tree tops to create a shadowy scene of dark green figures. He was hoping, also, that their captor had less than evil intentions for the sake of their welfare.

There was an elaborate lean-to that had been fixed to two trees supposedly for the purpose of stretching and drying animal hides. This told him that the man had been involved in fur trading and that probably there was a trading post nearby. As his mind wandered, he was interrupted by a surprise move by Japheth. He turned to the man with the spear and seemed to converse fluently with him. Ralph looked at Running Deer and without saying a word, conveyed the thought of having been taken.

The quarter moon was not in sight yet so darkness was beginning to enfold them. As they neared the door to the main building, a flicker of light emanated from within. Japheth was the first to go inside, then as if by a welcome gesture, the spear wielder motioned for them to enter. Sitting at a small table, was a brightly adorned black-haired woman with piercing blue eyes. Running Deer guessed her age to be in the mid-thirties and her unblemished skin revealed a light tan color.

Japheth had seated himself already, so Running Deer and Ralph were shone fur-lined seats near an apparent dining area. The first to speak was Japheth who first introduced Jed Desmond to Running Deer and Ralph. Then in a change of dialect, he introduced both of them to the man and woman. When Running Deer and Ralph reached out to shake their hand, they were not met with a customary greeting, but instead a slight bow with right hands to their heart.

It was difficult for Running Deer to understand such a greeting, but he was willing to accept it as a hopeful sign of welcome. By this time, four young children had assembled themselves in a corner of the cramped quarters beaming questioning eyes at the visitors. It was evident to Running Deer that these were not native Indians, yet he did not rule out the possibility that they were a mixed breed.

Japheth was conversing with the hostess as if the two had known each other for a while. After about three minutes, he turned to face Running Deer and Ralph and said "I want you to meet Diana Silver Fox, my sister, who is pleased to prepare a meal for my friends." He could detect the consternation in their faces, so he assured them that there would be plenty of time for explaining.

"By the way", he said, "Jed is not my sister's husband. He is a long time friend and caretaker. Diana's husband was killed in an ambush by unfriendly natives."

Jed did not have to be instructed, so he proceeded to prepare for a fire in the crude fireplace in order to cook their meal. When the fire was amply stoked with wood, Jed disappeared from them a few minutes, returning with a sizable cut of meat that appeared to be dried venison. While the meal preparation was taking place, Running Deer was anxious to find out if Diana could speak any English, so he moved closer to her and blurted right out "I beg your pardon, do you know English?"

In response to his query, she glanced at Japheth, as if seeking his approval before she answered the question. With a nod from her brother, she proceeded to unbutton her shirt at the neck revealing horrendous scars all about her throat. Running Deer understood this to mean that she could not speak. Japheth explained that during the attack by the natives that took her husband's life, there was an attempt to cut her throat and end her life too, but she was miraculously saved by faking death. The children were unharmed but left alone to be with their dying mother.

Japheth revealed that he was living in a nearby cabin at the time and happened on the scene shortly after the attackers had fled the scene. The motive for the killing was robbery. Japheth explained that Samuel Johnston, Diana's husband, had accumulated a large amount of animal pelts that were nearing the end of the drying process which would soon have been taken to the trading post for sale. It had been an unusually good hunting year created by exceptionally favorable weather conditions.

It was known by Samuel that there were unfriendly and hostile natives that lived to the north and east of them. A small skirmish had alerted him of their presence a few years prior. Since there hadn't been any trouble for quite a while, the ambush was quite a surprise. Running Deer's mind raced back to the incident in which Ananias White had lost his life in that violent storm. Although there was a difference in the two incidents—in both cases—a mother was left with young children to raise. In the best of times, the wilderness was no place to rear a family without a man.

He expressed his sympathy to Diana as best he could and made up his mind that there was more exploring to do concerning this family. He then summoned his buddy Ralph to join him for some serious planning.

"First things first", said Ralph, "the aroma from this here cooking pot has permeated my taste buds and I fear that my stomach is becoming angry."

Running Deer agreed that they would join the Johnstons in the evening meal. It was the highest form of hospitality and, besides, it had been a while since they had partaken of a scrumptious home-cooked meal. Diana had begun to set the round cypress table with her best hand-hewn plates and Chinese silverware that had been acquired a few years back from the trading post. There was ample seating to accommodate the guests because the hostess was visited frequently by her kinfolk. The nearest one, a sister, lived with her mother a few miles inland.

Their visits were limited to once a year, though, due to the hazardous conditions of the dense forest and the possibility of being set on by unfriendly natives or thieves. Their visit this year had been during the previous spring after the last winter's frost. She had not heard from her family since the last visit, but she had taken the view that "no news" was "good news". Outside news, she explained, was a rarity but occasionally hunters would stop by to share recent happenings.

Diana motioned for her guests to take a seat while she filled each plate with an ample serving of tenderized and stewed venison. Oven baked bread was placed in the middle of the table along with a knife to cut it. Jed produced a pottery jug which he had retrieved from the rear of the house that was dripping water. A wooden cup was set before each diner and filled to the brim with a red bubbly wine. It was his special blend which he had fermented from last year's grapes and cooled to perfection in the stream that flowed behind the cabin. Diana had boiled some nondescript greens which were dished out to have with the meat.

The hour was getting late while everyone savored their meal. There was small talk attempted among the group but Running Deer and Ralph were determined to not get involved with a discussion of their plans until they had finished their meal. Even so, Running Deer could not help but contemplate a conversation with Diana. He even wondered how this might happen, but he reasoned that even though she couldn't speak, she could hear and convey her part of a conversation through writing.

No thought had been given to arrangements for sleeping at the small cabin, but what he did not know was that his gracious hostess had already prepared accommodations for them. In the rear of the cabin, not visible from the eating area, was a row of pallets with comfortable corn shuck mattresses always available for unannounced visitors.

After everyone finished their meal, Jed moved quietly around the table to collect the utensils and plates. In very short order, the table appeared as if nothing had happened there. As if Diana had read his mind, she motioned for Running Deer and Ralph to join her at an ample square table on which she had placed a small oil lamp. The table had been converted from one of the seats at the dining table. There was papyrus placed in the center along with a writing quill and ink.

She smiled and looked at one and then the other. Ralph nodded in Running Deer's direction, indicating that he was the one who was loaded with questions. Running Deer took the hint and started by telling Diana how thankful they were for the meal and feebly tried to convey their appreciation for the hospitality overall.

With a slight smile and a hunch of the shoulders, she seemed to be saying to them "I am pleased that you are pleased, but I have done nothing special."

Ralph excused himself and announced that he was going to turn in. Japheth followed suit while Jed led the young children away to an area that was partitioned off from the other beds. This left Running Deer alone with Diana Silver Fox. Even though he was anxious to interrogate her, he considered himself to be at an awkward disadvantage. She seemed anxious to communicate, but he wondered how to break the ice. As the lamplight flickered causing shadows to play around her face, he was aware of her perpetual smile.

To break the silence, he asked how long she had been living at this location. She seemed pleased to reply and immediately began to write her answer with immaculate penmanship.

"I grew up in this place", she wrote. "my mother and father settled here around 1650 when it was very difficult to live with the Indian natives. Sometimes it was a matter of moving several times before it was thought safe enough to settle down. We were fortunate to have some half-breeds for neighbors. My father told me that his father, an early colonist, had fallen in love and had married my grandmother who was full blooded Croatoan."

"So your father", interrupted Running Deer, "was half Croatoan and half English?"

"That is true", she penned, "my father told me that on one or two occasions, my grandfather mentioned that his ancestors were driven from their homes by hostile savages. Their home was north of here near the Indian village of Manteo."

Even though the hour was late and he knew that he needed the rest, Running Deer was anxious to continue the awkward conversation with Diana. She sensed his weariness and wrote that they could continue to "talk" on the morrow. Even though his body was tired from the days happenings, his mind was like an insatiable sponge, anxious to soak up every tidbit of information that would form clues to help him in his quest. Diana showed him to his shuck-mattress bed. Afterwards, she retired to her own partitioned room that adjoined the living area.

At last, Running Deer was alone. He was careful to place his personal belongings, along with his clothes, underneath the bed. The night was quiet, the air invigorating, and a bright light from the waxing moon shined through a crack in the wall near the front entrance. He hadn't planned it, but the circumstances at hand, with events fresh in his mind, led him to try to put clues together from the past seven days.

He thought about the carving on the tree trunk, the non-native type burial site, and of course the ancient grist mill.

The only clue that previous researchers had talked about was the carving of the word "CROATOAN" on a tree trunk. This led folks to conclude that the small colony of Englishmen were captured and forcibly taken away to a Croatoan village. There they were killed or forced to become slaves for the tribe. After all, the natives were dependent upon their corn crops for sustenance. And further, some of the younger females were probably forced to intermarry with the young braves.

All of this was told to Running Deer by Chief Waccasaw. The problem with this theory was that there was never any evidence found in the years following that supported it. As for the unmarked grave, he was almost sure that an Englishman had been buried by his compatriots or family while on the run. After so many years, though, he despaired of finding any clues as to its owner. When his mind drifted back to the old water-powered mill, he envisioned an industrious Englishman, who had settled in that spot with his family after eluding some unfriendly natives. It was hard for him to imagine that all of the inhabitants of this new world would be an unfriendly sort.

Having given up on receiving supplies from the mother country, by the arrival of fellow Englishmen, he had no choice but to improvise for the survival of his family. He further supposed that the man probably had a wife and one or more children. Realizing that all of this was speculation, he still knew that all clues discovered should not be overlooked as they might become valuable to him. He had not given much thought as to what he would do when Ralph was no longer around, but he had already accepted the idea that Ralph's presence was part of the overall plan to help him fulfill his quest.

In any event, he felt that an important part of the journey was now behind him, so he would concentrate now on locating the old fort in the days ahead. "Tonight, I will take advantage of beautiful weather and a comfortable place to lay my head", he thought, "and then on the morrow, I will converse more with my gracious hostess. After that, I will go over our plans with Ralph before we set out toward the mainland."

Although there was loud snoring from one quarter, sleep came quickly. Sometime, in early morning, came the forlorn cry of a whippoorwill that awakened and startled the inhabitants. The sound was thought to be too loud to be genuine, but instead could be a signal between prowlers. Running Deer grabbed for his clothes which were at ready and at the same time reached for his trusty knife. He was not the first to exit the cabin, because Ralph was outside searching around the premises.

They both knew a whippoorwill sound, but there was something different about this one. The sound came a few hours before dawn, which is the usual time for their call. Running Deer re-entered the cabin to inform the others to be real quiet and not move around. After doing this, he joined Ralph on the outside to scout the area. A plan was devised to split up in case there was an attempt at ambush.

The light from the third quarter moon had subsided since it had moved closer to the horizon. While they listened, another signal came from farther away. Running Deer assumed that either the intruders had been surprised by the two as they exited from the cabin or there was an attempt to summon others from the dark woods to move in closer. He thought that it was essential to remain near the quarters in case there was an attempted raid.

Moments later, a figure suddenly appeared at his back accompanied by a loud raucous whooping noise. Taking advantage of the darkness, he turned to face his attacker and at the same time, moved quickly to one side. His assailant missed his mark by a few inches, giving Running Deer an advantage that would prove to be a defeat for his adversary. He quickly brandished his knife with his left hand while he landed a right fist to the solar plexus. The well placed right was not needed because the knife had dealt a mortal blow.

The quick reaction by Running Deer immobilized his attacker having the effect of saving his own life and possibly the lives of those in the cabin. In the meantime, his friend Ralph, was not so fortunate. Running Deer moved quickly through the darkness to join him and it appeared to Running Deer that a simultaneous attack had caught him by surprise. Hearing no signal from his partner, Ralph's attacker had quickly fled the scene.

Arriving at the scene of the ambush, he found that Ralph was still alive but in excruciating pain. So, without hesitation, he made his way to the cabin to seek help. As he approached the front of the cabin, he noticed all of the inhabitants except the children were standing near the doorway. To save valuable time, he instructed Japheth to fetch a lantern and follow him back to the fallen Ralph. Japheth, being very familiar with the interior of the cabin, spent very little time inside before he was back by Running Deer's side with the light. He motioned for Jed to follow them in case they needed his help.

As they approached the location where Ralph laid, they heard a groan which indicated that he was still alive but in much pain. Not knowing what they would find, they were ready to do whatever was necessary to save him. Running Deer and Ralph had become close friends but had managed to keep their feelings to themselves. It was times like this that would show the true meaning of a close friendship. It was he who reached Ralph first and he didn't like what he saw.

There was a puddle of blood underneath his prone body and evidence that his throat had been slit. His pupils were beginning to roll back in their socket and there was no movement except his right arm. He was attempting to reach for his throat but was too weak to place his hand there. Running Deer immediately sensed the seriousness of his wound and directed the other two to gently pick him up and head for the cabin. He would go on ahead and instruct Diana to prepare a comfortable place on which to lay him while they assessed the seriousness of his wound.

It didn't take long to see that he would not be able to lose much more blood if he was going to survive. Like a veteran caregiver, Diana soon gathered enough cloth strips to stanch the blood flow. The job before them now was to try to locate a doctor to sew up the wound. Time was of the essence because there was no way to tell how much blood had already been lost.

Japheth was the first to speak up and said "I know where a doctor is, but it will take almost a half day to reach him. Then it will take another half day to arrive back here."

"We have no choice", Running Deer said, "we must act quickly if we are to save his life."

At this point, Running Deer was helpless because of unfamiliarity of the area. As a result, he knew that he had no alternative but to trust Japheth with his friend's life. This was not a good feeling, but one he must live with. The fact that it would be a full four hours before daylight added grave concern. A special herbal tea prepared by Diana was now being ingested by Ralph and helping to abate the pain. In the meantime, the flow of blood had been slowed but not completely stopped by the crude tourniquet that had been applied by Diana.

Daybreak arrived and Japheth had not been able to reach the doctor. Traveling in the dark, he had strayed away from the old path, but he felt that his memory would not betray him. As the sun began to rise over the tree tops, he was able to correct his direction. A half hour was required to place him back on the right path where he would attempt to make up for lost time. Three more hours had passed before Dr. Johnson's compound came into view.

Dr. Phineas Johnson was in his seventh decade and had been in the same location for about forty of those years. His makeshift quarters was not located in a dense residential area but folks within a fifty mile radius was well familiar with his humanitarian deeds. He had received his training at the prestigious Boston Medical College and then had chosen the wilderness of North Carolina as his place of practice. No one ever completely understood the choice but it is certain that the need for medical care was lacking in this new area of colonization.

This thought was on the mind of Japheth as he ran up to the entrance of the cabin. A polite and petite woman answered a knock at the door. "Yes, what can I do for you?" was her greeting.

"I have come for the doctor", stammered Japheth. "There is a man at my sister's cabin who is badly hurt. His life depends on the doctor's attention."

The little lady acknowledged his concern and sought to calm him down. "The doctor is on a house call and is not expected back until noon." "However", she said, "he has left instructions for emergency help in his absence. If you will explain the nature of your friend's wounds, I might be able to instruct you on how to proceed with his care."

"The man is losing blood", replied Japheth, "I fear for his life if he is not attended to soon. In fact, it might already be too late."

"It is unfortunate", said the lady, "but even though we are fortunate to have Doctor Phineas in our neck of the woods, it is impossible to respond to all occurrences. We are fortunate, however, that he has written specific instructions for handling many wounds including animal attack, snake bite, or even an attack at the hands of savages. So if you will tell me what happened and try to explain the extent of the wound, I will follow the doctor's instructions, as best I can, to tell you what to do. Then, as soon as he arrives back here, I will relay the information to him so that he will be prepared when he reaches your sister's cabin."

"The Indian", began Japheth, "—and I am almost certain that he was a vicious savage—stealthily snuck up behind Ralph, the victim, and slit his throat before he was scared off by his friend, Running Deer. As soon as Running Deer reported the attack to us, we were able to pick him up from the dark woods and take him into the cabin. My sister, Diana, was able to slow the blood flow, but when I left the cabin to come here, I did not know the real extent of the wound. I do know that he was in excruciating pain."

Japheth, visibly shaken, hoped that he had not left out anything. One thing he did know, however, he was going to have to depend on the little lady.

She hurriedly began to instruct Japheth on how to attend to Ralph's wounds under the circumstances. Japheth listened closely but his concern for Ralph was intensifying by the minute. Even if he were able to follow the little lady's instructions closely, he would lose a lot of time on his return trip. Though his knowledge of his grandma's God was scanty, he lifted both hands to the sky and mumbled a plea for guidance. The morning sun had risen to a place in the heavens that it seemed to cast bright bars of light through the surrounding forest that was punctuated by the stately oaks that surrounded the doctor's cabin. The scene was reassuring to Japheth as he thanked the lady and turned to begin his four hour trip back. Maybe, with good luck, he could reduce that.

In the meantime, back in the deep woods, Ralph had lost more blood and was moving in and out of consciousness. The three adults were making him as comfortable as possible under the circumstances, but each had an unspoken grave concern that he would not last much longer. Few words were spoken as the children went about their daily chores. Many things ran through Running Deer's mind, but uppermost was the fate of his dear friend. Although he had not confided in Ralph as to the real reason for his journey, he felt that there was a reason that the two had met.

Alternative plans began to form in his mind, but at the same time, he was not willing to give up on Ralph. Fits of longing for sleep began to intrude but he managed to not give in to them. He had asked Diana to sleep some during the night because he knew that there wasn't anything more she could do to help. She reluctantly did so and now that she had awakened, she urged Running Deer to trust her to watch over Ralph while he, too, could get some much needed rest.

Afraid of what he might see, Running Deer looked reluctantly in on Ralph whose paling appearance had worsened, but he seemed to be breathing without undue labor. He could not know the real extent of damage and his only hope was that the doctor would be arriving soon. His eyelids were weighing heavy now and as he settled on the bed, sleep came to him suddenly. After Diana assured Jed that she could handle the situation, he also closed his eyes, but he refused to move from his location close by Ralph.

Though Running Deer slept soundly, at some point he began to dream. There was a vision of Chief Waccasaw who had appeared in a dark cloud. At first, he seemed far away, but as the scene began to materialize, his royal regalia gave contrast to the parting clouds. His headdress shined so that the dark clouds seemed to fade away. As Running Deer watched in awe, the chief placed his hand upon his shoulder and began to speak with strong but reassuring vigor.

"Do not be troubled, my son. Your friend will live, but he will not be able to continue journey with you."

As the chief spoke, all fear seemed to leave Running Deer and he no longer questioned his ability to go it alone. He had learned tremendously from their experiences together and would use this knowledge as he continued on his own to complete his journey. The dream did not awaken him, so he was able to continue sleeping without further interference, enabling him to gain much rest.

Japheth was making better progress on his return trip, but it would still be another two hours or so before he would arrive with the instructions for medical help. In the meantime, Dr. Johnson had arrived back from his house call a little earlier than he had expected. He was spent from his trip, but when apprised of Japheth's visit by the little lady, he felt that it was urgent enough for him to freshen up, pack his medical supplies and equipment, and set out to Diana's. He had been there before, but it had been a long time.

Dr. Johnson kept a small horse at his place that he used whenever the paths were open enough to allow it. He decided to saddle the horse so that he would be able to make more time on at least part of the journey. His chief concern was that he would be able to arrive in time to save the victim's life. In this wilderness setting, he had been confronted many times with serious wounds, but this time he knew that loss of much blood was his enemy. As he had done many times before, he turned his head toward the sky and asked for Godspeed and guidance to save another human life.

Back at the cabin, Diana was keeping close checks on the patient. He was having occasional fits of pain, but she managed to keep him still. His color was not good at all and her hope for help in time was beginning to wane. As much as she fought it, she could not keep from dozing off. Each time she awoke, she placed wet cloths on Ralph's forehead. She knew that it would help to abate the fever.

Running Deer was still sleeping soundly while the sun was approaching its high noon position. The children were told by their mother to do more than a fair share of their chores and to hold the noise down because of the worsening condition of their guest. Jed, in the meantime, without being told what to do, began to fix some vittles for the family. It was of utmost importance that everyone be kept in top physical shape. There had been times in the past when food supplies had to be rationed, but due to good weather and a good hunting season, everything was plentiful, so Jed prepared a scrumptious meal for the inhabitants and their guests.

Diana said that she wasn't hungry but would try to eat enough to stay alert. The children, however, was starving and was ready for one of their favorite meals prepared by Uncle Jed. By now, Running Deer had awakened, and was in the process of stretching his waking muscles. Japheth had not arrived back, but he reckoned that he should be coming soon, hopefully accompanied by the doctor.

After arising, Running Deer hastened to Diana's side to check on Ralph's condition. Not much had changed except he noticed that he was losing color. His flesh was paler due to additional loss of blood even though the flow had decreased. Lack of real medical knowledge had kept him from releasing any pressure on the tourniquet. He would sporadically groan with pain but the pangs were becoming weaker.

Running Deer managed to devour his meal and saw to it that Diana tried to eat while he watched over Ralph. The afternoon sun now was slowly moving around to the west and still no sign of Japheth and the doctor. Ralph was having periodic fits of delirium, but each time, they were weaker. Their hopes for his survival was lessening by the hour. He looked upon his friend and didn't like what he saw. As he turned around to place a fresh cloth on the wound, he heard unfamiliar hoof-beats in the distance.

Doc Johnson had traveled a more familiar route to the cabin and would arrive there before Japheth. Running Deer's spirit was lifted somewhat by the sound even though he wasn't sure that help was on the way. "Somehow", he thought, "a miracle must happen and just maybe a miracle was on it's way." The sounds were getting louder now and he moved quickly to the outside where he saw a man on horseback making his way toward the cabin. As the person moved closer, he recognized a black bag hanging from the side of the steed and decided that this must be his "miracle".

From his many years of experience, Doctor Johnson didn't waste time on formalities, but went straight into the cabin after tethering his horse. After a short exchange with Diana, he sat down beside Ralph and opened his bag. He removed the first aid bandage from the wound to assess the extent of it. Without making a comment, he reached into his bag and retrieved an instrument. He proceeded to clean the area and at the same time, he alerted Diana to prepare some warm water and stand by to help as he began to suture the long gash on Ralph's throat and neck.

He began to respond weakly to the activity going on, so the doc administered a sedative to lessen the pain. The process of cleaning the area was going smoothly with Diana's help. Running Deer felt helpless, but he remained close by while Jed saw to it that the children stayed out of view. In the meanwhile, Japheth was making his way back through the wilderness. He calculated that he was within a half hour of the cabin and not knowing that Doctor Johnson had taken a different route and had already arrived, he constantly listened for a sound that somehow he knew he wouldn't hear. After all, he had no way of knowing that the doc had already arrived at the house. He could only hope that help would arrive in time to save Ralph's life.

Back at Diana's, the clean-up had been done and Doc Johnson had begun the slow process of suturing the wound. Ralph was still out of it, but his vital signs remained fairly good. The doctor instructed Diana to mix a potion from a powdered substance that he handed her. The patient had lost so much blood that they would have to begin immediately to try to build his strength back. The doctor did not waste any time as he continued the suturing process, and at the same time, instructing Diana to administer the life saving potion to assist in keeping his vital signs up to par.

"He probably will live", the doctor said, "but his survival will depend upon the proper treatment in the days and weeks ahead."

There was a common sigh of relief as the words were spoken. Little thought was given as to why the incident had happened, while it was agreed by all that the outcome could have been much worse.

Due to the late hour, Dr. Johnson agreed to spend the night at the cabin after he had done all that he could and had seen that the patient was resting comfortably and all vital signs were passable under the circumstances. He would leave early the next morning after taking another look at Ralph and joining them in a hearty breakfast. Sometimes food was all the doctor received for his service and more than likely, that would be the case this time.

Running Deer requested a private word with the doc as the others were preparing for a much needed rest. The two of them walked outside into the darkening shadows created by the setting sun. Running Deer expressed his concern that the attack on his friend was not an isolated event, that others might be forthcoming. As the two were conferring, sounds of cracking bushes were heard in the distance. Running Deer, ever on the alert, ran inside to grab his knife and bow. Before he could open the door, he spotted Japheth jogging toward the cabin. He was surprised to see Doc Johnson standing there and did a double-take with a clearing of the eyes.

"You gave me a start", cried Running Deer, "unknowing if something had befallen you, we didn't know when to expect you." After expressing his elation at seeing him, he jokingly asked Japheth where he had been.

Before replying, he had spotted the doc's mount tethered around back. "I now know why", he said, "Doctor Johnson could not have possibly beaten me back here on foot." He also expressed his concern that he had worried all the way back that the doc would arrive too late to save Ralph's life. He then went inside to join Diane and the others while Running Deer and Doctor Johnson remained outside.

Running Deer gave Doctor Johnson a brief explanation of circumstances surrounding his and Ralph's appearance at the little wilderness cabin. He explained that the two of them were on a quest to locate an old fort near the head of the Chowanoke river. Without divulging details, he would only say that it was an historical quest.

Doctor Johnson interrupted him to say—"I have heard of such a place, but during my many years in the area, I have not done much exploring due to my work. Neither have I met anyone who has been there."

"I appreciate your dedicated work, especially under less than desirable conditions", said Running Deer, "and I want to especially thank you for saving the life of my friend. There is no doubt in my mind that he would not have made it without you. My concern now is that I will be pursuing my quest alone. I guess I become spoiled when I have a companion."

The doctor had anticipated his concern and meant to be straightforward with him. "You are correct", he said, "he will have to recuperate here with Diane for several weeks before he will be able to return to his trading post. After that time, he will be able to go it alone if he is careful, and I don't think he will have a problem retracing his way back."

Having come to terms with Ralph's welfare and immediate future, Running Deer wanted to pose a question. His gut feeling was that he was closer to his initial quest now and he would be able to reach the fort in a few more days if there were no more setbacks for him. He had learned a lot about self preservation in his travels with Ralph and he was sure the knowledge would be put to good use. His question for the old doctor was designed to probe him for information that he might possess that would help as he made his way northward.

Immediately after a description of the old fort that had served as quarters for the early English settlers, Doc Johnson surprised Running Deer by saying "I know the whereabouts of that site. In the early days of my practice, there were patients of mine that had seen the site—and especially—I remember treating a ninety five year old lady who claimed to be a descendant of a member of that colony."

Hearing this, Running Deer's curiosity was piqued. He wanted to know if there might be a living descendant of the old lady still around.

"Not that I know of", said the doc, "all of the family have passed away or moved."

It was not an answer that he had hoped for, but at least, he was more anxious to reach his goal where he was scheduled to rendezvous with the chief and receive further instructions to reach his goal.

After bidding Doctor Johnson a safe journey back and thanking him again, he placed some coins in his hands. The doc, in turn, placed a rolled up papyrus sheet in his hand saying "use this crude drawing, you might find it useful on your journey."

Running Deer graciously accepted the proffered gift. Dr. Johnson reined his steed in the direction of his travel and was finally on his way.

With the recent events still playing in his mind, Running Deer was anxious to get on his way, but first he felt an obligation to remain with Ralph until he was sure that he was on the road to recovery. There was a lingering question in his mind concerning the extent of Ralph's wound because it was common knowledge that a savage Indian ambush rarely failed to accomplish its purpose. Had he not been in close proximity when it happened, he had no doubt that the attack would have been fatal.

At any rate, he would not abandon his courageous friend until he was certain that he would be cared for while he was recuperating, and only then, would he break the news that he would be resuming the journey on his own. He had no fear, however, that Ralph would be able to find his way back to the trading post on his own. He entered the cabin expecting Ralph to still be under sedation, but he was met with the sound of groaning coming from the patient as Diane attempted to control him. The doctor had left instructions for such an occurrence and the caregiver proceeded to administer additional sedation. It was now beginning to work and Running Deer offered a sigh of relief. The children had been dutifully quiet while Japheth and Jed made sure that other chores were attended to.

While Ralph was again under sedation, Running Deer thought it might be a good time to get his thoughts together, so he retrieved his map from his backpack and spread it out on the table. At each opportunity, he had traced his progress and had made notes for reference. He felt a modicum of pride for his rise from an amateur hunter to an experienced traveler in uncharted wilderness. He did not want to under-estimate the danger of traveling alone, however, so he quickly erased the feeling from his mind.

While he studied the map, he attempted to calculate the amount of time it would take to reach his goal. Cognizant of the fact that when he reached the end of the first phase of his journey, he might still be a long way from his goal, he would still count it as progress. Allowing for unexpected slowdowns such as heavy undergrowth and bad weather, he decided that two weeks should put him in the vicinity. He still had not included the possibility of having to cross the river without the means of a canoe.

With a smile on his lips, he thought "I'll cross that river when I get there." The saying was an old adage that he had heard from his Pa many times in the past. The hour was getting late and Running Deer was beginning to feel an urge to rest, so he first checked on Ralph whom he had not heard a sound from, and afterwards he communicated with Diana to confirm the status of his condition. Then he retired to a comfortable bed which had been made ready by the girls. Due to the smallness of the cabin, he would be in close proximity of his friend if help was needed.

Before he fell asleep, Running Deer uttered a prayer for Ralph. This was reminiscent of the time in his youth when his mother taught him to say a prayer before retiring. This time he prayed fervently for Ralph's recovery before he said a prayer for his own safety and gratitude for Divine guidance. Sleep came quickly and after a night of restful slumber, he awakened to a beautiful brisk fall morning. There had not been a disturbance of any sort leaving him to believe that everyone else rested as well.

As soon as he donned his clothing, he moved to the place that Ralph lay. Diana smiled a "good morning" to show that she was pleased that he got a good night's rest even though he knew that she had not done the same while keeping vigil on Ralph. She began to write a short progress report on his condition because she knew that Running Deer would want an update. She stated that he had a restless night, but that she had managed to keep him medicated to keep him from moving about. She had heeded the doctor's instructions well and was satisfied that she would be able to guide him through rehabilitation.

She did not want to leave an impression that his recovery would be brief, however, so she let Running Deer know that it would be a lengthy process before he would be able to travel on his own. Barring any unexpected setbacks, though, she felt confident that he would recover from his wounds and be able to make his way back to the trading post before winter weather set in. Sometimes, the weather could be cruel at that time of year, but they had always managed to survive. Without proper preparation, though, they knew that times could become very hard when the temperature drops mercilessly low.

Running Deer felt incapable of expressing his true thanks for all that the little family had done because he knew that the whole ordeal could have been less bearable. He felt bad that he did not have anything of value to give Diana to make it easier for her. He felt that the least he could do would be to make a final trip into the deep woods and perhaps surprise a whitetail or at least bag a few rabbits. The scorching hot summer was over now and the cooler weather created a movement among the animals. The process of hunting would be easier and the preserving of the meat could be done better. Even so, years of experience had shown that survival comes at a cost.

He expressed his plan to Diana and she let her pleasure be known by flashing a warm smile. He began to arrange his hunting gear and announced that he would be leaving within the hour. He let it be known among the men that he preferred to hunt alone while assuring them that he would be alright. After all, he felt that he was a much better hunter because of the experience he had gained on his journey. Japheth and Jed both agreed and promised to stick around closely until he returned.

It was time to go now, so Running Deer set out alone on his way into the forest. He was careful to mark his trail as he went because he knew that it is an easy thing to become disoriented and not be able to find his way back. This would be a test for him because the area was entirely new. However, on a beautiful fall day, he figured that little could go wrong. He looked in on Ralph once more, who was sleeping heavily, and then looked at his compass to head north. He purposely chose this direction because, according to his map, the direction took him on a parallel course to the Chowanoke where animals would aptly be foraging.

It wasn't long before he was out of sight and sound of the cabin. He longed for a faithful dog companion which would help rouse an unexpected prey for him, but he was willing to accept the fact that whatever success he had, he would have to rely on his own skill at stalking. He reasoned also, that if he had a dog along, it might prolong the hunt. Moving easily now as he continued his course, there was a silence that was unlike anything that he had experienced in a long while. As he kept his eyes and ears attuned for any movement around him, he had time to think about his journey thus far.

All of the landmarks that he had discovered began to come to mind. He first thought about the crude grave that gave the appearance of a very old interment that must have been done in haste. It could very well be the resting place of a colonial refugee who had escaped marauding savages at the early compound. And then he thought about the markings on the trees that seemed to present clues for those who might seek to rescue them. It was a pattern of clues that he could not afford to overlook.

As he mused these things over, a crackling sound from above disturbed his thoughts. His keen since of sound directed his attention to a bobcat that had been lurking on the lower branch of a huge cypress tree. Drawing upon his earlier hunting instinct, Running Deer was not pleased with the possible threat of this animal to his person. Before the cat had a chance to leave his perch, however, he successfully launched an arrow that hit its mark causing the animal to fall to the ground, but not without protest. As the cat hit the soft woods floor, he immediately ran towards Running Deer in spite of his wound, shaking off the arrow in the process. As the enraged animal came closer, Running Deer sidestepped to gain refuge behind a tree. In doing so, he tripped on a vine as he turned to make a sharp turn backwards.

Losing some strength now, the huge bobcat made a final lunge towards its adversary. As Running Deer threw his arms up to protect his face, the animal fell prostrate on top of him. The hunter was pleased that his spear had hit its target, but nonetheless, his heart was still racing as a result of the confrontation. He stood up, straightened himself, and continued on his way. He decided to let the dead cat lie for the time being and possibly return later to retrieve his kill. The fur would make a nice trophy for his friends.

The business at hand now was to continue on his quest for food. It wasn't long before he had bagged a middle-aged buck deer that had grown a sizable rack. As he moved closer to the kill, he realized that it was too large for him to lug back to the cabin. So he made the decision to return to the cabin for help. They were surprised to see him so soon, but were elated to hear of his success. He decided to save the bobcat tale for another time. Japheth accompanied him back to the site of the kill, where they rigged a carrier out of a young sapling and then placed the ends on their shoulders to transport the deer to the cabin.

As they slowly made their way, at least three fat rabbits and one squirrel scooted along the ground ahead of them. "Your turn will come later", mused Running Deer, "but today you are spared." Arriving back at the cabin, they immediately began the process of dressing the deer. The venison would provide a sumptuous parting meal for Running Deer as well as plenty to spare to help with the transition of fall into winter. From the success of this one trip, he felt better about the welfare of those he was leaving behind. He would not let his mind dwell on his friend's recovery, but he was confident that he would be properly cared for. Jed was already involved in the process of skinning and dressing the deer with Japheth assisting.

While watching the two at work, he guessed that it wouldn't be long before the venison would be searing on the spit and filling the fall air with a pleasant aroma. This process, apparently, had been repeated many times before, so he did not offer his help at this time. Instead, he sought out Diana to enquire of Ralph's condition. Through movements of her hands and eyes, she responded that he was resting better now and was beginning to take on a little more food. She sensed his concern that she was having problems attending to Ralph's personal needs while he was in a helpless condition, so she put him at ease by letting him know that she had two male nurses for assistance.

Finally the deer was on the fire while special pieces were sizzling in the stew pot. The children were getting things in place in anticipation of one of their favorite meals. They, too, knew that this would be a special meal for their guest and wanted him to leave with a favored impression of their hospitality. Crude as it was, there was no question that this scene would go with Running Deer to be etched into his memory while he was far from them. There was little conversation during the meal because the hosts were apparently saddened by the fact that Running Deer would be leaving them soon. As for his part, there was no withholding of gratitude for the family's help in caring for his friend and making things much easier for him to strike out on his own. Thanks were expressed individually before he prepared to settle down for a much deserved rest.

The night went without incident, save once when Ralph moaned out loud, apparently from a bad dream, because after a close check by Diana and Running Deer, his vital signs seemed to be in order. Everyone arose early to see that their departing guest would be sent off in a proper manner. The first to arise was Diana because she wanted Running Deer to have a hearty breakfast to start the day. The children were the last to arise but still in time to say goodbye. They did not remember much about their father, but the youngest made a remark that if she had a father, she would want him to be like Running Deer. This amused Running Deer, but he couldn't help but have sympathy for them.

With all gear in place, Running Deer said a final goodbye to everyone while expressing his gratitude for having known them as his friends. He wasn't sure that Ralph was aware that he would be leaving without him, but he was fortunate to have his friend acknowledge him as he placed his arm around his shoulder and bade him goodbye. A fall rain-cloud was forming in the east but did not seem to be threatening for the next few hours. He turned to face the direction in which he would be going and then raised his right arm as a last farewell.

For the first few hours, he was able to make his way at a fairly good pace, but then the density of the brambles slowed him down considerably. He double-checked his compass and looked around to see if he might do a slight detour and still remain on course. As he soon discovered, it was just as well, because just beyond the thicket was an impenetrable swamp. He thought he had heard the sound of gators splashing nearby and now he knew why.

While watching a family of wading birds, he narrowly missed the jaws of a scaly monster as he did a skip to turn and back up. To try to remain on his predetermined course, he calculated that he should adjust his direction ninety degrees to the southwest until he was clear of the swamp, then correct his direction to the original setting. In order to continue in the original direction, he must set his heading ninety degrees back to the original path. It was a simple matter to become disoriented in the thick growth of trees, so he could not rush and use up valuable time.

Clouds were gathering now and the prospect of a storm was looming. He knew that the fall of the year produced unpredictable weather, so he was not entirely surprised when he heard rumbling of thunder coming from the direction of his travel. Ever alert, he began to look around for a suitable place for shelter. As he trudged on while scanning the surroundings, he heard the crack of a lightning bolt off to his right. He didn't panic, but he did not waste time either while he looked for shelter. He knew that he was in the midst of hundreds of tall pines which were perfect lightning rods.

So he began to look for any cave that he could find. Maybe, he thought, there was an abandoned stump that was not occupied by one or more of the forest animals. Immediately after the thought occurred, he spotted such an opening and made a run for it. Fortunately, the den was large enough for him and his gear, so after determining that he was the only inhabitant, he removed his backpack along with his bow and arrows and then spread his bear-skin bedroll to settle in for the duration.

No sooner had he settled himself into the cramped space, that the bottom fell out of the darkened sky. There was no way for him to know how long the deluge would last, so he relaxed and tried to make the best of it. Fortunately for him, the autumn temperature was still at a comfortable level, so he managed to keep himself dry and out of the path of the racing water. An hour went by with no let-up in the downpour. It was getting late in the evening, so he decided to make some adjustments in his position and settle down for the night. Hunger was gnawing at him but he decided to forgo any attempt to eat until the next morning, when hopefully, the rain would have subsided.

While he was deep in slumber, Chief Waccasaw appeared in a dream. The chief seemed to be smiling while delivering a message to Running Deer.

"I, Waccasaw, wish to congratulate you on the success of your journey thus far. You have met every adversity with courage and have learned valuable lessons on many occasions. Some of the things that you have learned will help you reach your goal of seeking knowledge of the fate of the lost colony. Keep up the excellent work and you will be rewarded in due time."

After this the vision disappeared like a vapor, and without awakening, he slept peacefully until he was awakened by a bright sun.

Sitting up in the shelter, he noticed that water from the flowing rainwater had almost covered his feet. Removing his moccasins, he maneuvered himself out into the open to discover that there was water all around him. It's a good thing, he thought, that the old tree stump was on higher ground. Looking around, he saw a couple of wader birds that had been forced inland by the flooding of a nearby body of water. His trained ear at once picked up the sound of rushing waters. He soon determined that the sound was directly in front of him.

It was time for breakfast and his stomach did not have to remind him that it had been almost twenty four hours since he had eaten. There was plenty of fresh water at hand to go with pieces of the dry food that Diana had so graciously supplied him with. He would take his time to satisfy his hunger before he would analyze his situation and seek to figure out what his next step would be. Not knowing the extent of the flooding around him, he knew that it might take considerable time to map out his route. He hung his moccasins on a limb to dry in the meantime.

Higher in the sky now, the huge round orb was warming the entire area. Running Deer thought it ironic that such a clear beautiful fall day could present such a problem for him. But he was buoyed by recalling the encouragement offered by the chief in his dream last night. His thoughts returned momentarily, to the condition of his friend Ralph. He and Ralph had been through a lot together and he felt a little bit guilty about abandoning him. Then he thought of the kindness and compassion of Diana Silver Fox and her family, and took comfort in knowing that Ralph had received excellent care and would be well enough to make the journey back to the trading post alone.

After finishing his meal, and laying his thoughts aside, he was ready to begin his final, and yet unknown, journey to locate the old abandoned fort site that would be crucial to ending his quest. There would be a face to face meeting with Chief Waccasaw and there he would receive instructions and possibly important clues for his successful quest. To reach the fort seemed to be an exciting task for him and he was anxious to be on the way. After donning his gear, he checked his map and compass before he walked away from the site.

Chapter Six

REMEMBERING THE WADING BIRDS AT the swamp site, Running Deer reckoned that there must be a body of water nearby. According to his map, there would have to be a river crossing before he would reach the fort. He had no way of knowing how soon that would be, but he had an intuition that the river was not very far away. For now, though, he would continue on the chosen path. At times he seemed to be following an ancient pathway and then it suddenly gave way to thick undergrowth. Half of the morning had vanished and it seemed that he had made very little progress. The warm glow of the sun was causing him to perspire heavily while his arms were beginning to tire.

He preserved his strength by using one arm and then the other. At times during his progress, he caught himself looking around to speak to his companion, and then he would suddenly realize that he was alone. It would take a while, he figured, to get used to the silence. The forest seemed unusually quiet, also, as if the animals had abandoned it. This situation was short lived, however, because a loud cracking sound seemed to permeate the whole area directly in front of him and to his right. His instinct told him to stop dead in his tracks and then quietly seek shelter.

It would not be an easy task since he found himself amidst a stand of tall loblolly pine. It had been a long time since he had shinnied a tree, especially when the first branch was located at thrice his height. As he was in the process of making a decision, the cracking noise came to a sudden stop. Apparently his presence had been discovered by the mysterious noise maker. At this point, his body was at ease while his mind was working overtime.

He scanned the area in a three sixty degree sweep, yet was unable to detect the source of the sound. It was a very eerie feeling given the density of his surroundings and a sudden onset of loneliness. It hadn't occurred to him that help was always available if he chose to use the magical powers available to him if he only chose to use them. Or at least, at a time like this, there was little time for thinking. It had been a decision of his to use the power only as a last resort. This might be one of those times, he thought, so he kept his options open.

As he struggled to assess his situation, a scantily dressed figure of immense proportions appeared from behind a huge swamp cypress. When Running Deer convinced himself that this was no apparition, he remained in a posture of readiness with his right hand on his trusty knife and his left around his spear shaft. He decided to let Shaggy make the first move. He didn't have to wait long before the hairy visitor began to hold out his hands and walk toward him. Relaxing a little, Running Deer took this to be a friendly gesture.

It was time now, he thought, to attempt some kind of communication, so he asked the strange person to identify himself. In an attempt to reply, the man mumbled an answer that appeared to be crude English. As he became bolder, he began to walk closer to Running Deer. On closer examination, the man had a long black beard that revealed deep set eyes that were scarcely viewable through his beard. His only clothing was an animal skin that was fastened loosely around his waist. At ten paces, his breath revealed that this was someone who lived entirely in the wild with very little contact with other humans.

In order to learn more about this strange anomaly, Running Deer stretched forth his hands to show that he was a friendly being also. By this time, the woods man managed to utter more words to further introduce himself.

"I'm called Trapper Tom", he said, "my shack is over by the river and I am hunting for food."

"But where is your weapon", replied Running Deer, "Surely you don't hunt with your bare hands, do you?"

"I left it behind the big tree yonder. I didn't want to approach you armed."

This amused Running Deer and he took the opportunity to invite Trapper to sit and talk. The mention of a nearby river had aroused curiosity in him so he wanted to know more about the immediate surroundings. He thought that here was an opportunity to talk with someone who was familiar with the area and might be able to help him with his journey.

The two located a clear dry area to sit, relax, and talk. Even sitting, the man was a head taller than Running Deer. First, Running Deer reached into his backpack and offered the stranger a strip of hardtack. There was no hesitation on the part of Trapper to accept the offering as he crammed one end into his ample jaws, which when opened, revealed a display of very few stained teeth. Around his waist, he carried a crude horn of a liquid substance attached to a leather cord. When a drink was offered to Running Deer, only then did he learn that it contained fermented grape wine. He declined the offer as he reached for his own decanter of fresh water.

Running Deer began the conversation by asking how long he had been in the area. "I am eighty years old", Tom replied, "and I have been in these woods most of my life."

"Then you should be very familiar with the forest", said Running Deer, "but do you know anything of the surrounding area such as the Chowanoke river as it winds toward the mainland, or have you heard of an ancient fort that was abandoned by early English settlers?"

"Not only have I heard of an old fort across the river. My grandpappy claimed that his parents were among the English who were inhabitants of that compound", said Tom.

"That is real interesting", Running Deer responded, "but have you ever heard of the Lost Colony?"

"I never learned to read", he sadly replied, "and neither of my parents have told such a story."

Running Deer was disappointed by his answer, but he sensed that there might be valuable information to be gained. So he continued the line of questioning, as best he could, seeking to learn more about this person. "How about your kin folks?", he asked, "do you have kin folks who live near you?"

"No", he replied, "but I had a cousin—son of my Aunt Safronia—who went to live in Virginny. I don't know if he is still alive. He left these parts when he was a young man. Said he wanted to git a eddication so's he could become a good farmer. There is no one left in the family, so I reckon I'll never hear from him again."

"So, it seems that you're a loner, then. Do you ever have a desire to move away from these parts and find out what the rest of the world is up to?"

"Well, to tell you the truth", said he, "I did want to explore some when I was younger, but my maw and paw lived to a ripe old age and after looking out for them `til they passed going on five or six year ago—just three months apart—did I decide that I might as well stick it out around here until I pass on."

While the conversation continued, the setting of the sun went almost unnoticed. The two agreed that they should be preparing to settle down for the night and await the dawning of a new day to do any further talking. Both of them walked around the area looking for a suitable spot to settle down for the night. By now, Running Deer was convinced that there was no harm in this old huntsman so he felt more at ease. Running Deer had gone hardly a hundred yards from the area when he spotted what looked like an ancient log cabin. As he moved closer to the site, he discovered that the forest growth had almost hid it from view.

It didn't take long to verify that the old place hadn't seen any inhabitants in a long, long time. Surprisingly, though, the frame work looked to be in good condition. He whistled for Tom who shortly joined him in front of the structure. The roof was partially intact, so they began to try the door to get an appraisal of the interior. The shutter windows had kept the weather out, so they were hoping to find a suitable place on the floor to bed down. Water had invaded the interior in a lot of places, but they were able to find a complete room with a dry wood floor. It appeared to be what was once a bedroom, but two old beds had deteriorated to the point that they were barely recognizable.

A decision was made to clear all of the debris from this room and use the floor bedding down. Further exploration turned up a table that was probably used for dining. Not far from the table was an old mud-chinked fireplace that was apparently used for heating and cooking. They entertained the idea of having a look-around outside the next morning to see if the old chimney was still in place. Not completely trusting the old man, Running Deer was careful to stay near his possessions, and especially his trusted map. He would welcome any help that he could get to make his journey easier, but he had learned long ago that he could not trust everyone that he met.

Pretty soon the two were sacked in and welcomed a peaceful night of rest. The night passed without incident and at break of dawn, the two arose to find a beautiful cloudless morning that was punctuated with the sound of bird songs that helped to usher in a new day, making it the fifteenth since he and Ralph had begun this leg of the journey. It seemed longer but he reckoned that the unfortunate circumstance surrounding the attack on Ralph had caused it to seem so. Before he would continue on his journey, he wanted to question Tom some more and to document all information that might become useful for him.

Unbeknownst to Running Deer, Tom had arisen earlier and had bagged a wild turkey which he was preparing for their breakfast. The smell of the roasting turkey excited his appetite and he was ready to partake of same. He couldn't help but think about the fact that he would soon be on his own again and would again miss the skill and companionship of a traveling partner. Nevertheless, he was aware that he had started out on this quest alone, and even though he valued the friendships that he had encountered on the way, he was ready to face the unknown again before he at last completed the journey that was set before him.

In less than thirty minutes, Tom announced that breakfast was ready, so the two of them made themselves comfortable while they enjoyed the wild game and a cup of Running Deer's favorite coffee. He was wise enough to bring along an ample supply of coffee beans that was given to him by the trader Ralph. After breakfast, they seated themselves comfortably around a makeshift table that was fashioned from an old tree stump.

Running Deer began by trying to tap into Tom's memory. He figured that if he used a methodical sequence of questioning, he would be able to dig deeper into the woodsman's past. "What do you remember about your parents while you were a young lad?", he queried the old man.

"Its been a long time", he said, "but I do remember more about my father than I do about my mother. You see, my mother died when she gave birth to my only sister. I was seven years old at the time and I remember that my pa took it real hard."

"So I suppose that your father taught you about your grandparents", stated Running Deer.

"Not much", responded Tom, "but I do recollect that he told me a little something about his grandmother. He said that she was half Indian because her daddy was a full blooded Croatan and her mama had English ancestry."

"That sounds very interesting", replied Running Deer, "Can you tell me more about this ancestry?"

"I'm afraid not", he said, "Papa didn't talk much after Mama died. He was always busy trying to feed and clothe Chloe—that's my sister's name—and me. Times were real hard back then, especially in the winter time."

"So where is your sister—uh, Chloe—now?"

"She wanted to get an eddication for herself, so she went over to the mainland when she was about sixteen and I aint seen her since. I always had a feeling that Chloe would get that eddication she wanted and make something of herself, but its been a long time and I have given up hope of ever seeing her again."

"I'm sorry to bring up sad memories", said Running Deer, "but I'm only trying to gain knowledge that might help me in my search for the truth."

"What truth?", interrupted Trapper Tom, "you must tell me something about yourself. Why you are here in this God forsaken wilderness and just what you are searching for."

"Well, it's a long story", said Running Deer, "and I can't go into all the details, but if you are truly interested—and I see that you must be—I will try to answer your question. I met a man once upon a river, who relayed to me a story about a group of people who had settled not far from here and had encountered a tribe of unfriendly natives. They set about to protect themselves—men, women, and children—from possible assaults by the natives. History has told us that they built a fort of sorts and proceeded to live out their lives until their friends could return from across the ocean to bring help with much needed food and supplies."

"To make a long story short", he continued, "after a prolonged period of three years, the friends did return but they could find no trace of the little colony of immigrants. In history, this event became known as The Lost Colony. The man that I met was known as Chief

Waccasaw. I was given an assignment by him to make this journey to find out the truth about the colony. My quest has brought me to this place and I must continue to search for the truth as to what really happened. Many theories have been put forth, but none satisfies the Chief."

After he had said this, Running Deer arose from his sitting position, after picking up the journal in which he had recorded the short recollection of Trapper Tom.

"I must be going now", he said, "it is getting late in the day and I want to take advantage of a beautiful day of travel. As you can see, there is not a cloud in the sky and the fall temperature is a walking man's delight."

After saying this, he reached for Trapper Tom's hand to bid him farewell. In response, the old man placed his right arm on Running Deer's back and gave him an affectionate hug.

"Its been a while," he said, "since I've encountered a man with your character and one who seems "hell bent" on succeeding. I wish you the best in your search, because you'll need all the luck you can muster while traveling alone in this God-forsaken wilderness. If you ever come back this way, I might see you again, cause Lord knows, at my age, I'm not gonna leave these parts."

With a nod, Running Deer turned to face the northwest and walked away from the old man. When he had walked about two hours, he approached a clearing that appeared to be the remains of an earlier settlement. He rid himself of the backpack and gear laying it beside him on the sparsely grassed ground at his feet. It was a good time to take a rest, he decided, while he pondered over the events of the last few days. But first things first, he thought, as he took a drink of the weaning supply of fresh water from his flask. Placing his head on his hands that were folded behind his neck, he reclined on his backpack and looked wistfully at the blue sky above him.

At that moment, a puff of a cloud appeared in his sight that began to reassemble itself into the shape of a native warrior with feathered headdress, and as he looked, the figure seemed to raise an arm with its right forefinger pointing toward the west. In his imagination, he took it to be a sign from his mentor, Chief Waccasaw. All else seemed to fade from his mind as he continued to gaze at the phenomenon. The little cloud faded and vanished as quickly as it had appeared. He then closed his eyes and began to think that what he had seen was just a figment of his imagination, that he should not take it as a message of some sort. After all, he reasoned within himself, cloud watching was a game that he used to play with other kids, and sometimes with the family. But something inside kept gnawing at him and telling him that he should heed the message in the cloud and alter his course slightly westward.

Donning his gear again, he looked up at the sun's position in the sky and reckoned that he had another two hours of daylight in which to travel. He reached into his pocket to retrieve his compass and faced forty five degrees westward from his original course. Undergrowth was very thick for the first thirty minutes but then he suddenly entered a clearing that resembled an old well trodden path. There was ruts from years past that was well preserved in the loamy soil. The path continued to lead pretty close to his compass setting, so he continued on and managed to travel farther than he expected before the shadows of dusk began to encompass him.

He kept walking, but now he began to look around to search out a suitable spot to spend the night. Unfortunately, there were no caves or uprooted stumps in which to make shelter, but he was not overly concerned because the weather was still in his favor. He didn't have to search long before his eyes spotted the remnants of a small building. From the position in which he was standing, there appeared to be a roof still in place.

Before he divested himself of his belongings, he continued to walk toward the spot for a closer inspection. Within fifteen feet or so of the building as he made his approach, he was surprised by the shrill cry of a mother fox as she scooted from the building leading her brood of three in tow. He felt bad that he had routed the family from their den in the shelter, but he also knew that they probably would not be back, so he began to appraise the shelter for a possible overnight stay.

For the most part, undergrowth had claimed the site, but he began to utilize his knife to clear the close-by perimeter. In about an hour, he had accomplished his task and had determined that he would be safe in case of inclement weather. The fall season was subtly making its appearance and he knew that wind and rain storms were unpredictable at this time of year. Anyway the sky was clear at the moment so he continued to clear a place to bed up for the night.

As he looked around inside, his eyes came upon what appeared to be a skeleton reposing in one corner. He immediately began to look around the area for any relics that might have been left by the owner of the white-washed remains. From the size of the skeleton, the person was estimated to be a male adult. Guessing further, he decided that whoever the unfortunate individual was, he either was hiding from an enemy or he had taken refuge from cold weather and had subsequently frozen to death.

Dusk was beginning to envelop the woods and this prompted Running Deer to concentrate on preparing a few victuals to keep his hunger at bay. On the morrow, he decided that there would be time to resume the investigation of his co-habitant. He wasn't comfortable at all with the idea of waking up in the middle of the night to stare at the remains of this mysterious person, so he gently placed his cape upon the bones. The temperature was not unbearable, but he decided to gather dry branches to burn for light and it would serve a double purpose of brewing some coffee while at the same time, it would help ward off an animal intrusion.

From experience, he knew that some animals in a desperate situation for food, would attack humans. Sleep came easily and he was not interrupted until the wee hours of morning when he awoke from a nightmare in which he imagined that native savages were attacking from all sides. He had already reached for his trusty knife before he realized that it was only a bad dream. It took some time for him to go back to sleep, and luckily, the remainder of the night was very restful.

He awoke at daybreak at the insistence of the sound of fowl that had taken up residence in the trees surrounding him. Rays from the sun had not made an appearance, but he felt recharged and ready to meet the new day with gusto. He arose from the floor of the little building and began to walk around the area outside for an early exploration of the place. After a few minutes, he came upon the decayed remains of what had been a well constructed canoe. He proceeded to clear the wild grape vines that had encased the canoe over the years. He decided to search for more relics that might have been left at the site along with the canoe. While he was in the process, it occurred to him that there was a good chance that a river was close by.

After chopping and dragging and pulling the vines aside, he was ready to flip the canoe over to see what might be directly underneath it. The developing rays from the morning sun began to squint through the tree tops now, and as a result, he caught the reflection of a small round object that was partially protruding from the newly revealed soil. He picked the object up to examine it closer. It turned out to be an old coin with some corrosion on one side and a remarkably new looking side on the obverse.

Unfortunately, any date that might have been on the coin was not discernible because of the tarnished condition. Nevertheless, the discovery of the coin inspired him to examine the soil further. He placed the coin with his map and other valuable pieces and then returned to the site to further explore the soil that was underneath the old canoe. After an hour's digging with a crude tool that he had put together using a sharp slab of stone, he decided that the coin was the only thing of historic value that he was going to find. A lot of work with very little pay. His thoughts now turned to his malnourished friend that he had left in the dilapidated shed.

The sun was getting higher in the sky and he was bathed with bright light that gave him a better perspective of his surroundings. An upset piece of timber fell from the top of the only door and barely missed his head. He had heard of the remaining spirits that remained with an old house, but with a wry smile, he dismissed the possibility and resumed his activities. But it did cause him to wonder how long the old shack had been there and how it had managed to stay upright through the years.

He would not allow himself to speculate on the age of the skeleton that resided therein. Curiosity overcame any other consideration of abandoning the site and continuing on his journey while the weather was pleasant and time was still left in the day. Instead, he carefully examined the interior taking an extra measure of care to not upset the bones which were still intact. Dim light began to permeate the inside and it became evident that part of the stranger's belongings were near his remains. The first thing that caught the eye of Running Deer was a deteriorating leather clutch that was near the right hand that rested on the floor.

It appeared to be fastened together with leather thongs which indicated that whatever it held was the most valuable personal belongings of its owner. Running Deer was tempted to open it to reveal its contents, but he decided to lay it aside for the time being while he continued to explore other areas inside. After careful investigation, it was evident that the only other relics left behind was a rusty fry pan and less than half a dozen cooking and heating utensils.

Running Deer determined that the cooking utensils were not of Indian origin and, therefore, must be of an early English manufacture. His conclusion was made on the basis that none were crafted from stone, as is the case of the crude utensils made by the Indians. Carefully entering all of this in his journal, he pondered his next step before leaving the site. Ordinarily, he would pack up and walk away to continue his quest, but there was one last problem left to solve.

He was torn between two choices. A gut feeling told him that his latest discovery might have important significance among the long list of clues which he had gathered on his journey so far. Therefore, he should spend more time in exploration before he continued on his way. The other choice would be to gather up what he had found, which he deemed important, and be on his way. It was not an easy decision, so to clear his mind, he retired to a shaded area underneath a very old cypress tree.

He extracted his map, made sure everything had been properly recorded, and then began to make notes on the margin. He hoped that the document would be decipherable once he reached his first-leg destination—the old fort. Once this was done, he began to think of the alternatives that faced him. If he were to leave at once, leaving the site just as he had found it, he wondered if all would be intact if he were to return at a later time. The answer came to him in a vision when Chief Waccasaw suddenly appeared and raised both arms that were pointed in a direction that Running Deer understood to mean that that was the direction in which he should go and that he was to leave right away. The vision was fleeting but he got the message.

Within the hour, he had gathered all of his belongings, had placed his quiver on his back, and was on his way through the deep underbrush. The discovery of the canoe at the shack caused him to think that a river must be close by, so he altered his original course and began to move slightly to the west. After about a half hour, he was beginning to see bushes and ground cover that grew where nearby water existed. Though forest sounds were in abundance, his ears were attuned to the possible sound of running water.

The change of tide had always been a fascinating phenomenon for him and he had always had a deep respect and admiration for a body of water. He knew others who had polluted the rivers and streams and still depended on them for the abundance of food that they provided. From his days as a very young lad, he remembered the many times that his grandpa had taken him fishing and had allowed him to hold the cane pole when the cork had suddenly been pulled under. His pa had taken him too, but most of the time, his older brothers got the most attention. So the memories of his grandpa had lingered longer.

The swampy area that he encountered soon became thick underbrush again, but he continued to hack his way in the same direction. It wasn't much longer before he stepped over a downed tree trunk and riled a sleeping water moccasin. If it wasn't for the lethargic state of the huge reptile, he was sure that he could have been a victim of its bite. All he could say was "Psheww" and then he backed off to a safe distance before he stopped and began to survey the area all around him. "Moccasins like to inhabit a wet area", he thought, "so maybe my predictions about a river are correct."

He decided to let the snake be and considered the confrontation a draw. It was hard to tell who was the most frightened—him or the moccasin. Before he had covered a hundred or so yards, he was sure that he heard the familiar sound of rippling water against a river bank. In a way, it was music to his ears, because he counted it favorable if he had found a river that was going the same way that he was going. The sound of the running water was more prominent now, so he zeroed in on its source. The undergrowth had become thick again, but there was a certain elation that he was headed in the right direction. He figured it was near low tide now because all of the water had drained from the little stream that was draining from the swamp.

Making his way toward the river, and as he worked his way through the thick underbrush, his mind was in the business of trying to guess how large the body of water would be. His thoughts also flashed back to a time not long ago when he navigated his canoe on the river between the White's place and the trading post. He remembered the pleasant side of the experience and the not so pleasant when he encountered the "river rats". A smile creased his lips as he thought that he was being too kind to put the two thieves in the same family as rats.

About forty minutes had elapsed when a flash like that of the sun on a smooth rock fetched him back into reality. He hurried through the last great clump of vines and gave a sigh of relief as he looked in all directions in front of him and to each side where his eyes took in a panorama that he did not expect to find. At the spot on which he was located, it was difficult to focus his eyes on the other side. Looking up and down the great body of water he could see that there were less wider places in the river as well as a bend not far from where he was standing.

There was no life to be seen in either direction, human or animal. The scene quickly changed, though, as he watched two widely spaced eyes just at the top of the water and making their way toward the bank. It was as if he had disturbed the silence, as he made his way toward the river's edge, and things were about to change. Running Deer kept his eyes focused on the moving head of a huge reptile. If the swimming behemoth had seen him, it was not evident, because there was no shift in direction as it made its way to the bank of the river.

Always the alert one, Running Deer made a decision to play cat and mouse with the huge predator. With spear and knife at the ready, he remained as still as possible and waited to see what the reptile was up to. By now, it was close enough for identification. It was probably the largest alligator that he had ever seen and he had seen a lot of them. It was too early, though, to assess its real size. Just before reaching the bank directly in front of him, the great gator silently switched directions and began to swim close by the bank in a stealthy manner.

Leaning over and looking up the river in the same direction, Running Deer spotted a huge multi-antlered buck deer that had emerged from the forest to lap water at the river's edge. Seeing the opportunity for food for himself, the race was now on to see who would win out—he or the gator. In the gator's mind, it was not a contest, because he sensed the movement of Running Deer at about the same time that he began to hoist his legs, making a dash out of the water to surprise the buck.

At the sight that followed, Running Deer was stopped in his tracks as he envisioned the battle of survival between predator and prey. He guessed the huge alligator to be about fifteen feet long and cared not to speculate about its weight. After reaching up to sever the lifeline, the gator had moved the heavy deer from the bank and out into the running water. He made notes of the action that included a mention of the enormous size of the participants.

Disheartened by the loss of food but heartened by the sight of the river and animal life, Running Deer decided to pause long enough to assess his whereabouts before moving on to hunt for food. He took a long look at his map, and after taking into consideration all of his course corrections, it was determined that if he followed the river bank in a northerly direction, he would be headed roughly toward his destination. He could not know the many turns that the river would take, but he was willing to follow it. He regretted that the canoe he discovered was not river worthy, so he continued on foot with a stomach that was fussing with pangs of hunger.

His guess that there would be other animals near the river paid off greatly when a medium sized rabbit appeared around a cypress trunk where he was munching on leaves of grass that covered the ground near the shore. Quieter than usual, he withdrew an arrow from his quiver, pulled back his bow, and scored a meal. He made quick work of the dressing and pretty soon the aroma of roasted rabbit permeated the woods around him. To supplement the wild meat, he gathered some of the same greens that provided a last meal for the rabbit.

He had some of Ralph's special coffee left in his pack, so he rounded out his meal with fresh brewed coffee. Shadows were lengthening around him now, so he figured he would be on his way again, and hopefully, he would find a decent place to make shelter for the night. It was much clearer of undergrowth near the river's edge, so he was able to move at a better pace than he had experienced farther inland. The next long bend of the river altered his course considerably towards the north. He could see far enough to tell that the river followed a straight course a long time before it would make a turn to the left.

Dusk was creeping all around now and he knew that he must soon find a suitable spot to spend the night. After working through a thick bramble patch, he suddenly came upon a clearing that he figured would fill the bill. There was no shelter but the area was dry and looked as though it had been used for the same purpose in the past. After ridding himself of his backpack and arrow quiver, he commenced to clear a spot to build a fire. There was plenty of dry branches, so the burning boughs began cracking in short order while the darting flames did their dancing number in the darkening night air.

The moon was in its last quarter and would not contribute much light tonight. At least the sky was cloudless for the time being and there was no rain in sight. After fixing a comfortable pad for his bed, his thoughts turned to his journal and another look at his map before the fire settled into embers. Making notes of his new course of direction, he was careful to mention his thoughts regarding the river. It was possible, he thought, that the river beside him now was the same body of water that he had entered at the beginning of his journey. His map was not clear enough to afford him this information. He thought it possible that he might be in uncharted territory. One thing he was sure about was the fact that others besides Indians had lived in and hunted the area in times past.

With only a reddish glow emanating from the embers now, he pushed the remaining ashes into a small lump, turned over on his side, and dozed off into the quiet restfulness of slumber. Before long—it could have been an hour or two—a weird barking sound pierced the still night air. He awoke suddenly, and then after reassuring himself of his surroundings, he sat up resting his torso with his arms outstretched to the ground, and looked around as he awaited to discover the source of the sound to repeat itself.

Silence pervaded the area again and there was no repetition of the disturbance that woke him up. It was not possible for him to return to sleep right away, so after about an hour of waiting and listening, he began to wonder if he had not interrupted a dream, that the sound was not real and only a figment of his imagination. Dream or not, he felt himself dozing off and soon was fast asleep again. Once again, after being shaken from deep slumber, the same sound—only louder—filled the area around him.

This time, though, it came from two directions. He was convinced that he had better prepare himself, stay on the alert, and be ready for a potential life-threatening attack by something or someone. Trying to analyze two different sounds, he came to the conclusion that the first could have come from an animal, but there was something different in the second. His mind drifted back to the attack by savages that almost took the life of his good friend Ralph. So he knew that there was a remnant of wild savages still in the dark recesses of the thicket and he might be getting too close to one of their villages.

Listening for any sound of movement around him, he was very aware of their stealthy ways. The time spent on his journey, thus far, had served to equip him with an extraordinary sense of self preservation, so he was not going to make it easy for a surprise attack. In the few seconds that it took to assemble these thoughts, his ears picked up the sound of someone or something making its way toward him. At the very same moment, two figures appeared. The dim light of the moon was casting an eerie glow upon them. Since one appeared from his left and the other from his right, his eyes were kept busy while he assessed the situation. There appeared to be twenty feet or so between him and the two strangers, which he had identified now, that might bring harm to him.

There was no room for misjudgment so he felt for his weapons to make sure that he was ready for any eventuality. Neither of the newcomers had uttered a sound since they made their appearance, so it was a standoff in introductions. As if by cue, the two made a deliberate step toward Running Deer. It was time now to make a decision whether to attempt to introduce himself or to enquire of the two. By now, it was evident that they were scantily clad and neither had chosen to change their position away from opposite sides. Running Deer recognized this as an ambush play, so he drew his knife with his left hand and grabbed his spear with the left.

Sensing that Running Deer meant business, the one on his right placed his hands—palm forward—in front of him and uttered a sound that was recognized as a gesture of friendship. The one on his left followed suit and both of them picked up pace while walking slowly towards him. Not knowing if the two could speak English, he figured that it might be a good time to find out.

"I'm Running Deer", he said, "to whom do I owe the pleasure of this acquaintance?" In saying this, he hoped that he had not gone over their head with his English.

"Me Moon Bear", said one, and immediately from the other, "John Beaver". We mean no harm, Moon Bear continued, we come from village close by here and was surprised to find white man alone in deep forest at night."

"It's a long story", replied Running Deer, "but I suppose I owe you an explanation. Since it is near dawn, why don't we build a fire to knock off the chill while we chat for a while."

The two interlopers agreed and hastily began to gather dry branches for the fire. Running Deer, in turn, began to clear a place on the moss covered ground. It wasn't long before the fire was crackling and cinders from the burning dry branches were wafting toward the clear autumn sky. After making themselves comfortable, Running Deer broke the ice by asking where they were from.

John Beaver was the first to speak, and by this, he appeared to be the spokesman for the two. "We live in a compound in the middle of the forest", he said as he pointed in a northeasterly direction, "and we are about two days away from there. We were preparing to go back there at dawn. We have not had much luck—as you can see by our kill—but we hope to make up for it on our way back."

"We have killed enough small game to keep our stomachs satisfied", echoed Moon Bear, "but on trips like this, we always hope to kill a deer or black bear to take back for the others."

After wishing them luck on their hunt, Running Deer was anxious to know if they were from a mixed breed or from all-Indian stock. So without appearing to be too nosey or personal, he threw this typical question at them—"I take it from the sound of your names that you must possess some Indian blood", he said, "but among your clan, is there also foreign blood?"

They gazed at each other with an inquisitive look and then John Beaver replied by saying, "We know little of our ancestry but there are older ones that live among us that might have an answer for you."

Running Deer was pleased by the reply, but then his next task that he contemplated was whether to seek out these oldsters that were mentioned and perhaps lose valuable time by doing so or dismiss it and possibly miss out on some very valuable information. "Tell me", he said, "I have heard of an old fort in these parts that was inhabited by early English settlers who were seeking to explore the area for possible colonization, have you heard of its existence?"

The two began to speak at the same time, but John Beaver took up the reply by saying "the story has been handed down through several generations that a compound of some sort or "fort" did exist on Roanoke Island, but no one in our family knows its exact location." "That is so", chimed in Moon Bear—and it never has been a great concern of the family's. I am a cousin to John Beaver here and when we were young, our grandparents would sit around a campfire and tell stories that had been handed down."

All this was worthy of note to Running Deer and he wanted to know if any of their grandparents were still living.

"Only our old grandmother", answered Moon Bear, "she is very old but her mind is sharp as a tack."

There was no question now in Running Deer's mind that he would indeed take the extra time to visit the old woman and perhaps extract some valuable information from her. It was times like these that he felt that the hardship of his journey was worth all his effort.

"I wonder", he said to the two woodsmen, "if you mind if I accompany you back to your place to sit a spell and have a talk with your grandma?"

"Not at all", said the two in unison, "we would be obliged to have you visit us. Visitors are few and far between in these parts."

As a condition set forth by them, he would not be able to interfere with their hunting on the way there.

"I understand clearly", said Running Deer, "I might even be a little helpful in this effort, as I've been known to hunt a little myself."

They all laughed and began immediately to make plans for the morrow. They all agreed that they should get as much shuteye as possible while it was still dark. At first dawn, they would arise early, prepare a scant breakfast and then go over a departure time and plans for hunting while they made their way to the compound.

In his mind, Running Deer had envisioned a crude compound including dwelling quarters and accompanying buildings to house livestock with room for storage. His main task for now would be to develop a closer friendship with the two of them. He hoped that he would be able to bag a fat buck to impress the hunters and their family. In the quietness of the forest, there was little to keep the three of them from dozing off. It was the loud "caw" of a cruising crow that penetrated the mist surrounding the campsite and brought Running Deer to a sudden awakening. As he gazed at his campmates, he was aware that it was going to take more than a crow to bring them out of a deep sleep. It was still a little early, he thought, so he decided to let them sleep a while longer. The extra time would allow him to make a few notes on his map and in his journal. He wanted to make sure, also, that the site was properly marked in case of a return visit by him.

By now, the woods surrounding them had become alive with divers sounds. The circling crows had become even louder while fishing birds could be heard in the distance preparing to try their luck in inland ponds as well as along the bank of the nearby river. They must have been plenteous because he could hear the flapping of their wings as they swooped toward a potential target. In the distance could be heard the indistinguishable sound of a human or the busy sound of animals conversing with their mates.

A look at the sky foretold a sunny day that did not, at the time, reveal a single cloud. Everyone was up by now, looking newly refreshed and ready to take on a new day. A heavy mist had formed at first daylight which would eventually move from the river nearby to fill the surrounding forest with a thick fog. He knew that an early morning fog would disappear after the sun rose higher into the early autumn sky. This would give the trio time to do some more planning so that, hopefully, little could be left to chance.

Beaver and Bear were adept at their calling but surprises could and would happen on almost all of their ventures into the forest. Now that they had a companion, they would exercise extra precaution. The forest had changed very little over the years so it wasn't very inviting to newcomers. The deep woods had been very good to them and their family, but they were always alert to the dangers lurking therein.

By this time, Running Deer had been confronted by many life threatening occurrences himself, but he was willing to learn from these more experienced hunters. After half an hour, the fog had been burned away and visibility was again in their favor. Since he was following now, Beaver and Bear headed off in a northerly direction which was fairly clear at the moment, but he knew that the situation would change before long. Right away, the more experienced hunters looked back at Running Deer with their hands placed over their mouths. This, of course, was a signal for him to be very quiet and be on the lookout for a foraging deer or smaller game that could be lurking nearby.

Though the woods thickened, Bear and Beaver were able to find the more traveled paths so that they could forego the noisy hacking of vines and undergrowth. After an hour, it was evident that the sky was less bright now and there was a distinct possibility of a rain cloud forming from the east. Bear and Beaver were still in sight so they turned to look at Running Deer and attempted to signal him to stay put so they could join him. He knew this was a way for the three of them to appraise the possible approaching rain and decide where to hunt for shelter. By now, he knew that this would not be a light rainfall, but more than likely it would be a frog-strangler.

After a few minutes, the three men assembled and began to discuss ways to look for safety in a shelter of some sort. Lightning was beginning to light up the sky in the distance and the rumble of thunder followed after the count of ten. This meant that the lightning was most active about ten miles away. The base of a tree was the worst possible place to be at a time like this, because the tall trees were natural lightning rods. Running Deer was open for suggestions, so he eagerly awaited a decision by one or both of his companions.

John Beaver was the first to speak and said—"if my memory serves me correctly, we should head back toward the river. There used to be a trapper's cabin in this vicinity and it might be our only hope." There was no argument following, so the three of them hastily made their way to the river.

Thunder and lightning were occurring closer together now, so it was becoming more urgent that they find shelter. Soaking wet by now, the trio approached the river bank and began to scan the edge of the river both ways. John Beaver's memory paid off eloquently as he pointed to his left where six eyes zoomed in on a small lean-to that looked to be the remnants of a former cabin. It was not easy to reach from where they were, but all agreed that a few scratches from thorns would be small pay for a safe haven from the worsening storm.

The plan was made for each of them to proceed toward their goal at their own method of clearance. Before long, though, an old path was discovered and all three of them were able to move closer to their potential haven from the storm. Bear was the first to arrive and began to appraise their chances of attaining safety from the now impending danger. Lucky for them, the make-shift roof was still intact and there was room underneath for all three. The downpour of rain, however, was not in their favor and managed to blow in from the many cracks in the old decaying walls.

Running Deer was thankful that the chosen spot was on a small knoll and that in case of a continuing downpour, it would not be flooded. He could not help but think of the flood that took the life of his friend, thus, he was acutely aware of the risks involved on a journey such as his.

John Beaver observed the calm demeanor of Running Deer and remarked "its good to know that you are one of us. Bear and I have confronted these situations many times because of the nature and length of our hunting trips. We are always aware that inclement weather and dangerous animals are things with which we must deal. It's the price you pay in the pursuit of survival."

Running Deer concurred and told them that he appreciated their friendship.

The deluge did not let up until it seemed that an hour had passed. Flashes of lightning was still brightening the sky followed by rolling thunder from out of the southwest. The clouds still obscured the sun, so they could not be sure if more rain was on the way or if it soon would clear up. As it turned out, though, there was another hour of the former. It was moving toward noon and the storm was relentless and looking as if there would be no let up any time soon. There was an obscured view of the river and they were aware of a rising tide where the busy midstream current was running at a fast pace carrying flotsam and uprooted logs with it.

Occasionally, an animal could be heard as they sought better shelter around them. As they peered out, a frightening bolt of lightning followed the top of a tall longleaf pine down to the forest floor just across the river opposite them. The heavy deafening peal of thunder followed. There was silence underneath the shelter after this occurred, but John Beaver and Bear looked at each other as if to say that they had never been caught before in a storm of this magnitude. Running Deer was a little uneasy himself, but he did not want to show his feelings. After all, he thought, someone had to help keep their spirits up.

After two long hours, that seemed like a whole day, the storm finally abated. The sky was still grey and dark clouds seemed to be rolling eastward. Hopefully, the sun would appear soon and begin to dry things out. It was a matter of sitting and waiting. While they waited, they began to contemplate their next move. There was no question that they would resume their hunting and move on toward Beaver and Bear's home. Running Deer was anxious to meet the old lady and have a chat with her. This could be a break that he would value later on, but on the other hand, it might be a waste of time. Hopefully, if it were to be the latter, he might still be able to move on to the old fort from there by making a few corrections in his course.

He needed time to assemble all his notes and place them in his journal. So far, he was able to keep all of them intact and he was still in possession of his map. Time was running out for any productive activity for this day, so his plans were changed to camp at the shelter for the night where they could refresh their body and their minds. It was just another day for Running Deer in his quest for knowledge. However, for Beaver and Bear, they were concerned that their delayed arrival at home might unduly create fear that they had possibly met with an untimely fate.

This would not be the first time that they would be late returning home, but there was so much depending on their hunting skills and success. The first business at hand would be to dry out the area and prepare for a fire site. The place was drenched from the storm, but the undergrowth was so thick that enough usable branches could be gathered for the fire. Food was the next concern. All of the men carried dried beef and cold biscuits to munch on, but according to their stomachs, it was time for serious food.

As hunters, the men knew that small animals sought shelter in a deluge, and as a result, they would be scampering about to resume their places in the woods after the storm was over. Acting on this premise, all three of them scattered out and began to scout the area for any action. The first unfortunate animal was a medium sized arahkun which left safety on the lower limb of a chestnut tree and plopped to the ground. A quick retrieval of an arrow from the quiver of Running Deer, and their potential feast was no longer a speculation. Coon meat, or as the Indian called arahkun, was somewhat of a delicacy among woods folk.

Nevertheless, Bear would not be happy until he had bagged a nice fat rabbit. All agreed that that would add flavor to the meal. He quickly, but stealthily, stalked the inland area and vowed within himself that he would not go for just any small animal that he might come upon. He drew upon his long-time honed hunting skills to seek game that was worth his efforts. After all, among a hunter's expertise, was a well-earned sense of pride. He would not say as much to his long time hunting partner, and especially not to his new found friend. A likely retort would be a reprimand for being choosy when your stomach's empty.

Bear was saved this fate when a fat fox squirrel became lodged in his sight. A swift reaction of his left hand stopped the rodent dead in its tracks. He returned to the site, and in a few minutes, the squirrel was skinned and ready for roasting.

"What's a banquet without dessert, boys," he said, "there's enough to go around."

The lingering clouds had now given way to sunlight, but a look at the sinking orange ball in the west told them that dusk would soon be settling in. The fire was beginning to crackle leaving red hot coals on which to roast the meat hanging from their make-shift spit. By the time that the sun had set, the diners were full and now it was time to clean up. There was very little left to leave for the carnivorous woods dwellers or the final clean-up by the vultures.

The fire was now stoked to provide light and also to alleviate a chill that would be forthcoming on this fall night. Running Deer had become more accustomed to John Beaver and Bear and he figured that they had earned his trust. They had not been inquisitive up to this point, but he decided that maybe it was time to share some of the information that he had gained up to this point in his journey. Not that either would be interested, but the more that they trusted him, he thought, the easier it would be to interview the old lady.

After the three were comfortably seated around the fire, Running Deer began the conversation by saying "I have become more acquainted with you two since we have spent this time together under less than favorable circumstances. I have learned to trust you and hope that you have come to trust me. I am going to share with you some of the reasons for my journey and also some of the information that I have managed to gain thus far."

The two hunters shifted themselves into a more comfortable position by the fire, indicating that they were eager to hear what Running Deer had to say. Ambition was not an important thing in their priorities since food gathering had always been at the forefront in their lives, but both of them remembered sitting at their parent's feet anxiously awaiting the next story. It was like the calm after the storm, since the quietness dominated the little area that they were fortunate in securing, while only a few hours before, they had been seeking shelter from a life-threatening storm. Their stomachs were sated from the wild game that they had just devoured, so they promised to stay awake if his story was interesting.

Running Deer continued by saying that there were others who would be interested in the results of his findings on this trip. Without mentioning names, he said that he had been sent out by an important person to gather information that would result in setting the record straight about an occurrence in past history that had never been resolved.

John Beaver interrupted by saying "you must be one of those arkyologists that used to roam around Ocracoke. I hear they've never been able to find many artyfacts."

"No, I am not an archeologist," Running Deer replied, "however, I have been able to dig up a few important clues", he said in jest.

He went on to mention the mixed breed people that he had encountered, the discovery of an old English coin, and the carving left on an old tree. While he was discussing these findings, he was hopeful that his listeners might have come across similar discoveries. For the most part, though, they were as attentive as elementary students in a classroom awaiting further elements of his story. When questioned by Running Deer, neither of them had run across any unexplainable discoveries. They did, however, admit that they had found several Indian artifacts like arrow heads, shards of cooking and eating ware, but nothing to link the early inhabitants to the visiting Englishmen.

"On second thought", Bear Said, "I recall our great granddaddy mentioning the name of a man that he knew who was endowed with savage traits but had bright blue eyes like a European or other foreigner would have. At the time that he said this, I was very young and did not take further opportunity to enquire further about this. The fate of the "so-called" lost colony has been a subject that has been mentioned from time to time, but never has been explored by family members."

"Yeah, he's right", echoed John Beaver, "it has never been a matter of concern amongst us. We jes' chalk it up to legend."

"Be that as it may," continued Running Deer, "the mystery has caused great concern among succeeding generations, and many have created their own ideas as to what their fate was, but no one has been able to prove their theory. So it has become my task to set the record straight. My mentor, Chief Waccasaw, has placed the responsibility on my shoulders. He has assured me that, with his help and others, the task will be completed. And with the information at hand, there will be no more speculation as to what took place in these very parts over two hundred years ago."

The exchange continued for another hour or so but there was nothing substantive gained from their conversation. The first to mention bedtime was Bear who suggested that they bank the fire coals and get as comfortable as possible for a good night's rest. There was a second by John Beaver that was followed closely by a nod from Running Deer. He had already read the sky and had decided that the morrow would be an excellent day for hiking and he was looking forward to it.

There was no dream this night for Running Deer and he was thankful that he was able to sleep straight through without interruption. He was the first to awake and was able to enliven the still smoldering coals on which he was able to heat some clear branch water for coffee. The running water that he had discovered was from an underground stream that was just a few yards from the brackish water of the river. Fresh water was a precious commodity and he considered himself fortunate to have found it.

Chapter Seven

BY THE TIME THAT THE coffee was ready and the aroma filled the campsite, John and Bear were beginning to stir. It was another half hour before daybreak, but all three of them were used to stirring early. A hunter knows the value of early morning hours so they were not strangers to rising early. Running Deer also knew that the days would be gradually shortening and he needed to take advantage of daylight hours and good weather. They took advantage of the few pieces of meat left over from the previous evening and soon were ready to move out.

Secure in the knowledge that John and Bear would be guiding this part of the journey, Running Deer was free to scan the area for any clues that might be useful for him. Donning their equipment, they moved out in a northerly direction. Running Deer followed closely behind as Beaver and Bear spread out within hearing distance of each other as they slowly and determinedly made their way in the general direction of their home site. They were not traveling along a familiar path but their instinct kept them in the right direction as it had done many times before. A seasoned hunter has acquired numerous ways to move about the forest without becoming lost.

Running Deer was willing to trust their guidance, yet occasionally, he would retrieve his compass from his backpack to reassure himself. The forest appeared to be a fine habitat for game, so he was hopeful that his friends would not be disappointed. There was a clear blue sky overhead and the forest was thick with a variety of longleaf and loblolly pine that were huge from many years of growth. Intermingled with the pines was a mixture of hardwoods that towered above the undergrowth nearer the ground. As they progressed through the woods, the movement of small animals could be heard as they scampered through the now-drying brush to seek food. The hunter's ears were alerted to the slightest sound but were able to differentiate between the smaller ones and others that were worth pursuing.

After an uneventful couple of hours, the sun was higher in the sky creating beams of bright sunlight that enveloped their surroundings. The woods was drying out more now making it more comfortable to proceed. By noon, it was hard to determine how far they had come, but the last hour had been easier going, so they agreed on a guess of three miles.

"How much longer?", asked Running Deer. The question did not receive a good answer.

The onward trek continued for another half hour before a loud hooting yell came from the direction in which John Beaver had headed. A similar yell emanated from another direction which Running Deer reckoned was a reply from Bear. He assumed that they would be meeting soon to carry out a predetermined plan for assistance. He figured that if John Beaver had killed a deer or other large animal, he would be able to offer his assistance. The distance separating them was farther than he had anticipated, so after about fifteen more minutes, he decided to try to make contact by yelling loudly himself.

An instant response from Beaver was so loud that it astounded Running Deer. He discovered that he was within fifty yards. Bear had arrived at the scene minutes before. Bear had dispatched a huge black bear sow with multiple shots from his bow. It clearly indicated that, for Beaver's sake, there had been no room for error. Three or more cubs had scampered away from the dreadful scene and were still circling the area. A decision was made to skin and gut the bear and to save the choice cuts to take to the family. The process took two hours but could have been done sooner had it not been for a learning process that was afforded Running Deer. He had never skinned a bear before, but had always admired a bearskin rug and the many other uses for the hide.

After taking time to cook part of the meat for a mid-day meal, the bounty was evenly divided among the three for further transport to the compound. The logistics of travel would be different for the remainder of the trip because they would not be concentrating on hunting. So the three set out together this time for the final leg of this trip. After navigating around and through thick vines and briers for two hours, the duo of John Beaver and Moon Bear figured that another hour remained on the trip back home.

The sun was beginning to sink in the west, obscuring their pathway, but the area was more familiar now and they knew that they would make it before dark. There was cheerful banter among the men, having almost completed a successful hunt—never mind the single prize. Bear and Beaver were looking forward to introducing their new friend to their elders. Though their folks had rarely left the area, they hoped that they would be helpful to Running Deer. Running Deer was hopeful, also, that his delayed trip would not be in vain.

Several small and medium sized rabbits and a lone red fox ran across their path, but this would be their lucky day. As they approached the log cabin, a scrawny yard dog ran out to greet them. From the looks of the mutt, Running Deer secretly hoped that this was not a sign of the condition of the inhabitants. It wasn't long before human heads began to look around the corner of the building. First, there were three, and then others rushed out to greet them. Among the crowd was four children ranging in age from about three to twelve. They were barefooted, but neatly dressed. After spotting Running Deer, the children slowed down and waited for the three to approach.

The older ones hesitated to speak, apparently waiting for Beaver to make the introduction. He was the first to speak after he nodded for the other two to shed their loads. Facing one of the older women, he pointed to Running Deer and said: "This is a traveler that we met near the river who wants to make an acquaintance of our family. His name is Running Deer and he tells us his name has been adopted from an Indian name, but that he is a white man on a quest for knowledge. We want you to welcome him into our household for a short visit. As you can see, we are bringing bear meat from our hunt, so lets prepare a scrumptious meal for our guest. After which, he is desirous of having a talk with our elders."

The women nodded in agreement and immediately began to prepare for the feast.

Beaver directed Running Deer to a small creek a few hundred yards from the cabin where he could take a much needed bath in privacy. The temperature of the water was surprisingly warm for the season. This was a special treat for him since his pathway through the forest had afforded very few opportunities for refreshment. As he basked in the clear tepid water, his mind wandered from where he had begun the journey to a place where it might end. He tried to piece together all the clues that he had happened upon and how much more would be needed before his journey would be complete and his search for knowledge satisfied.

He was suddenly awakened from his daydreaming state when he heard a loud clang from the direction of the compound. He figured that it was supper time, so he hastened to dry himself off, don his clothes and rejoin the others. Without realizing how much time had transpired, he came upon a huge table that was already set with a feast to behold. His eyes gazed upon a table that was far more resplendent than he had ever beheld anywhere much less on his journey. The aroma of food was such that he would place it against any that he had ever savored. There were more people present now that represented a wide range of ages.

All of the children aged about sixteen downward were seated at a separate table. A quick glance around the scene told Running Deer that most all of the inhabitants were dark complexioned, with raised cheek bones to show a possible Indian connection, but in contrast to those features, were added a decided display of bright blue eyes. He reasoned that he shouldn't jump to any conclusions, but he couldn't help but think that there was an emergence there of Caucasian and native Indian blood.

The table was set in a festive manner with ample, yet not fancy bowls, full of what appeared to be venison and lighter game meat with a gravy boat residing in the middle of it all. Green beans, shelled peas, and browned squash fritters complimented the meat. Before a utensil was raised, the elder of the group that occupied a seat at the end of the table, raised his hands to the heavens and then slowly placed them on the table to offer thanks to the Creator for the provision of food. There was nary a slight snicker from any of the children until after the Amen.

The meal began quietly and then John Beaver broke the silence. Turning to Running Deer, he asked if he would like to tell the family about how he happened to be in these parts, and then he would be free to ask questions of the others. In doing so, he explained that it had been many seasons since they had had a visitor and that it was a real pleasure to have him as their guest. Several nods followed and all eyes turned toward Running Deer to listen to his story. Sensing a genuine friendship that was shown by their actions and hospitality, he felt free to relate, in some detail, a story of his journey so far.

Between bites of the tasty vittles, he related to his listeners, the reason for his quest and some of the memorable events that he had encountered so far. At the tables, all ears seemed to be attuned to what Running Deer had to say. In many ways, this was not a routine meal. In the first place, it was a welcome home for Moon Bear and John Beaver. The fact that they had brought a guest with them from the hunt created an air of excitement among the adults as well as the children. The elders had been able to tutor the children by reading to them but they were limited due to their own upbringing.

One of the boys, a sixteen year old, was especially attentive to Running Deer's story. He listened in wide-eyed amazement as he learned of visitors from across the ocean and how they managed to become lost in such a short period of time. After the meal, the young man made his way to Running Deer and introduced himself as Thaddeus, grandson of Moon Bear. He wanted to hear more of his adventures and wondered if he would find time to talk more. Running Deer explained to him that he must be on his way soon, but perhaps he could take a few more minutes before bedtime to talk. The youngster shook his hand and nodded in appreciation.

I must seek out the eldest of the clan, Running Deer thought, who might have knowledge that was handed down from their ancestors. As the diners moved away from the eating area, the women immediately began the clean-up chores while the men assembled in a common area to smoke and talk. Running Deer felt obligated to join them, but secretly hoped that they would break up soon and allow him to talk to Talitha who was introduced as Bear's grandmother.

She was ninety seven years old and was purported to be the keeper of the family history. After about an hour, his wish was granted, so he made his way to a corner of the cabin where she sat rocking and reading an old and tattered Bible. "Pleased to make your acquaintance", gushed Running Deer, "you have heard my name and I have been told that you are Talitha."

Slightly more than an inaudible grunt was heard as she turned to look him in the eye. "Talitha Bankhead", she finally uttered as she pointed toward a cane-bottomed chair in the corner. "My daughter, Fair Moon, was Bear's mother. She died of the fever ten years ago."

"I'm sorry to hear that," Running Deer said. I know that you miss her."

At first looking downward, then raising her eyes to the ceiling, she pointed a long finger upward and said "She's with Great Spirit—she'll be fine."

Sensing an opportunity to question the old lady about her heritage, he asked if there was English blood in her background. Without hesitating, she explained that her daddy had said that he had come from a mixed blood of white man and Indian ancestors. She went on to explain that she did not know the source of either because her daddy never went into detail about it.

"Do you have any written history such as an old Bible record that might contain any more information about your grandparents," said Running Deer, "that might give us a clue about your ancestry?"

"There is an old document", she said, "but I have not been able to make heads nor tails of it. My reading is limited, but you are welcome to look at it if you care to."

A sense of encouragement swept over Running Deer as he thought that this would be the first time on his journey that he had had an opportunity to possibly find a clue or an answer from a written document. "Yes ma'm, I would care to," he responded, "and I wish to apologize if I seem to be intruding in your personal affairs."

"You're the first man that has intruded in over forty years," said she with a toothless smile, "so go ahead and help yourself." The old woman shuffled into her bedroom to retrieve the "document" as she referred to it, and shortly returned to her favorite spot, the old creaky rocking chair. "Here it is", she said as she handed the yellowing keepsake to Running Deer, "but be careful how you handle it, because it might fall apart."

"I shall be very careful", he responded, "because I have a feeling that it is very important to you."

"Oh, it is", she retorted, "it was given to me by my pa and he said to guard it with my life."

Very carefully, Running Deer untied a brownish red ribbon from around the rolled up document and slowly unrolled it, at the same time literally holding his breath. It looked to be several pages in length and the scribbling appeared to be legible.

"This makes the second time it has been unrolled," she said, "you're the first one that has shown any interest in its contents. Part of it, I have not seen, because no one here has cared about it. If you find anything interesting about our family, I will be obliged if you will tell the younguns. Some day, they might like to pass it along to their children."

Running Deer promised to do that, but at the moment, he was anxious to get on with the business at hand.

There was a few introductory lines at the top of the first page that named the author and the names of those to whom it was addressed. The best that he could make of the first name was "Jepthah Lasie, descendent of James Lasie and Secotan, late of Hatterask". It continued on to state that "these words are written so that our descendents might learn of their ancestry for posterity". Running Deer was extremely careful as he placed weights on each end of the pages so that it could be more easily deciphered.

Miraculously, most of the words on the first page were discernible and showed an excellent handwriting skill. As he read on, he discovered that the bulk of the entry had to do with names and dates. Mixed with English names were a number of Indian sounding names. Some of the names were not decipherable by him but he continued to read all of it as he carefully unrolled the voluminous scroll. Out of the corner of his eye, he noticed that Talitha had closed her eyes and the rocking had ceased.

Thinking that she was taking a nap, he began to read to himself so as not to disturb her. When he reached the end of the long list of names, he came across some writing that appeared to have changed from the original. It looked as if more than one person had participated in writing it. As his eyes scanned the heading of the document, he came across a date of 1599 in one corner. This confirms, he thought, that this is a very old record and that it remains legible in fairly good condition. The words appeared in Early English, and to Running Deer, it was equivalent to discovering a gold mine.

The first line began—"These words are written to inform the reader that my grandfather, James Lasie, and others managed to escape from the little English outpost on the mainland before it was overtaken by savages. We made our escape through the help of a friendly Indian, who to this day, remains nameless. As he pushed our canoes out into the Chowanoke, an arrow that was meant for us, went straight to his heart." As Running Deer paused to take in all this, his attention was again directed to Talitha in the old rocking chair. He was hoping to be able to talk with her about what he had just read, but was taken aback when he discovered that the old lady was no longer breathing.

He placed a marker at the point that he had stopped reading and then reached over to feel her pulse. He was unable to detect a movement, so he looked around to see to whom he was going to announce this shocking discovery. There was no adult in the immediate vicinity, and he didn't want to upset the children, so he looked around for Beaver or Bear. He found both of them outside the cabin preparing the bear's hide for drying and tanning. Dusk was beginning to envelope the area but they were taking advantage of the remaining rays from the setting sun.

At first introduction, he sensed a closeness in this family, so he struggled with the words to say at a time like this. He finally made up his mind, so he simply stated that he had noticed that Talitha was real still and he was afraid that there was something wrong with her.

Bear said "she's just taking a nap as she usually does when she settles down in that rocking chair."

"At any rate", said Running Dear, "I'd be obliged if you'd check on her because she was real attentive when I began reading the old document."

So Bear motioned for Beaver to stop what he was doing and go check on the old lady. Beaver laid his flaying tools aside to accompany Running Deer into the cabin to check on her. What he found there verified that Talitha had indeed passed away peacefully while listening to Running Deer read from the old document. If there was any sound at all from her, he was unable to hear it because he was so deeply interested in its contents. The two of them returned to the yard to apprise Bear of what he had known all along.

"Don't say a word", Beaver said, "let me handle the sad chore of breaking the news to the rest. The children will take this real hard, so I need time to figure out a way to break the news to them."

Running Deer agreed and said that he would steal off to a place by himself to continue reading. He wanted to read it slowly so that he could soak up this very important piece of history, and at the same time, jot down parts of it that he thought would be critical to his research. He would wait until all members of the family were aware of what had happened in their midst to their loved one, and then he would join in to help in any way that an outsider could. Beaver thanked him and told him that he would let him know when to rejoin them.

As he read further through the document, he came upon more evidence that the Bankheads were indeed descendents of mixed English and Siouxan blood. Thereon was a notation that a great-grandfather on Talitha's side of the family was a full-blooded Croatoan Indian. The discovery was so revealing that he knew that he should write the information down and not trust to memory. So he reached into his backpack and retrieved a sheet of papyrus and a quill.

As he began to write, Bear walked up to him to make an announcement that all was well with the family and he was welcome to come and be a part of the mourning and memorial process. All had agreed that they no longer considered him a stranger. He marked his place once again and put away his writing material. He followed Bear back to the cabin where he began to speak to each member of the family to express his sorrow for the loss of a family member that he knew meant a great deal to them for a long, long time. He learned from an entry in the old document that she soon would have been ninety nine years old.

He considered her to be a significant link in the history of her clan, and also because she had been the caretaker of the written source of history that he now had in his possession for reading. He had no intention of keeping the document but felt an obligation to impress upon the others to guard it so that it would be available to pass on down to her heirs. There was no doubt in his mind that that would have been her last will and testament.

John Beaver and Moon Bear, who were now the elders of the family, met apart from the others to make plans for the old woman's burial. Running Deer assumed that there would be a Christian burial, but he awaited their announcement as he sought a few minutes alone at the outer perimeter of the cabin. Beaver and Bear soon returned to make an announcement to the family. There had been no written will left by Talitha, but they had heard her say on a few occasions that she didn't care for the burial ceremony that her ancestors used. They conducted last rites for their members and had a formal burial known as "communal burial" or ossuary.

Her stated request was for simple family last rites and an individual grave which would also contain her personal possessions such as shell beads and her beloved peacock hat pins to be placed in her "pine box" with her. Nothing fancy, she had said, just a few rocks on top of the mound and a simple oak wood cross. She was a believer in earthly spirits as expressed in nature, but she also looked forward to her life in the hereafter.

Bear wiped a tear from his eye and allowed that "surely we can do no less than these simple wishes."

After the decision was firmed as to type of burial, the women of the family were anxious to prepare the body for burial. There was a procedure that the family had followed for many years. When a family member passed away, a mixture of assorted herbs was quickly gathered to use as an ointment to help preserve the body. There was traditionally a short wake period before the final burial. Most of the women, including the younger ones, were involved in the process. Running Deer let them know that he did not want to get in their way, but would be available if they needed him. This is as close as he had been to a death in the family since his grandfather had passed away when he was a mere lad.

It was bedtime and it looked as if all the necessary chores had been taken care of, so he bade the family goodnight and retired to his bed. He was extremely tired in body and spirit, so he looked forward to a restful night's sleep. It was not to be though, because a dream invaded his quiet slumber, which he later referred to as a nightmare. The dream consisted of two parts. In the first part, there was a scene of a number of Indians who were gathered around a brightly burning fire as if they were in an important tribal powwow. He could not understand their language but knew that whatever they were saying could affect him or someone he knew.

Just as if a play had moved into a second act, the next scene showed several white people tied to stakes with the Indian children appearing from the nearby woods with armloads of brush. Others had already dropped their loads around the stakes that held the captives. The strange thing about this second part was that there was also a number of white women who were standing around the area looking on passively.

This was the part that he deemed a nightmare. As the burning flames reached the trussed captive men, there was no audible screams coming from them, but instead they stretched out their arms as if to bid their wives and children to join them.

As the women and children began walking toward the men, Running Deer awoke with a cry of "No, No, No.". He began to look around to see if he had awakened anyone, and when he determined that he had not, he realized that it was only a dream—a terrible dream. He tried to go back to sleep, but lying awake, he attempted to interpret his dream. After about an hour, he gave up and drifted back to sleep. The next thing he knew, the sun was shining brightly through a crack in the closed window and he heard voices coming from the exterior that sounded like the burial ceremony for Talitha was already under way.

He donned his clothes and quietly joined the family just before he heard a hearty "Amen" said by John Beaver and then an echoed Amen from everyone gathered there. Then it was time to inter the body, so he watched as the children came by the casket one at a time, where they placed Talitha's favorite beads and other items by her side. It was a very touching ceremony and one that Running Deer reckoned that he would remember all his life. It came time for the men and older boys to cover the casket with the dark loamy soil and later to decorate the mound with pebbles gathered from a local stream. Then later, a fitting wooden cross would mark the spot where she laid in rest. It was done just as she had requested.

It was time now, Running Deer thought, that he should continue on his journey alone. But first, he would begin at the point where he had left off, in reading the old document. It was such an interesting piece of history that he thought it would surely help him in his quest. He would leave the household with their mourning which he guessed would last for at least a week or two. They would then get back to living life as usual except for the presence of Talitha.

The morning was half over now, he had finished reading the document, so he decided to have one more meal with the family and then be on his way. Anyway, he had been invited to do so, and who was he to refuse their kind hospitality. The fall weather was becoming more evident, so he was constantly aware of the fact that storms could appear anytime. For the time, though, the clouds did not look menacing. For him, it had not been more evident than now, that he should step up his efforts to move on toward the old fort ruins. He would be alone now and would be able to move more diligently toward his goal.

Gathering his belongings, he carefully armed himself with bow, arrows, knife and spear. From his experiences so far, almost anything could and more than likely would happen in the deep woods. His trusty compass in hand, he bade everyone farewell with a special hug for the children and promised to stop by and see them again if his travels brought him back their way. Deep in his heart, though, he knew that he would never see them again. There was a deep fondness in his heart for most of the characters that he had chanced to meet, but through it all, he knew there was a higher purpose. Parting was always sweet sorrow, but he had learned to live with it.

With a simple twist of his body, he stepped out into the unknown once more. The weather was still in his favor, but he knew that soon he would be experiencing a chill in the air, so he might have to keep on the lookout for an additional animal fur. John Beaver and Moon Bear had told him of the presence of black bears in the area and he knew that a bearskin provided a mighty fine covering. But for the present, he was intent on moving on toward his goal.

Chapter Eight

FOR AN HOUR OR SO, the lack of tough underbrush was in his favor. But then, he encountered a swampy area which slowed him down considerably. He spent perhaps another hour attempting to find his way around it without compromising his sense of direction. Finally he acceded to the very unfavorable conditions and decided to take it on headfirst. If there was water in the swamp, he deduced that there might be an easier way to navigate around it. At any rate, it wouldn't be the first time that he had guessed wrong.

He retrieved his trusty knife, which he had remembered to sharpen back at the cabin, and began to hack through the thick myriad of vines. The undergrowth was so thick that even after an hour of solid hacking and working his way through the network, he could look back and see where he had started. Even though he didn't want to, he decided to take a break while he quenched his thirst. If he were to come upon fresh water, he would be able to refill his canteen which was very essential to his sustenance.

He reckoned that there was only three hours or so left in the day before darkness would set in, so he resumed the arduous task of working his way through the forest. Continuing on through the swampland, he was interrupted by the unmistakable sound of a she bear. The noise produced by the crackling of branches and the movement of his knife against the vines had upset the relative quietness of the surrounding area. As he listened and moved very quietly toward the area of the growling sound, it suddenly became quiet again. He knew from this that he must be near the source.

Then the growling resumed from a place at his back. He turned quickly and saw that he had aroused a medium sized black mother bear with three cubs in tow. He shook off a sudden pang of fear and readied himself for the attack. He wasn't in favor of separating a momma from her kids, but he had little choice. It was a matter of him or her, so he decided in favor of himself. Besides, the cubs were getting to be a good size now and they more than likely had had the proper hands-on training to take care of themselves.

He readied his bow, pulled back the arrow, and released a lethal blow into the big gal's heart. The bear continued to advance toward him, but at a twenty yard distance, began to stagger and finally fall to the forest floor. Taking no chances, he drew his knife and approached the dying bear with care. By this time, the three juvenile balls of fur had beat it back into the woods. Running Deer was a realist when it came to an incident of this sort, so he would not rule out the possibility of the head of the family being somewhere close by. He knew that if this was the case, he had problems ahead.

He decided to wait a few minutes before commencing the arduous duty of butchering and skinning his prize. The sun was about two hours before setting now, so he decided to quickly scout around for a place to bed down for the night. This was a priority for him at the moment plus he needed a suitable location to attend to the dead bear. It wasn't a perfect spot, but he settled on a place beneath a huge cypress tree. The presence of the cypress trees around him suggested that he was near a stream or at least a swamp that contained pockets of fresh water.

After removing his backpack and gear, he began to search around the area as usual for nice dry branches for which to start a fire when the time came for supper. The meal that he had partaken of before he left the Bankheads had satisfied his hunger at the time, but he was beginning to get a mite hungry after working so hard. He was soon able to gather enough branches for the fire, so after clearing a place for it, he began to explore the immediate area in search of a water supply.

Before he had gone fifty yards from his base, he came upon a quiet flow of water that was bubbling up at the center of a small pond that spread out in a circle that highlighted a tranquil swamp scene. There were no bird calls, no frog croaks, or slithering of moccasins. Given the quietness of the place, he thought of it as a garden. A plenteous supply of fresh, cool water caused him to gaze upward into the tree tops, hoping to spy ripe fruit hanging from their branches. That was not the case, however, so he came out of his reverie and suddenly thought of the dead bear that he was going to have to deal with.

He knelt at the edge of the fresh water pond to sate his thirst. He could not believe how sweet and cool the water was and he already had plans to fill his water canteens and perhaps craft another firkin to add to his available containers. He had no way of knowing how much farther he had to go before he would reach the final goal of the first leg of his journey. He would, however, take enough time while he was there to summarize his actions so far so that he would be better prepared when he set out the next morning.

Back at the campsite, he rigged a rack on which to hang the bear to make his job easier. This was accomplished by cutting some vines that were plentiful in the area. He used the vines to shape the rack while they were supported by the lower tree branches and stakes driven into the ground. He sharpened his knife on a nearby stone and began the tedious work of removing the bears entrails. Then using the experience taught to him by former hunting friends, he carefully removed the choice portions of meat.

He knew that he couldn't rush the process, but the very sight of the meat caused his stomach to growl. When he had removed all of the finer portions of meat, he was ready to start the fire to begin the cooking process. The evening was drawing nigh now, and while the sun began its final daily descent into the horizon, the fire made up for the lost light. The smell of the meat cooking was a most welcome aroma, and even his stomach seemed to sense what was about to happen.

The weather continued in his favor and he was looking forward to sleeping in the open. The possible presence of more bears had not left his mind, so he made a practical decision to keep the fire going on into the night. He remembered that his pa had told him that bears didn't like to be around fires. He felt so satisfied after the meal that he wanted to stay up later to bring his journal up to date and to prepare plans for the morrow. The heavy meal had the effect of making him sleepy, so he had to brew coffee to keep him awake after the sun had set.

He gathered another armload of dry branches to feed the fire and then he began to add notes to his journal. There were some notations to go on his map and another look at where he reckoned himself to be in relation to his destination. The crackling fire and the coffee was not enough to keep him awake for long, so after an hour or so, he added a few branches and proceeded to make himself comfortable for bed. Sleep came quickly, but he was awakened after what he perceived to be just minutes, by a deep growling noise.

Grabbing his spear and knife, he jumped up and quickly surveyed the campsite. The fire had subsided and in the dim light he saw the outline of a huge black bear that had gotten the scent of the fresh meat and was already proceeding to scatter it on the ground. Running Deer considered himself lucky that the bear had been drawn to the meat before there had been an attempt to attack him. He proceeded cautiously in the direction of the animal with his spear poised and his left hand holding his knife. He had not tackled a bear of this size in all of his hunting experience, but he felt capable of defending himself.

He quickly made the decision to attempt to scare the bear away rather than wound him and possibly create a worse scenario. Unfortunately the foraging animal was not going to be intimidated, so he continued on his destructive path. This situation did not please Running Deer, so he was faced with only two courses of action. He would quietly gather his possessions and leave the skin and fresh meat behind or he would summon all of his hunting acumen and try to kill the beast.

Accepting the latter choice would prove to be one of the worst decisions that he had ever made. Anger at the loss of his mate had made the bear even more ferocious. Instead of backing off at the sight of his approaching adversary, he rushed forward to attack Running Deer. As the spear was held back to gain more thrusting power, the onrushing animal stretched both claws into a position to bring his threatening opponent down. Not being able to release his spear, Running Deer was now in a situation that required bringing all of his life saving skills into place which left no time for posturing.

Using all of the agility that he could muster, he quickly moved to one side and prevented the full force of his attacker's claws from swatting him in the face. While posturing for his next move, he felt a warm trickle moving down his neck and into his clothes. He knew that he was wounded, but did not know to what extent. He had no time now to assess the magnitude of his wound, instead he was faced with another attack imminently because the huge hulk had repositioned itself for the kill. The adrenalin rush of mere survival was now felt by

Running Deer, so he reached to get to his knife which had fallen to the ground. Disregarding the ominous claws of a snorting male bear, he swung for the jugular. He was right on target, but the eventual fatal blow did not stop the raging ursine.

He had been proud of the fact that he had been forced to use the help of Akimko only a few times on his journey, but now he thought, there is a real need for help if I'm going to survive. Turning his head aside, he gave the high pitched whistle signal, and immediately heard the whirring wings of his helper, Akimko. In a way unexplainable by Running Deer, the great bird was chasing the wounded bear from the campsite.

After the commotion had settled, Running Deer turned his attention to his wound. The bleeding wound was in a location that he could not see, so he stripped himself clear of his upper garment, and only then did he realize the magnitude of it. His clothes were soaked in crimson and he was beginning to feel weak from the loss of blood. He had heard of an old Indian medicinal recipe for using leaves as a compress for slowing the flow of blood, but had never used it. Looking desperately around the area, he searched for a leaf that resembled the one used for the purpose. His eyes immediately came upon a large plant with heart shaped leaves that was growing nearby.

The idea came to him that he could place the large leaves on the wound which he discovered was on his neck above his left shoulder. It certainly would be worth a try and he knew that he had to begin somewhere. In order to hold the leaves in place, he proceeded to shred a shirt so that he could use the material to wrap around his neck. Not wanting to return to his former friends' cabin that he had left just hours before, he decided to make himself a comfortable pallet on the ground where he could lie down and wait for the bleeding to stop.

Either from sheer exhaustion or weakness from the loss of blood, he drifted off to sleep. He had tried to fight sleep as long as he could, but was overcome by a drowsiness that he could not handle. While in deep sleep, Chief Waccasaw appeared to him—first, like a figure among the clouds and then standing at his side.

His first words were "Fear not, Running Deer, I have been following your progress and I am very pleased with what I have seen. Continue on the path that you have taken and before many moons have passed, you will arrive at your first goal. When you arrive, remember your instructions on how to summon me and there we will have important conversation. So, stay the course. Do not worry about bear wound."

The sudden appearance of the chief was too real to be an apparition, so Running Deer was anxious to converse with him. But before he could utter his first word, the chief disappeared into the surrounding scenery and was no longer in his sight. He slept the balance of the night without event and awoke to a beautiful sun drenched morning. The wound was not the first of his concerns, but became a close second as he turned his neck to survey the area around him. He quickly placed his hand there to find out if the bleeding had stopped. There was no wetness, so he assumed that the leaf compress had worked and he proceeded to unwrap the binding that held the self-administered medicinal wrap against the wound.

To his surprise and relief, the wound required very little cleaning so he decided to leave any covering off so that it would heal quicker. There was a slight pain, especially as he moved his head around, but he was fortunate that the vicious claws had not struck near an artery. He suddenly recalled the mysterious meeting with Chief Waccasaw, and then decided that maybe—just maybe—the chief might have been responsible for saving his life. As the day drew on, he was feeling like his old self and considered the confrontation with the bear to be only a slight impediment to his goal.

He cleaned up his campsite, gathered the hide and what remained of the meat, and was now on his way again. If the weather continued as it was, he would be able to cover a lot of ground this day. The underbrush and thick vines had given way to clear forest floor and he felt that he must be getting nearer to a river and perhaps some civilization. His map had shown scattered houses or huts if he had chosen the correct direction. But before he moved on, he retrieved his map, made a few notations, gathered his gear, and made sure his protective weapons were at the ready.

After a quick reading of his compass, he headed in a direction that he hoped would move him closer to the old fort by the end of the day. He had two important things going for him, among others, the weather and less undergrowth—at least as far as he could determine. There was an inner yearning for company, even a dog, but he understood the responsibility that would be his and knew that that was probably the reason that he traveled alone on this segment of his journey. He had an over-riding desire to complete his quest successfully for the Chief, and of course, he felt that the information gained by his journey would benefit the people who would learn from it.

These thoughts clouded his mind as he walked farther into the forest and helped him to forget the healing wound that was on his neck. Occasionally he would be reminded of this when he turned his head to scan the area around him. As the day wore on, the bright overhead sunshine had turned into shadows around him to remind him that even though he was making good progress, he would have to stop in a very few hours to again search for a suitable spot to set up camp for the night.

Another occurrence that sneaked up on him was the slight darkening of the sky. The tree canopy was less dense making it easier to view the clouds that were gathering. The situation prodded him to begin looking sooner than he intended. Another 380 degree turn revealed the shape of a small hut or lean-to that was nestled in a grove of loblolly trees to the south. He figured, with good luck, he would reach the location within a half-hour.

The change of course prompted him to leave gash marks on the trees as he made his way toward the site. He had learned that precautions of this nature might come in handy in case he would have to back-track. After a quarter hour, he obtained a better view of the little wooden structure and it was turning out to be larger than he had first thought. In case it was occupied, he kept his ears attuned to any sound that might emanate from the site. The vines were becoming a little more difficult to navigate through, so in order to stay on his course, he had to hack his way through. This action kept him another thirty minutes or so before he emerged into a clearer path.

Stopping for a few minutes to rest, he now could see the site clearer and one of the first things he saw at the rear of the building was an up-ended canoe sitting on a makeshift table or cross boards on legs. At this distance, he couldn't make out if it was a skin covered hull or had been hued out of a log. He was making much better progress now, which was good, because the darkened sky was becoming more ominous—particularly in the west where the clouds had gathered and had formed a solid blackness.

Occasionally there was a flash of light that seemed to bring relief to the darkness. As he moved closer to his goal, loud peals of thunder were beginning to be heard as if in concert with each bolt of lightning. Immediately in front of him, he heard a ripple of moving water. He walked around in front of the old structure and saw that it was a combination hunting and fishing lodge that appeared to have been occasionally used. The door was closed, but not locked, so he rapped upon the weather-beaten surface of the door before he went ahead and opened it. There was no reply from within, so he slowly pushed the door open and looked all around.

On the inside was a crude makeshift bed accommodating a mattress that seemed to be filled with corn shucks. There was a makeshift table which afforded a dining area and an old lantern which contained about a half tank of some kind of oil. It looked as though someone had occupied it in the not too distant past. This was not going to keep him from taking advantage of this shelter in a storm. He returned to the outside and was met by a fierce wind and a few drops of rain. This prompted him to begin gathering fallen boughs and branches so that he would be able to keep dry and prepare food for himself.

At first, it was easy to find dry pieces but the situation soon changed. The thunder and lightning had intensified, and with it, the downpour followed. He managed to gather enough material to bring inside where there was a centrally located fire pit that had been used many times before. In combination with the darkening sky and the lateness of the day, things began to take on an ominous look around him, but he was glad to be inside and partially protected from the gathering storm. Some of the branches were not entirely dry and they began to crackle loudly as they burned.

As he sat for a few minutes enjoying the warmth and light of the fire, his eyes began to scan the room around him. He noticed a few cooking utensils, a couple of pieces of pottery, but what really caught his eye was an object that looked like a book of some sort. "That's very interesting", he thought, but decided to check it out later. Now was the time to dry out his clothes and sleeping quarters so that he could refresh himself after a tiresome day in the deep forest. He was used to travelling alone but he wanted to be in good shape for the balance of his journey. He had a gut feeling that he was nearing the end of the first leg of his journey, so he needed time to review and assess his findings thus far.

By now, the rain was pounding the little shack with a force that was akin to a light hurricane. The thunder and lightning was unrelenting as it accompanied the incessant and worsening downpour. Running Deer had ridden out a few nor'easters and a frightening flood but nothing as unsettling as this. He felt fortunate to have found shelter, but wasn't sure it was going to stay intact. He was helpless as far as reinforcing the little shack, so he was left with no alternative but to hang on. The temperature had dropped since the rain had started, but the fire was providing some comfort.

It was hard to concentrate on his thoughts or make any notes in his journal, so he folded his arms, covered his legs, and prepared himself mentally for the duration of the storm. Fall was the season for uncertain weather and this would be no exception. His attention again shifted to the old book that was lying on a shelf, so he reached over to pick it up, taking care not to mishandle it in case it was in a delicate condition and might fall apart. Luckily, it did not fall apart, but he noticed that some of the pages were protruding from their places at the center of the book. This at once told him that the manuscript was well read and perhaps had been opened many times.

A first glance at the cover did not reveal a title, so he proceeded to open it to the first page. Paper mites had taken their toll on the frontispiece, but part of a word that resembled "colony" was all that remained. The rain was still pounding on the little cabin, but the thunder and lightning had begun to subside. He added a few more branches to the dwindling fire, settled back, and began to turn the pages of the old book. When he turned to the next page, he discovered that it was handwritten in Old English style. A cursory flip of the pages revealed that the pages were full and were in fairly good condition.

Going back to the first page, he began to read the first line: *To the reader of these words, I wish to declare this to be my true journal. I shall attempt to record my daily activities as well as the history of my family as handed down to me from my grandfather. My own father and mother died at an early age due to a terrible plague so I never knew them. My desire is that these words will be passed down through my descendants so that the family's heritage will live on.* This short preface was signed: *Merriweather Applebee.* It was dated May 8, in the year of our Lord, 1610.

The name did not register with Running Deer, but he felt sure that the contents of the book would be very interesting to him and may become an important clue to his quest. It was getting late now and the recent activities had taken a toll on his body and mind, so it was an easy decision to put his mind to rest so that he could relax and gain much needed relaxation for his tired body. While he was concentrating on the contents of the book, the storm had run its course and tranquility had returned to the area. This, he appreciated, because he was beginning to wonder if his humble abode was going to be able to survive the harsh weather conditions.

The fall temperature had not completely arrived yet, so he proceeded to stoke the little fire, prepare himself a litter and catch some much needed shuteye. The only thoughts remaining on his mind was the discovery of the old journal, but he laid those aside for now and before many minutes had transpired, he was fast asleep. Some time during the night, Running Deer was aroused from a deep slumber. While he sat up straight in his bed, he realized that he had experienced a frightening nightmare.

It seems that he was hacking his way through dense foliage when a brightly dressed Indian warrior confronted him face to face. As he was reaching for his knife, the brave produced a bow that held a shining arrow. As he gazed at the arrow, he was unable to move his hand toward his knife. Just as the arrow was pulled back into its position for discharge, he awoke from the hideous dream. The fear was so intense that he was unable to return to sleep.

After a few minutes, he decided to place the remaining branches on the fire and then re-open the journal. He had decided to return to it the next morning, anyway, so he reasoned that he would be able to return to sleep after reading a while longer. Following the introduction on the first two pages, the writer began a list of names that turned out to be a form of a genealogy. The list was rather lengthy, so before he had finished that part, he found himself getting sleepy again, so he carefully laid the book aside, and before much longer, he was fast asleep again.

The next morning, he awoke to a bright sunny day with not a sign of a cloud in the sky. The forest had become alive with a strange mixture of bird song and chatter of scampering animals. The contrast of the evening before was so stark that he seemed to be in a different place. After a meager breakfast of dry meat and coffee, he walked a few feet to a marshy river bank where he could get a closer look at the body of water that ran alongside the cabin. When he had cleared the dense growth along the river bank, he was able to take in its enormous width.

A little closer to the water, he was able to look in both directions. As far as he could tell, there were no bends for miles. He returned to the cabin where he examined his map to see if he could determine his location. It wasn't long before he calculated that he had reached the great Chowanoke. A few more computations showed that he must be near the old fort that would place him at the end of the first leg of his journey. He was so certain of this that he placed the map back into its container and then settled down in a comfortable position to read more from the ancient journal.

Running Deer had mixed feelings about whether to take the old manuscript with him to protect it from potential harm, or leave it and hope that the owner had intentions of returning to retrieve it. It didn't take long to decide, because he felt that the cabin had been inhabited in the not too distant past and that the owner would more than likely return. He had no intentions of staying around, though, so he continued with the reading. He had not taken the time to determine where the writer had fit into the genealogical list, but he would soon learn the relationship.

The next paragraph began: "My great grandfather, Phineas Lawson, related to me the story of how his grandmother, Sitting Dove, was married to a white man who claimed to have been a crewman on an English schooner." There were also stories of friends that had been ambushed and killed by bloodthirsty warriors. It was only through the intervention of some of the native women that a handful of the whites were allowed to live. The journal moved from handed down stories from the family to a chronological entry of events experienced by the writer. Some of the material was scanned over quickly while other portions were read with care.

The Old English style of writing was a little difficult to read at times, but for the most part, it was easily put together. Merriweather went on to say that his life had been that of a wanderer and that he had spent much of his life hunting and fishing. There were stories of short interactions with his kin, but only one stood out among all others. It seems that his cousin, Norfleet Hastings, had chosen to live with a tribe of Indians in the river area. He wrote that Norfleet did not admit to it, but the reason for this choice as determined by his siblings was because he had more than a platonic relationship with a young Croatoan maiden. No mention was made as to whether they were ever united in marriage, but it was reported by others of his family that children were seen around the Indian village that bore an amazing resemblance to his cousin.

He read the journal completely, but did not find any further reference to the English and Indian relationship. So he placed the book back on the shelf as he had found it and immediately began to think about his next move. Since the growth along the river bank appeared to be fairly navigable, his decision was to don his traveling gear and protective equipment and proceed along the river bank northward. He was careful to leave the site as he had found it so that if and whenever the owner returned, there would be nothing amiss. He had a fleeting flashback of his confrontation with the bear, but he soon brushed the thought away from his mind while beginning to move on.

Movement was fairly easy compared with the trip on the previous day. Occasionally he would move closer to the water to look up the river in one direction and then down the other. A couple of hours into the journey, nothing had changed. The great body of water was just as broad as it was when he began and there appeared to be no bend in sight. He suddenly ran into thick vines which prompted him to move inward a ways before he was able to proceed without difficulty. Taking care not to alter his direction, he resorted to his compass to keep on track.

His intention was to move back into the direction of the river whenever possible because he was convinced that a route by the river would eventually take him to his goal. As he mulled these things over in his mind while he walked, he almost missed a strange sight at his left. There was a dark clump of something lying on the woods floor that seemed out of place. On closer inspection, he saw that it was a human body that was folded over in fetal form lying on a scattering of leaves. The first thing that he looked for was a sign of life, but soon discovered that there was none.

Carefully, he turned the body over and saw it was that of a male, perhaps slightly past middle age. He was amply clothed, so there appeared to be no sign of foul play or attack by an animal, also he must have died recently because there was no sign of a discovery by a vulture. Further investigation showed that the mystery person had come from a direction that would put him heading toward the hut that Running Deer had just recently vacated. So, the next thought was that maybe he was its owner and also the author of the journal—Merriweather Applebee. Another document found on the body confirmed that supposition.

Another thought that surfaced on his mind was the question of a proper burial for the man. Searching further into the deceased man's clothes did not reveal any mention of his next of kin. Running Deer felt a closeness to the corpse, especially since he had read a very revealing story of part of his life. He mused that maybe he, himself, knew more about him than his closest kin, because a person usually includes a lot of personal information when he takes to pen to write his memoirs or genealogical history.

Running Deer remembered that he had seen a spade with a broken handle back at the hut, so he began to back-track to retrieve it. It would make it a much easier task to give this man the decent burial that he deserved. On his way back to the hut, he began to think of ways to give Merriweather, whom he had never met, a proper Christian burial. He remembered his own grandfather's burial and was impressed by the kind words spoken at the funeral by the old preacher. Running Deer wasn't good at quoting the Bible, but he remembered a few of the words that was uttered as he was slowly lowered into the cold ground. "I will use these words", he thought, "and I will be ever thankful that I will have prevented the wild animals and vultures from mutilating this man's body".

He made the trip back to the site in about an hour, and upon arriving there, he began to take a closer look around the area again. The only other items that he found was a few cooking utensils, but since he was certain that he had found its owner, he walked around to the rear of the cabin to take a closer look at the old canoe. As he checked its sturdiness by turning it right side up, he found that it was in excellent condition. The thought occurred to him that since the owner had deceased and didn't appear to have any close relatives, it might have been placed there for him by Providence to use while he navigated his way up the river.

So he loaded two boards that he removed from the rear of the building, placed them and the spade in the canoe and then proceeded to the edge of the river. It occurred to him that the paddles were missing so he went back to the shack to look for them. It would be very difficult to navigate the river's powerful stream without them. The paddles were nowhere to be seen, so he began to think of a way to devise substitutes for them. He soon located two boards that were of adequate length and carefully hued for himself a pair of usable oars. In the interest of saving time, he hurried the process along so that he could return to the site of the body and proceed to give it a decent interment before sunset.

He was pleased with his progress for the day, even after taking into account, all the events that had transpired. He was satisfied that, near the burial site, there would be an excellent place to bed down for the night. The weather was amazingly calm after the storm, so he was satisfied that he could make good time beginning on the morrow and for several days following, especially since he would be travelling on the river. Equipped with mobile power now, Running Deer proceeded to the river where he launched the old canoe and proceeded up the river against the ebbing tide back to the proposed burial site.

It suddenly occurred to him that he would be making a little better time with the canoe and it would be difficult for him to find the site since he had not provided a landmark near the river bank before he left. The only rational thing left to do would be to estimate the location, and if he missed it, he could explore the area in an effort to find it. The brush along the shoreline was not filled with vines, so the task might not be as difficult as he thought. About an hour had elapsed when he decided to pull the canoe into the shore. Luckily, the falling tide had left a sloping shoreline so that he could exit the canoe and manually pull it up into the cypress knees that lined the bank.

Upon reaching the dry land, he discovered that a well travelled path made its way in both directions through the woods. His intuition instructed him to go back toward the shack for several minutes, and then if he didn't succeed in finding the spot, he would turn around and head back in the other direction. He first would leave an adequate landmark to bring him back to the canoe.

In less than fifteen minutes, he came upon the site, so he immediately began his return to the canoe and then made a decision to re-enter the river and back-track to the burial site. Time and distance calculation was easier now, so in just a few minutes he again pulled the boat up to the bank. This time, he was right on target, so he secured the canoe at the edge of the woods and proceeded to unload the material that he had brought with him for the burial.

After clearing a suitable place in which to inter the body, he began the process of removing the soil from the ground. Lucky for him, it was a sandy loam and fairly free of roots, however, with the use of his crude equipment, it was very tiring work. With a determination to give Merriweather a proper burial, he toiled on until the grave was to his liking. Including short breaks, the digging process was over in about two hours. He regretted that he did not have a pine box in which to place the body, but under the circumstances, it would be impossible.

A waning sun was making its way to the far horizon and Running Deer was ready to commit a stranger to the soil. In a way, though, he felt closer to this person than anyone else he had met on his long journey. After reading his journal, he had gained more knowledge about him and his aspirations than he would acquire from a lifetime of conversations. So it was with a feeling of sadness that the two of them had not met before. With this thought and others racing through his mind, he gently lifted the body and proceeded to lay it into the bottom of the grave. But before he began to replace the soil, he uttered the words that he remembered from his grandfather's funeral: "In the sweat of thy face shalt thou eat bread, 'til thou return unto the ground; for out of it wast thou taken. For dust thou art, and unto dust shalt thou return". All this said as if the stately trees of the forest were participants and then he added a robust "Amen".

After placing the makeshift cross at the head of the covered grave, he began to search around the site for dry branches to use as fuel for a campfire. The procedure took longer than usual because of the earlier heavy rain. Nevertheless, after about an hour, he was able to gather enough branches for the fire. When the coals were ready, he retrieved a few pieces of bear meat from his pack and cooked them on a spit over the glowing embers. Having satisfied his hunger, he decided to once again look at his map and try to assess his whereabouts. Since he would be travelling by boat now, he figured that he would be able to make much better time.

As for his positioning on the river, it was too early to make any sense of it, because the river was extremely wide and there was no bend in sight. An uneventful night allowed Running Deer to gain some much needed sleep. When he awoke the next morning, he felt refreshed and ready to tackle whatever the new day had in store for him. His first task was to tidy up around the site in respect for his departed fellow man. All was accomplished in about thirty minutes and he had made his way toward his new mode of transportation and the river. In case he would ever have to come back by this place again, he looked around on the river bank for landmarks that he could record.

Chapter nine

SHOVING OFF FROM THE RIVER'S edge, his eyes were diverted to the top of the water where more than a few strange eyes were observing the action from the sanctuary of the reeds growing close by. It didn't take him long to figure out that the river was densely populated by alligators waiting to snap up any morsel to fill their enormous gullets. The splashing and dipping of the makeshift oars excited them at first, but as soon as he had moved a little further out into the current, the scene quickly turned to one of tranquility with nothing but the rush of the current and occasional dipping of the oars as the canoe made its way up-river.

Reading from the tide mark on the river bank, he calculated that he could make good progress for approximately six more hours as he followed the tide coming in. After about two hours on his journey, Running Deer had come to a sharp bend in the river. Not only was the bend acutely sharp, its banks were not as far apart. On the opposite side, his eyes beheld a couple of whitetail does that were quietly grazing along a narrow, sandy shore. As a hunter who used stealth as part of his prowess, he decided to see how close he could get to the deer before they would scoot back into the woods. If he were successful, he thought, he could at least bag one of them to help sustain him as he proceeded on his journey.

He felt that he could not afford to pass up any opportunity that came his way. Using minimum working of his paddle, he managed to make his way stealthily toward the unsuspecting animals. He had to be in absolute readiness now, so he quietly placed his bow and arrow at his feet so he could retrieve it at any moment. As he moved closer to them, they seemed to be aware of an approaching predator, but had not yet begun to abandon their stance. The brackish water was an important part of their daily diet and they were willing to wait until the last moment to spring back into the woods.

Only one of them was able to make it back because Running Deer's lethal arrow point had made its way into the other's heart. There was hardly a struggle, so he pulled the boat up on the narrow strip of sand and proceeded to pull the mortally wounded deer on board. Since it was still early in the day, he decided to continue along with the current, because if he were caught in a tide change, it would be difficult for him to navigate with the extra cargo on board. After another hour, the river became wider and another straight long stretch was in sight.

There was no clearing in sight on either side of the river, so he decided to continue on until about an hour before sunset and then he would have to hack out a clearing—if need be—to set up camp for the night. Fortunately, the growth along the edge of the river was not as thick and wild as he had previously encountered, so he guessed that he could clear a campsite much quicker. He was going to need the extra time to dress the doe, but he wasn't too concerned about his meal. As far as the excess meat was concerned, it didn't take him long to decide to leave the remnants of the bear meat behind because he would be unable to transport both.

As a matter of fact—if he had his druthers—he would rather have smaller game, such as a rabbit, for a change of diet. After setting foot on shore, he pulled the canoe up closer to the bank and secured it to a cypress branch. He then began to explore into the nearby wood canopy for a suitable place to clear. After a short trek into the woods adjacent to the landing site, he was fortunate to find a spot that could be easily cleared. It was always a major concern of his that his campfire would not spread and start a larger woods fire. There would be no problem here as the ground was easy to clear and no grass cover to fuel a fire.

The first task before him was to bring the dead doe ashore and then proceed to dress it. This chore took about forty five minutes and he was proud of the skill that he had gained at butchering and skinning wild game. He scattered the entrails into the woods around him and some into the river for the gators and then began the delicate procedure of removing the choice cuts. As soon as the dressing and cleaning process was accomplished, he quickly gathered the dry branches necessary for the fire. It was about another half hour before sunset, so he began the cooking process by starting the fire and setting up a crude spit on which to roast the meat.

As soon as the burning dry branches began to crackle, he decided to look around the area for a low spot that might contain fresh water. His own supply was almost diminished, so it was always wise to seek out nearby sources. Soon he came upon a small creek that rippled with clear, cool water. He proceeded to fill his flask and would return to the spot before leaving the next day. The coals from the fire were simmering now, so Running Deer began the process of hanging the venison strips above the orange glow to which he added more branches to provide light to the darkening area around him.

The sun had set and he counted himself fortunate to have experienced another good day on his journey. Following a scrumptious meal of venison, his only regret being that he was unable to recognize any wild greens to supplement the meat. He knew that he should consume a balanced diet in order to maintain his strength and stamina, but there was a very limited variety on the forest floor that he had access to and was familiar with. He was thankful, however, that he was able to obtain fresh meat.

The next hour was spent in updating his map and journal, making notes, and preparing himself for the next day's journey. Satisfied that he was on the right course, of paramount importance, was to watch for the tide to ebb, so that he could join the incoming current for a good part of the day. His eye would constantly be on the next bend in the river as he would try to determine how much closer he was to his destination. He was proud of his efforts thus far, especially the fact that he had only needed the assistance of the majestic Akimko on a very few occasions and the Chief, only once. He felt that he had gained valuable knowledge along the way that would help him carry out Waccasaw's assignment.

A sated stomach caused him to doze off and soon after, while in deep sleep, he was awakened by the sound of a red fox that was scampering back and forth around the perimeter of the site. The smell of cooked meat had attracted a loner that was working its way cautiously toward the campfire. Running Deer reached for his knife that he kept handy for such events and waited for the sound to come closer. The sly visitor was not easy to scare off, so it looked as if Running Deer was going to have to forfeit some much needed sleep to play games with the intruder.

Fortunately, he did not have to deal with the fox. As soon as he sprang up from his bed, the animal dashed off into the surrounding woods and soon was lost from sight. Of course, there was no guarantee that the hungry fox would not return, so he resumed his much needed rest, except this time he placed his knife and archery equipment close by in case a larger animal might have the same idea. The balance of the night went without further disturbance and he awoke to a beautiful cloudless sky that complemented the mild, brisk autumn air.

After clearing the area, as was his habit to leave an area as clean or cleaner than he had found it, he loaded his gear and the balance of the fresh venison in the canoe and pushed off into another day's adventure. He had in mind to try a new drying process for the meat at the end of the day, because he knew that the weather wasn't yet cool enough to preserve the meat for very long. But for now, he would follow the river and the slowly moving current as far as it would take him toward his goal.

The rushing water brought to mind pleasant memories of fishing, so already in his mind, he was thinking of ways to fashion some type of crude fishing gear. He thought about those day trips on the river with his grandfather and the times that they would cook their catch right there on the river bank. The thought was so fresh in his mind that he could almost smell the fish cooking. It wasn't hard to daydream while floating down the river so his mind drifted alternately between his memories and the task at hand.

He was so sure that he was going in the right direction that he had forgotten to take a look at his compass. The compass was off about forty five degrees, but in a flashback, he remembered that the big river possessed many bends and that he could not rely entirely upon any constant reading. So, with this in mind, he calculated that since he began in the right direction, that if he would follow his reckoning, he would be on target. He hugged close to shore to keep his pace in line with his thinking. If he were to allow himself to be allured to the faster running water, he might tire himself quicker and still might not be much closer to his goal. He had learned long ago that smart thinking and perseverance was worth much more than eagerness.

In less than an hour, the river had revealed a very sharp bend that almost over-corrected his previous compass readings. He asked himself why he didn't just follow the river and forget about the compass, but then again, he thought it possible that he may be on the wrong river. After a closer look at his map, he brushed these thoughts off as foolishness because he had relied on his map and instinct thus far, so he was not going to change. Fortunately the current had only abated slightly, indicating that the tide would become closer to the flood stage and then reverse its course. This in mind, and a cursory look at the sky, he hoped he would be able to coordinate the daylight hours with that time to begin looking for another campsite.

As he drifted along a beautiful panorama, he would not let himself even think about the possibility of not arriving at the old fort site before the rigors of winter would set in. These kinds of thoughts, if they momentarily appeared, would be overtaken by the memories of what he had already achieved under somewhat difficult circumstances. His grandest achievement, he thought, was that he had asked very little help from the sources that was made available to him. I am, he mused to himself, part of two worlds. I am a white man accustomed to the wilderness, but I have been taught to think like a native Indian.

The river was not as wide at this point, but the water had a sheen like that of a looking glass and was lined with verdant lush marsh reeds and inviting pale green outcropping. The wary person that he was, Running Deer had to convince himself that the beauty of the place was not fraught with some unknown danger that awaited him around the next bend. It had been a good while now since he had seen a real live person, so perhaps, he longed for companionship. On the other hand, he knew from past experience that he could make more progress traveling alone.

Looking over his left shoulder, he noticed that the bright rays of the sun had reduced themselves to a soft yellow palette of soothing orange that engulfed the western sky. As the large round orb aligned itself with the river in front of him, he stretched out his left hand toward the sun and measured two hands toward the water to reveal that there was approximately one more hour of daylight left. The tide had slowed considerably, so he was pleased that his initial calculation was right on time. Not to cut himself short on time, he began scanning both sides of the river to locate an opening in which to pull up and attempt to set up camp.

It was the opposite side of the river that revealed a clear entrance through the underbrush to allow him to land the canoe and prepare to locate a campsite. This was accomplished half an hour after he saw the spot, leaving him an additional thirty minutes to begin gathering the necessary material for his fire. The forest at this point was covered with a ground moss which required very little clearing, so more time was used for gathering additional dry tree branches for fuel.

As he began to move around the area, his eyes had missed a pair of elevated eye sockets that had been watching him come ashore. The huge gator considered this an invasion of his territory, so he let it be known by emitting a deep growl from its humongous lungs. Running Deer was startled by the sound, whereupon he instinctively wheeled away toward the safety of the forest. No amount of acrobatics was going to deter the huge reptile from holding its place, so Running Deer was faced with the problem of convincing it to return to the water. From past experience, he had learned that alligators when disturbed, were reluctant to return to a location.

Precious time was lost as he attempted to convince the gator to slither back into the water. However, after much prodding, the mission was accomplished. The meeting of the alligator was not factored into his time schedule, so he was late getting started with his chores. The camp was quickly set up and he was ready to barbecue a piece of bear meat. Greens around the camp looked enticing, so he carefully selected enough to supplement the caloric content of the bear meat. Coffee was always a favorite with a meal, so he crushed a few beans and brewed up a decent cup.

Darkness had settled over the campsite now, so he threw on a few more branches to provide light in which to update his journal. For the last couple of days, the only significant discovery was the old journal that told of its writer being raised by a family of Indians. This information might prove to be a very important discovery as he begins to put together the pieces that will eventually solve the mystery of the missing colonists. He dared not rule anything out at this point, but the closer he gets to the beginning point—the old abandoned fort, his excitement grows daily.

Days were at their longest now and he was able to accomplish much writing before darkness came and made it more difficult. He would not rule out the arduous travel ahead of him, but he was more confident that he was on the right course, and with perseverance, his long sought after goal was within reach. The embers from the fire finally died out, but not before he had put together a rather comfortable pallet on which to lay his head.

Sleep came quickly because he was more fatigued than he realized. There would be no dream to interfere with his rest this night so he awoke refreshed to face a beautiful sunrise that had also awakened the senses of the neighboring songbirds that surrounded the campsite. Many species were singing their favorite songs while the mockingbirds were having a heyday. Frogs were croaking at the edge of the river while some were scattered among the tree branches. It was as if the small animal kingdom was aware of the presence of a listener and wanted to make it known by presenting a concert. While each sang in their own key, it was a splendid display of nature's harmony.

Running Deer celebrated the occasion by brewing a fresh cup of coffee and downing a couple of scones. It was his intention to get started early and take advantage of the remarkable weather. Since he was waterborne now, he could move much faster with a great deal less effort than hacking his way over land. He pushed off into the river about seven o'clock which coincided with the tide change. He calculated that with the weather, daylight, and the tide going for him, he would be able to traverse twenty or twenty five miles on this beautiful day. Each new bend in the river was a new experience and he wondered how many more bends he would have to turn before he would reach his destination. For today, though, everything seemed to be going his way.

By the time the sun was overhead, the river had widened and there was no bend in sight. Even though it took little effort to move with the current, the heat from the sun had caused him to perspire enough to dampen his garments throughout. The temptation to pull on shore to dry his clothes was overwhelmed by the desire to keep moving while the tide was on his side. He figured that in another hour, the tide would begin to ebb and change directions. He decided to take advantage of the free ride for now and then, in the next several minutes, he would keep his eyes open for a decent clearing that would afford him a short stopover.

As he scanned first one side and then the other, he did a double take to his right where he thought he noticed a movement. The river was very wide at this point, so he reasoned that his eyes were playing tricks on him, which was not an unusual phenomenon with woods all around him while he was alone. Nevertheless, he placed his oar into the canoe and continued to focus on the area near the opposite bank. Even though it had been several days since he had seen another person, he knew that inevitably, there would be others that he would meet as he proceeded. His only concern was whether they would be friend or foe. He did not expect to meet any savages along the way, but in his mind, he knew that that was always a possibility.

As he watched, the movement ceased, but he wondered if this was indeed, someone watching him. The standoff continued for about thirty more minutes before Running Deer decided to continue on his way up the river. No sooner had he pushed the canoe ahead, that he noticed an additional movement that seemed to join the first and then begin rowing toward him in the middle of the river. Remembering his run-ins in an earlier setting, he instinctively began to check his protective gear in case of a confrontation with unfriendly river runners, and at the same time telling him not to panic. He knew he was outnumbered if these strangers turned out to be robbers or unfriendly river rats, but he had been up against these odds before. It also occurred to him that the strangers may be friendly fishermen or hunters that were surprised as he to be meeting on the river.

Running Deer continued on his course up the river while he kept an eye on the progress of the craft that was approaching from his side. As he continued to check out a clearing, he kept a constant lookout as the two boats drew nearer to him. At about the same time that he spotted an open clearing on his left, he heard a welcoming "Ho" from the approaching strangers. Though the sound was friendly, he was not going to relax from his protective posture. Also, he wondered if the clearing that he spotted could be a campsite that was already set up and was being used by the strangers.

So he decided to drop anchor and wait. Since there was still a ten minute gap between them, he was pleased that the two river men, which he was able to make out now, did not split up in an attempt to approach him from both sides. Such a change of perception would definitely have the appearance of a trap if they were less than honorable men. The two continued to approach Running Deer running close together and side by side. A closer glimpse of their cargo revealed a bounty of several furs and hides, so he knew that they were probably honest hunters. An astute observation had shown Running Deer that the forest was teeming with wild game and that there were few hunters in comparison that took advantage of it.

He reckoned that a sparse population was the answer and perhaps few men were interested in the harsh life that accompanied a deep woods hunter. Nevertheless, he had come across a few in his travels thus far, and maybe he would encounter more as he approached the environs of the mainland. The trappers were approaching now and he was able to make out their features. One of the men was stocky and sported a beard that reached down to his chest. The only other features he could make out was a bulbous red nose and sharp, blue eyes. The other was unshaven, tall and lanky. He surmised his height by the length of his torso. The only one wearing a hat was the bearded one.

The first to speak was Running Deer, but he was hoping it would be the other way around. After all, the two had rowed all the way across the wide expanse of water to approach him. Neither of the three held weapons in their hands, but Running Deer was in a position to access his if need be.

"My name is Running Deer—what's yours?"

There was a slight hesitation as the two looked at one another as if to see who would go first. Long Beard spoke first without holding out his hand. "You have an Indian name, but you don't look like a savage. I'm Charlie Boon and this here's Sam Drayton", he said as he turned facing his partner.

The lanky one stood up and verified his height as he struggled to balance his boat. Neither thought it was necessary to shake hands.

After the introductions were accomplished, Running Deer proceeded to explain who he was and why the Indian name. He didn't think it was necessary to go into detail, but he figured that he could satisfy Charlie's question. After the introductions were concluded and all was convinced that there was no animosity or suspicion of implied danger, the conversation shifted to the discussion of a possibly shared campsite. The three agreed to pull ashore and proceed to seek out a suitable clearing. The sun was beginning to set now and showed that the direction of the river had changed since the last evening.

Running Deer had made considerable progress since he started out in the morning. The river had narrowed somewhat and there was an approaching bend a few hundred yards away. A slight clearing on the bank and a further investigation revealed that someone had used the site before. There was even an old lean-to that former users had put together and had left intact. A glance at the sky revealed that there was no sign of approaching rain, but the shelter would certainly come in handy if storm clouds did appear.

The two trappers spread their pallets close together while Running Deer chose to occupy a spot on the perimeter so he could be more aware of any unexpected event. Not that he was afraid of the two strangers, but he learned long ago that it was better to be safe than sorry. Charlie Boon was the most talkative of the two, so most of the conversation took place between he and Running Deer. Before Running Deer could ask where they had come from, Charlie volunteered the information. He and Sam were from the mainland near the head of the Chowanoke river. They had been on and around the river hunting and trapping for the last two weeks. A trip of this sort lasted from two to four weeks depending on the abundance of game that they encountered. This trip had not been very productive, particularly in the value of the pelts, so they would continue on for another week.

Running Deer grabbed an opportunity to ask about their family connections. Sam was the first to speak up and said that he came from a mixed blood of English and Native American stock. "My mother was full-blooded Scotch and my father, a Waccamaw chief. My mother died when I was three years old and she left my father to care for six children. All the children except me were adopted by a wealthy farm couple who made sure that the children were properly educated. The couple had no children of their own, so it wasn't a problem with the finances. I would have joined them, but my father insisted that since I was the oldest and would be able to do my share of the work, he would be able to keep me. I never knew that I had brothers and sisters until my father was getting up in years when he told me. He told me that he wanted to make sure that he had one son that would be trained to be a hunter like himself in order to carry on the tradition of the family. He handed down some of the history of his Indian heritage and told of the early exploration by the English settlers."

At that point, Running Deer interrupted to say—"my only reason for making this trip is to find the secret of a missing colony of Europeans who made an attempt at settlement in this very area."

He went on to say that he was looking for an old fort on the mainland which the explorers used for an outpost. Sam listened to what Running Deer had to say, but merely replied that he had never heard the story. So, somewhat disappointed, Running Deer thanked him for the conversation and remarked that he would go ahead and turn in for the evening. They planned to resume their conversation the next morning, and after that, he would be on his way.

The next day broke revealing a bright morning sun, a shimmering river, and a greeting from the animals and birds with their potpourri of sounds. The sound of the birds reminded Running Deer of his conception of a rain forest teeming with wild life. He had slept well—waking only once from a shallow dream. His two new acquaintances slept soundly through the night, also, because they, too, awoke refreshed—and as the saying goes—bright eyed and bushy tailed. The saying was a hand-me-down from his grandfather. One of those tidbits of language that was always used but never explained.

At any rate, Sam said that "you can tell how the day's gonna go by how you feel in the morning."

He quietly began to gather his things together hoping to return to the river early to take advantage of the rising tide. His hope of soon reaching his destination had taken on new life and seemed to renew each time he reached a new bend in the river. Charlie and Sam began to stir so Running Deer stopped what he was doing in order to greet them on this new day. They, too, were bright eyed and ready to tackle another day of hunting. So, after a few minutes of chatting with each other, Running Deer was ready to push off for another day of discovery. He bade Charlie and Sam farewell and was on his way.

After thirty minutes or so, he was at another bend in the river that took a wide swing to his right. He took a look at his compass and calculated that he was now heading due north. There was a long stretch of water facing him that seemed to be going in a straight direction for miles. The current was still running strong and he seemed to be moving at a fast pace. It took some effort to hold his boat in a straight path. Observing the river banks, he guessed that it would be at least four hours before high tide. Everything seemed to be going his way now and he had ample time to think about what he had observed so far and also time to contemplate the near future.

The future was more on his mind because he was anxious to arrive at the place that marked the beginning of an unsolved mystery. He had been charged with the awesome duty of solving the mystery so that the knowledge attained by him would be shared with his neighbors and the world. He would be able to report to the old chief Waccasaw that he had indeed uncovered clues that no one else had been able to find. Strangely, he had no desire for credit or recognition for himself, so he was able to proceed under little or no duress.

While a potpourri of thoughts were running through his mind, he was distracted from a movement close by that seemed to be following him. The lapping of the gentle waves on the sides of his canoe had concealed a slight belligerent sound that emanated from the nearer shore. A huge alligator had slithered off the muddy bank and was making its way toward him. He had been able to deal with an occasional hungry gator, but this fella was able to upset his canoe if he was hungry and appeared to be mad enough. Just as he turned to look into the direction of the oncoming menace, he dropped his oar into the boat leaving the canoe to float on its own.

He grabbed for his spear and positioned himself so that he would not be upset and thrown from the craft. The monstrous reptile lunged toward him while arcing his long tail for a sideswipe at the boat. It was at this instance that Running Deer discovered the true size of his assailant. His spear grazed the scaly upper portion of the gator's head near his right eye but failed to stop him from thrashing about. In fact, this fellow was more infuriated than he was before. As the tail began its swipe toward the canoe, Running Deer braced himself for the impact. Fortunately, his attacker sideswiped the lower edge of the canoe and scraped the bottom with a terrifying scratching sound.

The near miss afforded Running Deer the time to grab his oar and head the canoe toward the bank. This action surprised the gator and supposedly he had left the scene of action, but Running Deer discovered in short order that she had not given up. He had determined the gender of the reptile when he looked toward the bank and saw the rest of the family, including about six smaller members making their way toward him. Not wanting to get involved in a family fight, he changed courses and made his way as fast as he could toward the opposite shore.

The river was about one hundred yards across at this point and he figured that he had time to elude his attacker and find a safe place to pull ashore where he could assess his near escape and plan his next move. His luck did not persevere, however, because directly ahead of him he spotted that same pair of ominous eyes peering at him. He wasn't sure that he could withstand another swipe by the giant swimmer, so he decided that it was time to beckon help. It had been a good while since he had need to summon help from Akimko, but he figured that this was one of those times that he needed to.

The huge bird had not failed him in the past, so he gave the high pitched whistle and waited momentarily for a swooshing sound to arrive from overhead. The timing could not have been a second off because his attacker, madder than ever, had already curled for another swipe at his boat. Akimko arrived at the same time and began to extend its claws aiming directly toward the gator's eyes. As soon as contact was made, the gator straightened out and began to dive down into the deep water beneath the canoe. The rest of the family followed suit swimming in a direction toward the shore. Just as quick as Akimko had made its appearance, it disappeared into the mist that hung over the river.

The commotion had used up about a half hour's time while the current was beginning to slow. He figured that he could float about another thirty minutes, so he headed toward the middle of the stream where the current was the strongest. Running Deer had begun to feel that he was nearing his destination but had been distracted by the encounter with the mammoth reptile. He thought if his luck would hold out a while longer, he could concentrate on his mission and be able to—once and for all—solve the problem of the missing colony. At least, this is what he was hoping for because he never started a new day without optimism.

He was able to travel a while longer than he had calculated, so this had given him time to scan both banks looking for a feasible camping site. Like an answer to prayer, a short bend in the river revealed a clear opening just as he made the turn. He headed the canoe toward the open area about the same time that the tide had ebbed. He was elated because he wouldn't have to spend a lot of time clearing a spot for a fire. He noticed as he pulled the boat toward the shore, that the area looked as if it had been used many times before. As a result, he looked around the area for possible company. There was none in sight, however, so he figured that there was none around.

After securing the canoe, he began to offload material and provisions that he would need. Just around a bushy area, there appeared a lean-to that looked in fairly good condition. He surmised that it must have been used in the not too distant past and guessed that the owner or owners would not mind his using it for an overnight stay. When he had finished placing all his stuff under the lean-to, he began to look around the area to gather fuel for his campfire. Before he had gone fifty feet, he ran into an unarmed man who looked as if he was lost.

The man was dressed scantily and looked as if he hadn't shaved in a very long time. Running Deer wanted to appear friendly so that he wouldn't scare him off, so he held out his hands as if to greet the man with a handshake. Reluctantly, the man offered his hand in return without uttering a sound.

"My name is Running Deer—what's yours?" At first, he did not answer, but Running Deer continued to look him in the eye as if he expected a reply.

"Lonesome Cloud", he replied in a soft tone, "I am looking for my people."

The man wore moccasins, and around his middle, he wore a sash which was tied around an animal skin cloak. Running Deer wanted to ask more about his people that he was searching for, but decided to offer him food instead, planning to continue the conversation later at a more appropriate time. The dried bear meat was a welcome sight for Lonesome Cloud and he didn't hesitate to accept the small chunk that Running Deer held out to him.

The sun was about to meet the tree tops and could be seen as a huge orange ball as it was setting on the river ahead of them. The sky resembled a painter's palette with its myriad assortment of colors. Running Deer was pleased with his progress thus far and was particularly pleased that the fall weather had not produced any threatening wind or rain in a good while.

His interest now was directed toward the new stranger who had arrived on the scene and just what it might mean to his overall journey. He was sure that some or all of these questions might be answered if he could induce him to talk. In any event, he would give it his best shot and accept whatever the results would turn out to be. Lonesome Cloud appeared to appreciate the gift of food and began to help his benefactor gather dry branches for the campfire. It was a good ten minutes before he said anything when he asked Running Deer if there was anything else he could do to help.

Running Deer assured him that there was nothing else needed so it was a few minutes before sunset that they lit the fire and had it glowing brightly around the site. Soon the flames would die down and they would place the coffee pot on the hot embers to percolate. They continued to munch on the dried meat and partake of the dwindling supply of corn scones that he had left in his pack. This would be no banquet but in the deep dark woods it sufficed for a meal. A very scanty meal, he thought, but he would turn his attention to better things for tomorrow.

After they had eaten and had conversed very little, they rekindled the fire while Running Deer attempted to break the ice in an effort to get his guest to open up. He was somewhat surprised when Lonesome Cloud began to tell him about his family. It wasn't long before the conversation really became interesting to Running Deer when Lonesome Cloud began to explain that he was born of a Native Indian father and a European mother. He was one of a family of four siblings. He and a brother were the older of the group with several years between them and the arrival of two sisters.

Before he continued with his family history, Running Deer eagerly wanted to ask questions about his mother. He wanted to know where she had come from and how she had met his father.

"I was getting to that", the man said, "but first, I want to tell you about the rest of my family because I am very proud of them."

"I apologize for rushing you," said Running Deer, "but I will explain later why I am so anxious to know about your mother. Please go ahead and I promise not to interrupt."

"I have told you of my brothers and sisters," he said, "now I want to tell you about my grandparents and great grandparents."

He went on to explain that his grandparents on his father's side were full blooded Siouxans, while his mother's parents came from two old mainland families that descended from the English.

"My maternal great grandparents were directly descended from English colonists who had escaped their native captors and led lives of seclusion, and of course, on my grandfather's side, his parents were natives of the Croatan tribe. I have heard my grandfather speak of them on many occasions. According to my grandfather, my ancestors had escaped from a stockade that belonged to a warring tribe, but had been overtaken by a friendlier tribe while roaming the forest for food. In order to survive the harsh winters in the wilderness, which they were not accustomed to, they continued to work and live with them."

"As the years went by, their friendship grew and the two groups began to intermarry. As the merged group grew larger, their villages began to expand. Some of the mixed-race males began to explore farther and farther away. My family was a product of one of those wandering groups."

Running Deer was amazed at this man's knowledge of his ancestors. He thought that this had to be a confirmation of his own beliefs about the missing colonists and a very good clue toward solving the mystery.

"That sure is an interesting story," he said, "I no longer need to enquire about your mother because what you have told me settles much of my curiosity. It certainly seems that I am beginning to put pieces of the puzzle together which lies at the root of my quest. The time has flown so quickly, so let's secure the campfire and settle in for some much needed energy renewal."

"I am with you", uttered his new friend, "I am much overdue for some rest from scouring these woods looking for game."

So the two made quick work of their clean-up and left a small flame from their fire to help ward off dangerous predators. Running Deer, at times was a light sleeper, but he was also careful about not being surprised. He considered himself real lucky so far, given his surroundings and some of the close calls, so this night he felt good about his progress thus far and was anxious to proceed on his journey beginning tomorrow.

Sleep came easy for both of them and it would have been a perfect night but for one interruption. Shortly before midnight, a blood curdling scream emanated from an area of the forest near them. Running Deer raised his torso up from his sleeping pallet while Lonesome Cloud rose upright on his feet. He placed his hand in front of his mouth to warn Running Deer to keep silent. At the same time, he raised his left hand pointing to an area in which he had sensed that the eerie sound was coming from.

For a time that seemed to be about two minutes, there was not another sound. Then it occurred to them that a crackling sound on the woods floor was getting louder instead of fading. This prompted Running Deer to silently reach for his trusty spear and hunting knife. Following this movement, the crackling sound suddenly stopped. There was still no sight of the intruder, but both men were prepared to take on whatever it was. Suddenly a huge cat-like animal sprang from its camouflaged surroundings and made a bee line toward the closer target.

It so happened that Running Deer was the target and at precisely the same time that the cat sprang, he sidestepped, which had the effect of propelling the beast directly toward Lonesome Cloud who was in the process of positioning his knife directly in front of him which met its mark as the animal reared to the side and hit the ground with a heavy thud. Both men let out a sigh of relief as they viewed a larger than normal wildcat or lynx that looked as if it hadn't eaten in days. Hunger, notwithstanding, was not a deterrent to the cat's prowess. Even after it was wounded by Lonesome Cloud's skillful attack, it recovered quickly from its lying position and seemed to be choosing its prey again.

This time it was Lonesome Cloud who had changed stances and motioned for Running Deer to attack from the side. With all his agility and strength, Lonesome Cloud could have starred in a bull fighting ring of old Spain. Without a moment to spare, he moved quickly to the side as if parrying his enemy as Running Deer moved in for the mortal wound. There was no question as to which man would receive the valuable pelt. After all, the kill would make Lonesome Cloud's day and Running Deer was not in the business of fur trading.

Since the night was cool, it was decided that they should wait until the next morning to skin the animal. Also, after an hour's interruption from sleep, they needed to return to their rest. Running Deer had planned to leave early the next morning, but he made a decision to stay at the site long enough to help his friend get situated with the animal skinning and then part ways at a decent hour. The night seemed to have passed quickly, but there was plenty of solid sleep to refresh their minds and bodies.

After the flaying chores were over, a very meager breakfast with some hot coffee gave them the energy needed for a new days journey. Lonesome Cloud revealed that he was about two days away from his home and, of course, Running Deer could only guess what was left for him, so he was anxious to resume his traveling. After initial help from Running Deer, Lonesome Cloud thanked him and assured him that he would be alright with the remaining work to be done. So Running Deer gave his friend a hearty handshake and thanked him for sharing his life story, and he then proceeded to load his canoe once again for a resumption of his journey up the river.

He pushed off into the midstream and began to take advantage of the rising tide and swift current. The stream was not very wide at this point, so he quickly entered the fast flowing water. There was very little change of scenery for the first half hour, so he had time to contemplate his progress for the day ahead of him. With the use of his trusty compass, he assured himself that he was heading in the right direction. He figured that with all the interruptions that he had encountered since beginning his journey, maybe things would turn in his favor now and he would be able to reach his destination before many days would pass.

The destination that he was heading for was very important for him because it involved a meeting with the Chief and receiving instructions for what could be the second and final leg of his journey. In one way, he had enjoyed his journey thus far because he had always dreamed of traveling into strange territory, especially where there was a river involved, yet he was anxious to fulfill his duty for the Chief. His trip so far had offered many clues that he had managed to acquire along the way. He was certainly not sure as to how valuable they would be, but he knew also that it was important to gain as much information as possible so it would enable him to piece the puzzle together and be able to carry out his task.

Time passed quickly for him as he spent this time daydreaming on the quiet river. The sounds seemed to have been muted while the canoe floated up the glassy smooth river. Not even a frog could be heard along the bank. Midday was approaching and he could still see the place down river where he had begun his day's trip. That would not be the case for long because a bend in the river was coming up within the next half hour. There was no way to know how sharp the bend would be or in which direction he would be heading. One thing was sure, though, the trip would not be as boring. He welcomed the turns in the river because each turn in direction seemed to bring a new adventure.

As he approached the bend, the river widened so he negotiated his way toward the center. When he reached midstream, he was surprised by what he saw on both sides of the river as he looked from one side to the other. The scene revealed a mixture of crude houses—some constructed of wood planks, some with logs, and still others like wigwams. As fall was imminently approaching, there were billows of smoke rising in the still air from most dwellings. As he took it all in, he began to wonder if he was nearing the mainland and would soon approach the old palisade that had been the object of his quest for the last several weeks.

From what he saw, he knew that he would be contacting more strangers and it was a natural inclination to wonder if they would be friendly folks. So far, this had not been a problem with him, indeed most had been friendly, but he couldn't help but think about a small percentage that might not be, as he had been warned. The current flow in the river was slower now so he had to exert a little more effort on his oar to maintain his place in the stream and still make progress.

As he moved slowly along, he was able to see activity now as children and their pet dog frolicked along the river bank. He guessed that the settlement had been established for quite a while, so it was his hope that there had been contact with the mainland. Perhaps trade had been going on with the native inhabitants. While all of these thoughts were running through his mind, he hadn't noticed a canoe holding two passengers approaching his craft from the rear.

'Oh-Oh,' he said to himself, 'here comes my welcoming party.' There was nothing he could do but await their arrival. Both boatmen were using oars, so it seemed that they were anxious to check him out. As they got a little closer, he could see that both of them were wearing skins only around the middle and a band of some material around their head. It was too early to know if they were Indian warriors or just friendly town folks. While nearing Running Deer's canoe, the two seemed to slow their approach while they sized him up. He did not attempt to reach for a weapon, so they moved in and held their hands in front of them to indicate that they were, indeed, friendly. He will discover later the reason for their cautious approach.

The first to speak was Running Deer who tested them on their knowledge of the English language. The first thing he said was "My name is Running Deer, what's yours?"

The smaller of the two gave the first reply. "My name is Swift River and this here is Butch Legree." Then the other held out his hand and said "I see you're not a fur trader, so what brings you up the river?"

Running Deer sensed that there was a reason for such an abrupt question, so he began by stretching forth his right hand to the one called Swift River and stated simply that he had business on the mainland and if they would honor him by letting him set up camp for the night, he would be much obliged and he would explain further what his business was. At first, the two were hesitant to trust Running Deer, but after the introductions were accomplished, they welcomed him to their compound—but not before explaining to him their reason for displaying some mistrust.

It seems that just a few weeks before, a stranger had entered their compound and after hanging around for a few days had stolen food, supplies, and had kidnapped or convinced one of their young women to leave at night with him. They had spent some time in pursuit but had given up after it was decided that he had too much headway on them. They explained that theirs was a close-knit community and that they didn't take too well to strangers who attempted to upset that arrangement.

Running Deer thought about their story and proceeded to assure them that he had nothing but honorable intentions and that he had met many friends on his journey thus far and would consider it a pleasure of his to add their folks to that list. Sensing his honesty, the two villagers warmed up to him and began helping him unload his gear as they pulled up to their dock.

Right away, Running Deer saw that he could dispense with the idea of having to gather wood for a fire or even having to sleep in the open. At the end of a long earthen path, he spotted small children running and playing as they watched the sun set in the west. 'This is a happy clan', he thought, and was thankful to be watching such activity at this stage of his journey.

There was one large house—not a longhouse as is typical of a native settlement—and several smaller buildings surrounding the area. With their arms loaded, the two men led him directly toward the larger building. As he approached the building, he took notice of its construction. It was not a typical log building but was covered with split logs and daubed with clay for sealing. It was very professionally done showing an exhibition of pride for the builders.

As they entered the wide front door, Running Deer was astounded as he gazed first at the left front portion in which an immaculately clean kitchen was set up. There were pots, pans, and utensils neatly hung over a large butcher block table in the center of the room. Adjacent to this area was a room including a long table flanked by a comfortable looking sitting bench that ran the entire length on both sides. He realized that he was hungry when he ran his gaze from the kitchen to the dining area. They continued walking toward the rear of the building where he was in for more surprises as they progressed.

On either side of a central hallway there were rooms that he considered to be bedrooms for important people or special guests. As they proceeded along the hallway, the rooms became smaller but still were ample size for bedrooms. Running Deer could not help but think of the building as an accommodation used for traveling folks. Perhaps as an alternate source of income for the villagers. He quickly dismissed this thought when he realized that this may not be a profitable enterprise in this location.

His hosts stopped abruptly at a room and motioned for him to enter ahead of them. As soon as he had had a chance to look around, he was amazed at the furnishings that were neatly displayed around the room. The centerpiece, of course, was a comfortable looking bed that happened to catch his attention. It looked to be handcrafted by using hewn wood cut from the forest and finished with some sort of colorful brown stain. The thick mattress was probably filled with corn shucks mixed with some sort of down. He couldn't resist pressing his hand on it to test its softness.

All of his gear was placed in a corner of the room while the one called Butch welcomed him as a special guest. He realized that these were a special people by the way they were treating a complete stranger. His original intention was to spend the night and continue on his journey early in the morning at daybreak. He calculated that the tide would be just about right then to start him off for the day. But there was something about this place that made him want to spend more time to get to know them better.

There was still some sunlight left and after stretching a bit, he was invited to join the two for a walk around the area. After leaving the large building, all of the others paled in comparison. Most of them were no less sturdy, but looked as though they were provided for the younger native families or for the working class. There was no clear answer yet, but he was anxious to complete a tour of the village. There was nothing to lose, he thought, and might be a chance to rack up some more clues. So Running Deer and his hosts proceeded to walk through the area and it wasn't long before he received one of his answers.

Swift River took on the role of tour director and explained that almost everyone in the compound was related and that it had been that way for six generations. He went on to say that all of the inhabitants contributed to the upkeep of the village in which everyone shared alike. He cited some winters that had been particularly hard but with everyone's assistance in providing for food and heat, the population had grown along the river in spite of sickness in some years.

Running Deer wanted to know if there were any English blood in their ancestry. "I am sure there is", replied Swift River, "but I want you to talk with our oldest inhabitant about that. I feel sure that he can answer that and will be willing to discuss it with you."

He went on to explain that the old patriarch was their family historian and he could answer any question that he had about their early beginnings. "I hope that I am able to introduce you to Uncle Thaddeus, however, he has been a little under the weather lately and hasn't been easy to talk to. Perhaps you can persuade him to answer your questions."

The sun was sinking lower now and due to the shorter days of fall, winter would soon be approaching, so Running Deer suggested that they wait until the next day to attempt it. Another trip by his canoe would assure him that all was well with his transportation and the few items that he had left there. He returned to the great house just in time to smell the aroma of roasting venison. Also, he detected the distinct pungent smell of meat flavored greens. His salivary glands were getting a workout while his stomach was growling due to the anticipation of another scrumptious meal. He would use the time awaiting the call to dinner by looking over his map and notes to make sure he was still traveling in the right direction toward the larger goal.

Since he had been on the river, he had discovered that many different turns in direction had thrown him off course, but generally he was satisfied that he was correct. There was one area in the river that he had not encountered, but he believed that soon he would discover an enormously wide area as he approached the mainland. The document had shown such an area and he felt that it would soon come into view. Depending on the wind, he thought, he might be confronted by some rough waves. In an occurrence of that nature, he figured that he could hug the shoreline and still make progress.

While he was contemplating those possibilities, a young maiden with long dark hair surprised him with a tug on the arm and an invitation to join her at meal. This was quite a surprise for Running Deer, but he wasn't about to decline such a request. The young lady introduced herself as Morning Dove and explained that Butch Legree had told her that Running Deer was his name and that he was a special guest of theirs. She said that she would be honored if he would sit beside her at the meal.

Since he had begun his journey, he had not been attracted to anyone of the opposite sex, so several things began to run through his mind. His hosts had been friendly enough but he began to ponder the possibility of a set-up. 'I don't have time for this,' he thought, 'but I will take my chances and accept her friendly gesture.' "Why yes," he said, "I'd be delighted to join you."

Immediately she began to show him where he could wash up and then join her at the table. By this time, the smell of food was almost overpowering, so he didn't waste any time as he re-joined Morning Dove at the layout. The only thing that bothered him at this point was whether his manners was up to the task. He had been living in the woods for so long that he was afraid that he had forgotten many of the things that his mother and grandmother had taught him. Even though he wasn't trying to impress this young maiden, he didn't want to appear completely out of touch with the opposite sex.

Butch Legree and Swift River sat nearby with a smile on their face. The girl ladled a huge helping of meat into Running Deer's plate while he reached for a hunk of bread. The still smoking greens was next which covered the rest of his plate. Morning Dove provided the answer to his unspoken question when she stated that the meat was fresh bear meat that had been slowly roasted around an oak wood fire. He smiled as he replied "thank you, it looks and tastes delicious."

The robust drink was undetermined but he was satisfied that it was a popular fermented grape concoction just like his grandpa used to let him sample out behind the barn. As he continued to enjoy his meal, his hostess occasionally threw a glance his way from the corner of her eye. This made him uneasy and surprisingly made him uncomfortable. Nevertheless, as mealtime wore on, the uneasiness turned into a feeling that he hadn't experienced for a long, long time, so he began to look at her with an approving smile. He was afraid he was eating too fast, so he began to take longer drinks and smaller bites. This way, he thought, he would not be the first to finish his meal.

As he finished his meal which was accomplished with very little conversation, he reached for a fancy lace-bordered napkin that was placed by his plate. He wiped his mouth clear of excess food that accumulated during his meal. He laid the napkin aside and turned to Morning Dove to thank her for a very scrumptious meal and also for being such a fine hostess. He said that he had enjoyed her company and would remember it for a long, long time. When she turned to face him, he noticed a difference in her complexion. She was clearly blushing from the attention he gave her and the comments he had made.

Morning Dove didn't realize it, but there was an equal reaction on Running Deer's part. Maybe it was because of his rugged appearance that the blush did not show. His first thought was 'what do I do now?' It was certainly a first for him since he had begun his journey, so he realized that he was still attracted by the opposite sex and he didn't recall the Chief warning him of such an occurrence. Before he could offer his help to clean up after the meal, Morning Dove touched him on his arm and excused herself to attend to dish cleaning. There was something about her smile that triggered a feeling in Running Deer that he had never felt before. As he walked away to converse with the men, he vowed to himself to put the thought aside so that he could continue on his important quest without being sidetracked by boyish ambitions.

He caught up with Butch and Swift River who had already made plans to introduce him to a few of the other men. It was very nigh dusk now so the group headed for a campfire that had recently been lit. There were benches aligned around the fire making it the most comfortable sitting that he had had since his journey began. In fact, the whole encounter since arriving had included a lot of firsts. As they sat around the campfire, there was some small talk before they got around to the more serious discussion about helping Running Deer pursue his immediate quest which was to locate the old historic site where the early English settlers had supposedly spent their last hours on the island.

It was suggested by Butch Legree that Running Deer have a conversation with an old woman who had lived at the complex for a number of years. In fact, he said that he thought that she was one of the first settlers to come there. Running Deer agreed that it might be a good idea and asked if Butch could set up a meeting between the two of them. "I will do that now", he said, as he walked away.

Swift River, alone with Running Deer, felt it was wise to tell him that the old woman probably knew a lot more than she allowed, but sometimes it was hard to get her to open up. At her age, it was beginning to be a little harder to get her to engage in a conversation, so Swift River felt it his duty to accompany him when they meet. It had been a few months since he had seen her, but he had received reports that her health was failing and that her willingness to communicate might be impaired.

When Butch returned in about thirty minutes, he was not a bearer of good news. A person who was close to the woman had told him that her health had indeed deteriorated and that she was not expected to live very much longer. Discussion had already begun among her closest friends as to who should receive her belongings. She owned very little except one valuable piece that had been handed down to her from several generations of ancestors. The ancient artifact was a family Bible which he thought might be a valuable tool to help Running Deer in his quest for clues. The access to this information was a grave concern for him because his access to it might be in jeopardy due to the condition of the old woman and the uncertainty of who would obtain her belongings. He was sure of one thing, however, he was not going to miss another chance to possibly find valuable clues if he could help it.

After Butch made his announcement, the three of them talked it over and a decision was made that Running Deer would stick around for a few days to await the outcome. He decided that it could be his last chance to gain valuable insight into or knowledge about the Lost Colony. He wanted very much to succeed so that he would have a good report to deliver to the chief. While he was mulling these things over, he caught a glimpse of Morning Dove as she made her way slowly toward them. It was if she already knew that he would be spending another night, because as she edged toward them, she began to hold her arm out to Running Deer.

"Come", she said "I want to show you to your bed and make things comfortable for you—because you are our special guest, you know." Running Deer blushed as he touched her arm. She was more beautiful than he had realized from the previous meeting. 'I don't want to appear shy' he thought, so before he walked away with her, he nodded at his friends and tossed a half smile their way.

He would have loved to get to know her better, but as soon as she had shown him his meager quarters and accommodations, she smiled, wished him a good night, and disappeared into the darkness of the building. Before he undressed for bed, he sat on the edge of the bed while he was alone and tried to piece everything together that had happened since he had been at the compound. Foremost in his thinking was the friendliness of the inhabitants in trying to make everything pleasant for him. He still hoped to get a lesson in genealogy before he left, so he began to prepare for bed and a welcomed night's rest. Though he had gotten used to sleeping under the stars, he didn't complain about the more comfortable feeling of a real bed.

The night went well until he was awakened by a big boom at mid-morning. There was no window near his bed, but he began to see flashes of light from another area of the room. There was no question about what was happening when he heard a driving downpour on the outside. There had been no mention nor had there been any sign of a storm on the horizon as he gazed into the previous evening sky as was his custom. It wasn't long before Butch Legree came by his room to inform him that there might be some flooding along the river bank if the rain continued through the night.

He informed Running Deer that it was nothing to be alarmed about because it happened just about every fall and there had only been two occasions where the water had become a real problem. He assured him that they had always gotten through such weather without any loss of life. The words of Butch were not very consoling, but Running Deer knew that he had been through some tough scrapes and he felt that he could survive whatever happens now. There was very little sleep the rest of the night and he awoke at the sound of rain still battering the roof and outside wall of the building.

There was very little light at dawn and very little abatement of the deluge. He made his way to the front of the building, then looked in the distance toward the river, where to his surprise the water had risen over its banks and was making its way toward the buildings. His first thought was to seek out his two friends and try to determine what to do next. When he found them, they had already anticipated what might happen and was scurrying around moving valuable belongings to higher ground. They instructed him that he had better do the same and then come back and join them. There was a grim look on their faces and he knew that they were to be taken seriously.

There were a few articles of clothing and dried food that was left in his canoe, so he decided to take care of that first. To his amazement, the boat was upright, but the branch that it had been tied to had broken causing the craft to follow the water as it moved inward to shore. He quickly moved it to the edge of the rising water and tied it to a sturdier post. After he retrieved his belongings, he quickly made his way to the long building. On his way there, he came across an elderly woman who was struggling with an armload of what appeared to be her clothes and was trying to make her way to dry ground. He told her to not worry, that he would be right back to help her. The words were comforting to her but he could tell that she was not completely convinced.

Running Deer secured his stuff in an alcove above the bedroom and then kept his promise to assist the frightened woman. About the same time that he arrived back, he saw the little one room shack break apart and suspected that the same might be happening all around the place. He didn't have time to worry about that now because his first priority was to rescue the lady and get her to drier ground where other friends could assist and console her. When he arrived back at the location where the woman was now in hysterics, he quickly took her in his arms and headed back toward higher ground.

He came across two other women who were trying to keep their belongings dry and asked if they would take another poor soul in until the weather subsided and then he would try to help her rebuild her place. The two agreed to help but they would need extra food. So Running Deer agreed to find food and bring it back to them. After consoling the three women, he took a look around and saw that the water was getting higher. Promising to return and bring food, he hurriedly went looking for Butch and Swift River.

After looking around for about fifteen minutes, he came across the two men making their rounds to warn the inhabitants to grab all they could tote and head for higher ground. He nodded toward Running Deer and said "I'm beginning to rethink what I told you earlier. We have never seen one like this before. The water is higher than it has ever been and it is still rising." They feared for the lives of the young children and the older adults who weren't able to fend for themselves. Most of the inhabitants had been notified and there was a flurry of activity as the people headed into the forest to escape the onrushing water.

In less than an hour the tide had changed and the water began to flow back to the river leaving flotsam and floating branches in its wake. The surrounding area resembled a war zone. The rain had not completely stopped but there was a glimmer of sun rays appearing through the clouds. The good news was that the freak rainstorm had about run its course and the sky appeared to be clearing. He remembered the promise that he made to the three women and began to search for food that he could take to them.

After the frightening storm had subsided, the invading water had returned to its place inside the banks of the Chowanoke, so it was time to assess the damage and get on with the business at hand. It was a meager life fraught with the uncertainty of the seasons and the lack of basic health needs, but the people that inhabited the colony were a happy lot who took care of their neighbors and held any kind of evil in disdain. Running Deer had sensed this quality among them when he first came to know them. He was still hoping to talk with the old lady with the priceless journal.

A thorough search by the men found only one person who had been injured by the storm. One of the children was running back home from play and tripped over a young tree branch that was blown over in the path. He had landed on his arm and had broken it near the wrist. He was in considerable pain, but the resident medicine man had fabricated a splint for him and one of the women had concocted an herbal tea to lessen his pain. All of the major buildings were still intact but some of the shelters and pens for the animals were destroyed or badly damaged.

Dusk was creeping in all around which didn't leave much light to round up the animals and return them to an enclosure. The swine were running wild and it looked as if most of the others were hanging around their owners cabins for feeding time. Running Deer lent a hand and was happy to do so because not only was he happy to help but he was looking forward to a big plate of ham and eggs come morning. He heard a familiar call and looked around to determine from what direction it was coming. He recognized the voice of Swift River, and then sensing the direction from which it came, he began to run in that direction.

When he arrived at the scene, he discovered that his friend had located a child who had strayed too close to a puddle of water and was on the verge of drowning. He began at once to perform first aid on the youngster and before long the child began to spit and sputter. All the while, Swift River was standing by with dry clothes if Running Deer was successful in bringing the child to life. The mother was hysterical and in her condition was unable to help. When her little daughter opened her eyes and began to look around, the woman was beside herself with happiness. She promised Running Deer and Swift River that she would repay them for their unselfish and lifesaving deed.

The two men decided to make one more round in the complex to make sure everything else and everyone was secure. It took an hour to go around, and after finding everything else intact, they decided to head for the dining area to take their place with the others who had already gathered and were partially seated. Running Deer didn't realize how fatigued he was until he cleaned himself up and sat down to eat. He felt that he had worked for this meal and didn't feel that he was imposing. Therefore, he was going to sit down, relax, and enjoy what he perceived to be the best meal yet.

He didn't think it coincidental that Morning Dove came and sat next to him at the table. She turned to face him while displaying her shining white teeth. He thought that he had never seen a face quite as beautiful. He returned the smile but could not suppress the crimson color that was creeping over his face. The serving dishes were loaded with tantalizing meats both wild and home grown. And, of course, there were two or three green vegetables along with freshly baked bread. He noticed a dish that he could not identify but guessed that it was a dessert that was made especially for this meal.

One of the elders gave thanks for the food and then the serving dishes were passed around the table. One of the women saw to it that the children were served as well at their special table. Running Deer was impressed that the children were so well behaved. There were few words exchanged between Morning Dove and himself, so it didn't take long to finish his meal. He excused himself, arose from the table and went back to his room. Before preparing himself for bed, he reached for his notebook to enter the important events of the day. He thought of the day soon that he would arrive at the old fort site and meet the chief again face-to-face.

There would be a lot to talk about and he hoped that he would be up to the task. His notes would make it much easier, he thought, to answer the questions that would surely be brought up in the conversation. Laying his notes aside, he reclined on the comfortable bed that he knew that Morning Dove had prepared for him. He was not surprised that his thoughts returned to her, but as he closed his eyes, all of these thoughts left his mind as he drifted off to sleep.

He awoke the next morning feeling newly invigorated from a well deserved rest. The aroma of ham cooking perked his nasal glands. The sun had already arisen in the eastern sky and there was a sound of grown-up voices throughout the area. He hurriedly donned his clothes and was awaiting his call to breakfast. No sooner had he sat down on the edge of the bed that he was greeted and alerted by Morning Dove standing next to him.

"Breakfast is awaiting," she said, "come and join me at the table."

"Why, thank you," he responded, "I'll be more than happy to be your guest at meal."

She smiled at his unashamed response and then led the way to the great kitchen. Through daily habit, everyone had the same place at the table, but this time the place on Morning Dove's left was given up in deference to her guest. Running Deer had been taking account of the table manners of these people and he felt that he had learned enough to show himself approved. These people lived in the backwoods, but were certainly not backward in their ways.

He was trying with all of his might to not let the girl enter his psyche, but it was becoming a more difficult task to accomplish. At any rate, he thought, I will handle this myself and not have to consult the chief. He had come a long way handling things himself and he felt up to the task of going it alone without embarrassing himself or anyone else.

As the meal progressed, there was some small talk between the two of them and others, but most everyone concentrated on the delicious morning meal. Toward the end of his meal, his mind began to wander back to the old woman who held the key to the clan's history. He hoped that her health had not deteriorated further and that he would be able to interview her before he left to go on the last leg of his journey and on to his goal. After one of the diners stood up to leave the table, it wasn't long before others followed. Before Running Deer stood, Morning Dove surprised him by asking what his plans were for the day. She continued by saying that she would like very much to show him around the place. After all, his tour had been cut short by circumstances, so how could he refuse. There was no reasonable excuse.

The weather could not have been better. Autumn was coming up and it seemed like previews of coming attractions. Squirrels and other small animals were scampering in and out of the ground cover gathering material for their winter nests. According to the talk around the compound, there was a possibility of a harsh winter this year and the activity among the animals seemed to bear that out. It seemed that animals were better predicters of the weather than humans were. At any rate, there were tasks to be accomplished throughout the fall months in order to be prepared for the winter.

Morning Dove chose to take Running Deer further into the interior of the woods along a well-trod path. In the immediate vicinity, underbrush had been cleared away, but as the path continued, the brush and trees became thicker. A mid-sized doe suddenly surprised them as she sprang across their path. In tow were three large-eyed fawns that were going through a foraging lesson from their mother. The sudden action of the deer family gave Morning Dove a start causing her to reach for Running Deer's hand. As their hands met, a strange feeling of major proportions came over him. He had never felt this way before and he was in no hurry to let go after the animals disappeared.

So they continued hand-in-hand until they came upon a beautiful crystal clear lake. Morning Dove motioned toward a make-shift swing and the two made their way over to take a seat. Confronting them was a beautiful view and after they had taken in the scenery, eventually, their eyes met. Running Deer had no problem with looking a person in the eye, but this time he was staring into the face of a beautiful wood nymph. At least that was his thoughts as he gazed longingly into those pools of green. Neither uttered a word until a rabbit scooted in front of them to hide in the lush green grass. Morning Dove laughed at the sight and soon her laugh became contagious. It was she that said "well, let us continue our tour. There are lots of things that I want to show you."

Having been smitten by her looks and her boldness, he was not about to refuse her request. When they had been surprised by the rabbit, they had let go of each other's hand and now they were walking through a narrow one-person path with Morning Dove in the lead. It wasn't long, though, before the path widened upon entering a clearing that led up to a beautiful round crystal clear lake. As they walked closer to the lake, Running Deer could see that it was inhabited by multitudes of fish and was clear almost to the bottom. Fishing gear was available at several locations around the lake but there was no one else there.

Morning Dove explained that early inhabitants of the compound had left instructions that the lake would be enjoyed by everyone who cared to use it with the condition that it would be left at all times in a condition that others—native or stranger—could enjoy it as well. The first thing that entered his mind was the memory of his fishing with his grandpa on the Shalot river. There were times, he could recall, that fish were so plentiful and bold that they just jumped into the boat.

They reached for a pole and a fresh earthworm out of a container that was always available. The worms were wriggling around in a clump of fresh dark soil. As soon as their bait was secured on the hook, they threw their line out near a cluster of lily pads that was floating atop the quiet clear water. Occasionally, they watched a fish help itself to a visiting insect that had landed on top of the water. Running Deer was the first to feel a tug on his line, but in the next few seconds, Morning Dove had set a hook and was in the process of pulling a healthy black bass onto shore.

Running Deer was not quiet so lucky because in his excitement he had jerked the pole too quickly and had lost his fish. His luck changed when he pulled in two smaller bass but they decided right away to release all the fish back into the lake with the exception of two nice red drum specimens that she caught and promised to prepare for their supper. He cut a beargrass leaf, ran it through the gills of both fish, and then on a decision to cut their tour short, headed back to the compound.

Emboldened by the girl's friendliness, conversation ran more freely among the two explorers as they walked back together. During their conversation, there were already plans afloat for another rendezvous on the following day to continue their walk around the area. He had tentatively planned to leave the next day because of his anxiety to get on with his task. His feelings toward a person of another gender was not bothersome but was not entirely unexpected. In his mind, he knew what his priorities should be, but he couldn't dismiss the fact that a change had subtly materialized and he, a member of the human race, could not treat it lightly. At any rate, he knew he must clear his head and come back down to earth.

Arriving back at the compound, Morning Dove gently squeezed his hand, took the fish, and headed toward the kitchen. Running Deer went to his room to clean up and get ready for the evening meal. He wondered where the time had gone to, but he figured that that was always the case when you're having fun. After he had cleaned up, he sat on the edge of his bed and then couldn't remember falling asleep after he was awakened by a tug at his sleeve by Morning Dove. The meal was ready and had become apparent by the smell of fried fish drifting in through the quiet atmosphere. His stomach suddenly reminded him that he was quite ready for some victuals.

Morning Dove seated him at the table where there was a goodly layout of assorted food, but she had placed the two fish in his and her plates. The others at the table did not question this arrangement because they knew why the fish were there and some of the younger diners giggled at the sight. Running Deer was slightly embarrassed, but soon returned their playfulness with a smile of his own while he proceeded to devour the delicious roasted fish meat.

Before he got up from the table, he tried to think of an adequate way to thank Morning Dove for the meal and an exceptionally wonderful afternoon but he knew he was going to have to break away so that he could make plans for his departure. The weather had returned to normal after the storm, so he figured he had better take advantage of it and resume his journey. His plans were slightly altered, however, as Morning Dove took his hand and said "come, go with me to the large oak tree at the edge of the forest—remember, I haven't finished showing you around our place."

Here was a request that could not be refused, he thought, especially a request that was accompanied by a radiant smile that was accentuated by those two cool and limpid green eyes. He lamented the decision that he would not be able to help with the kitchen clean-up. He did not want a guilty conscience from enjoying such a scrumptious meal and not offering his help in some manner with the chores. Before his thoughts ended, he was interrupted by Morning Dove as if she knew what he was thinking.

"Don't worry about the kitchen chores", she said, "we always take turns and today is my day off. The men are never allowed to help."

He was not able to argue the point, so hand in hand, they walked off toward the ancient tree. Shadows were lengthening and the huge orange colored sun made its way downward to the top of the trees in the distance. There was not a cloud in the sky—not even a white puff. Grazing animals could be seen along the edge of the dense growth of mixed hardwoods and long leaf pines. Soon they would be returning to their dens, nests, burrows, and assorted resting and nesting areas for the night. The quietness was exhilarating and Running Deer struggled for words to make conversation with the equally shy Morning Dove. It wasn't long before a huge water oak came into view that displayed gnarled and expansive branches that were visible from the distance.

Little did Running Deer realize that what he was about to see would change a great deal of his plans. As they neared the copse that was accentuated by the great tree, Running Deer was amazed at the contrast in size that all the other trees presented. He turned to his companion with questioning eyes but decided not to ask questions. Before long, he thought, he would learn the answers. Almost as if on cue, Morning Dove began to explain that the ancient oak had been in existence as long as her people had occupied the area, and very possibly, many years before.

"There was an old legend," she explained, "that told the story of the first settlers in the area. Let us move into the area under the spreading branches and I will relate to you the story that has been handed down by many generations."

As they moved closer to the tree, all of the other trees round about seemed to pale in comparison. When they entered the canopy of branches, sunlight seemed to vanish from view. In the shade of the giant tree, there was a sense of tranquility. The rough bark that covered a horizontal low-lying branch had been worn smooth by the many visitors who had sat there to discuss business, romance, or just to while away the time. One could only imagine how many generations of people that might have utilized the seat.

When Morning Dove began her story, she told how the branches of the tree came to be bent in such a grotesque shape. She related the story of how Indian explorers would bend the branches of young tender trees to help them mark paths for traveling, hunting, or making war. She explained that the branches retained their new position as the tree grew.

"This", said she, "is one of those trees from long ago." She continued by saying that the path was also used by the English settlers who became friends with the natives and later began to intermarry with them.

The story was becoming real interesting to Running Deer, so he begged Morning Dove to continue. He wanted to ask her if she had ever heard of the lost colony of English settlers, but decided to hold that for later so she could go on with her story.

As for her own family, she said "my great great grandfather was an English settler and my great great grandmother was an Indian princess. Her name was Wontosa, but the name Rolling Waters was given to her by her close friends and family. Names related to nature were used quite often by the natives and it was a tradition that is still practiced today but not quite as much. Legend has it that she was very lithe in frame and most beautiful in appearance."

Running Deer's face flushed as he blurted out "Well, Morning Dove, you certainly inherited your great great grandmother's features. She must have been extremely friendly, also." She thanked him for his kind words, and smiling, she said that she appreciated the comparison.

Moving on with her story, she said that her English ancestor was not known for being a handsome man, but was unsurpassed in hunting skills and was an excellent provider. "My great pa-pa, as he was known, kept ample food around the home as well as the finest fir outer garments for Rolling Waters. I will move quickly through the family line and you will be one of the very few who has heard the story of my family. I do hope that you are not bored with my rambling on."

"Not at all," replied Running Deer, "I have become very interested in family histories and I appreciate you sharing yours with me."

She began again starting with her great grandparents who were mixed breeds and on down through her parents and siblings. She hesitated only when she related the story of her father who had left her mother to elope with a girl whom he had known for only a short period of time. It turned out that the "hussy" came to the complex selling sweet scents and other woman related products to all the adult female inhabitants. "That's as far as I want to go", said Morning Dove, "but the separation devastated my mother and led to her untimely death brought on by grief after just a few months. I haven't heard from my father since it happened, but I suspect that he and his "honey" fled to the mainland."

Running Deer tried to think of words to express his sympathy to her but was unable to compose the right words. He hoped that the expression in his eyes would somehow suffice. He also hoped that she would bring something out in her story that would help him to later fulfill his goal, but it didn't happen. He already knew about the English and the natives intermarrying, but he was looking for a specific incident or thing that would convince him that he was successful. He felt that he had the insight that would let him know whenever that occurred.

Shadows had disappeared and a huge round moon was appearing in the east when they decided to stroll back toward the compound. It had been a most delightful and relaxing rendezvous with the lovely Morning Dove and he looked forward to the walk back. 'I must break myself away from this enchantment that I find myself in, he mused, because there are more important things ahead that must be dealt with.

They arrived back at the compound shortly, and after a few parting words, they separated and went toward their respective sleeping quarters. Running Deer lit the crude lamp and decided to take some time to bring his notes up to date and make plans for the next day. The weather looked real promising and he was looking forward to taking advantage of it. He took a look at his map which was updated, and began to write out his tentative traveling schedule. One thing that was now in his favor was the terrain. This would mean that he could make much better time going forward.

After a restful night and an early breakfast with Butch and Swift River, he wanted to consult one of the elders of the compound to get an idea of the distance to the mainland, and from that, he would have a better idea as to how long it would take for him to arrive at his goal, the old fort. He wasn't sure what to look for, but he was taking the word of Chief Waccasaw as to its existence. Anyway, he thought, he must arrive there before he could begin to finalize his quest. After an hour or so, he caught himself nodding, so he decided to retire for the night. He had no trouble falling asleep, but sometime during the night in deep sleep, he began to dream about the chief.

Waccasaw was standing before him with one arm extended and pointing in a direction that appeared to be due west because the sun appeared as a reddish ball that was hanging just over the distant tree tops. He was very relieved by the appearance because it seemed to show a distinct direction for him to follow. The dream ended abruptly, awakening him, but he was soon fast asleep again to sleep peacefully for the balance of the night. He awoke to a bright sunlight that was casting long shadows throughout the surroundings. The grown-ups were up and milling around, and here and there, a child or two were beginning their daily routine of racing each other in the wide open spaces.

The smell of smoked ham was wafting through the fresh morning air which made the decision to leave early a little bit harder. He felt spoiled and a tad guilty of taking advantage of his short stay at the village. He never dreamed of finding such a location and such caring people at any stage of his journey. But, to the contrary, judging from the early stages, it was going to be a lonely trek through an unforgiving forest where there would be no one to talk to. And what better luck could have befallen him, than meeting these kind folks that reside in this place on the river and it would possibly take years, he thought, to erase the memory of Morning Dove. At the thought of her name, he wondered if she felt the same way about him.

He quickly dismissed such thoughts from his mind and began to think about preparations for leaving. A few of his provisions were still in his canoe which would save time in packing. His personal belongings including some clothing, charts, journal, and map were stashed safely under the bed in which he had been sleeping. No one but Morning Dove had made his bed so he knew that all of these were safe. He wanted to say goodbye to all of the folks that he had met, and in case he had missed anyone, he would ask Morning Dove to convey his parting wish to them.

He dared not leave without having one more meal with them, so he made his way to the dining area. There he met Morning Dove and without giving it a thought, he asked her to join him for his last meal.

"I am sorry", she said, "but I must join my family on the other side of the table."

He tried not to show his disappointment when he said "that's quite alright, I am leaving today and I won't have the opportunity to tell all of my friends goodbye, so will you please do that for me. I shall ever be obliged."

She smiled and replied "of course I will, and maybe some day, we will cross paths again. Please accept my thanks for being such a wonderful and deserving guest."

Such a statement stroked his ego, but he couldn't figure out why it was so. He was an ordinary person with normal wishes and desires and had done nothing to repay all of the kindness shown him. Then, on the other hand, he thought, "I have not created any trouble for anyone nor have I failed to help one in need." Back to the real world, his mind was once again focused on the day ahead of him. After packing everything, he pushed and pulled the canoe quietly back into the Chowanoke.

The tide again was in his favor when he entered the midstream current. He took one last glance back at the little village and then turned his sights toward the mainland and the object of his quest. He was looking forward to meeting the chief there to receive instructions for the final leg of his journey. He hadn't the slightest inkling of what it would be like, but he hoped for a smoother voyage.

The thought had barely left his mind when he spotted a lone occupant in a canoe that was heading toward him. His mind began to explore the possibilities of trouble heading his way, but he could think of no enemies that he had made by stopping at the village, so he was left to wonder. As he was about to find out, though, more than one feather had been rankled by his close association with the beautiful young half-breed. The strange figure eased his boat alongside Running Deer minus the usual greeting. The stranger's motive was displayed at once by a show of anger as he brazenly grabbed the oar from Running Deer and began to attach a tow rope to his canoe.

Before Running Deer had time to protest, he was knocked completely out by an oar that was wielded by an unseen assailant. The second person had been hidden by lying in the bottom of their canoe and covered with a large animal hide. Before he could recover, his hands were bound behind him and he was placed in his canoe while being towed to the river bank. When he awoke, he was lying on the ground near a small hunter's cabin. One of his captors had splashed a pan of water in his face while his partner was rifling through his belongings. While he regained his senses, he also realized that he was the victim of a robbery.

It didn't take long for the thieves to realize that the furs that they were expecting did not exist. They concluded that they had apprehended a lone traveler who was of no profit to them. He thought he was off the hook until the younger of the two asked him about his relationship with Morning Dove back at the compound.

"I just became a friend", he said, "I had no other motive". The thought entered his mind that he was entering into an entirely new experience—that of having to defend himself against a jealous lover. Morning Dove had never let it be known to him that she had any romantic relationship with anyone, although he had wondered why it was not so. Maybe, he thought, given her honest character, she was afraid to. While he pondered these strange thoughts, he was awaiting a response from his answer.

"I will accept your answer", the ruffian said, "but I warn you—if I ever see you in these parts again, I will teach you a lesson you won't soon forget."

With that said, he led him back to the water and his canoe, where he was given a hefty shove and sent on his way. 'Today will not be easily forgotten', he mused, 'but I will not let two thugs deter me from my goal'.

Chapter Ten

T HE WATER WAS REAL CALM this day and the current was gaining in strength as he entered the middle of the stream. The river was beginning to widen at this point and far in the distance it remained straight without a bend in sight. The sun was directly overhead now which increased the heat on the surface of the water. Fall was swiftly approaching, fish were jumping in the water around him, while small wisps of smoke could be seen arising throughout the forest on both sides. He planned to keep his course and navigate as far up the river as possible before he would start looking for a proper camping site. He was thankful for the weather and hoped it would continue to remain seasonal in temperature and not rain for a few days so that he could make real time on this leg of his journey. He was in an uplifted mood now having put the Morning Dove affair behind him with the help of the interlopers, so he could concentrate on the greater task.

After two hours of paddling upstream with the help of the rising tide, he could tell that he had made progress by the changing of the scenery around him. He was noticing different tree species in the forest and a narrowing of the river. In his sight was a bend which would alter his direction of travel again. Beyond this the unknown lay, yet for no specific reason, he was satisfied that he was headed in the right direction.

Almost two hours passed before he realized that more open area could be seen beyond the banks, but there was still no sign of habitation. He was not sure, but he thought that he could see evidence of crops growing. At this time of the year, most of the corn would have been harvested, but in the low marsh areas, there were signs of a coming rice harvest. Blackbirds were circling the fields, exhibiting their noisy cacophonous accompaniment. These were rice birds and they were busily engaged in taking charge of their share of the harvest.

All at once, figures appeared from the adjoining forest with fowl guns aimed at the marauding birds. In a few seconds, there was not one fowl left in the field. Apparently the routing had been successful, but Running Deer couldn't help but wonder if they would not return soon. After all, his grandfather had taught him that the growing of a rice crop was fraught with many problems. As soon as the birds had disappeared, the gun-toting figures disappeared into the woods.

All of this activity had awakened Running Deer to the possibility that he was nearing the mainland bringing him closer to his destination. Although he was still wary of what the new day would bring, he had an inner feeling that real soon he would be in the presence of Chief Waccasaw to learn his role for the final task of the journey. As he pondered these thoughts, the sky began to darken and there was a strange feeling of a storm approaching. Because of this, he began to evaluate his chances of making it to the shore before the rain started.

The sky continued to darken and an ominous rumbling of thunder began to appear from a distance. The direction of the thunder soon became more defined as bright streaks of lightning began to permeate the darkening clouds. A sense of urgency came upon Running Deer as he looked from one bank to another to assess his chances of taking cover from the pending storm. This would be one of those late summer events that provided little warning. He did not spot a shelter, but there was more of a clearing on the lee side, so he headed the canoe straight across to that side.

Before he made shore, the clouds began to release its heavy deluge on the area. His valuable cargo was protected from the rain, but he, himself, was becoming soaked. After a few minutes of desperate paddling, he made it to shore, pulled the canoe on the hill, and made it to the shelter of a huge oak tree that had been uprooted from a previous storm. He thought he was the only inhabitant until a small black bear ran past him to seek other quarters. He began to look around for other animals that had sought shelter there, but he soon decided that he was the sole inhabitant. The downpour of rain intensified while lightning illuminated the darkness all around him.

Running Deer had been through some bad storms, but he thought 'this has to be the worst that I will have to endure.' Trees all around him were victims of the powerful lightning strikes, so he knew that he was not going anywhere until it was over. There was nothing he could do but sit the storm out, so he pulled himself into the driest spot that he could find without being too uncomfortable and began to contemplate his next move after the storm was over. He had plenty of time to think about it because the thunder and lightning continued for what seemed an eternity. He had lost track of time but thought it must be near nighttime.

There was no need to think about a campfire because he knew he would be unable to scrounge any dry wood. He was thankful for his shelter and was safe, so far, from a possible lightning strike, but all of these thoughts quickly came to an end when he noticed that the river was nearing flood stage and moving rapidly in his direction. At the sight of the oncoming water, he knew that he was going to have to act quickly to find another dry spot. He began to look around as the deluge continued and his eyes went immediately to a small abandoned shack that sat a short distance from the downed tree. A minute or so before the flood water reached him, he was able to dart out to make his way to the shack.

The new shelter was a welcomed discovery for him and most of the boarding was still intact. There was still no let-up in the downpour but the thunder and lightning seemed to be moving away. There was darkness all around now so he knew that the sun had set. Luckily a few pieces of wood was left by the last inhabitant and Running Deer hoped it would be dry enough to build a small fire. He was still soaking wet and had no dry clothes to change into, so he decided to attempt to light the fire and try to dry his clothes on a makeshift rack that he fashioned from loose boards that were lying on the floor.

He managed to light a fire but knew it would be short-lived because there were no dry branches and probably wouldn't be for quite a while. Nonetheless, the token fire would give him a chance to dry off somewhat and start the process of drying his drenched clothes. There would not be a chance to bring his journal up to date, so he would look forward to tomorrow where he was counting on a bright sunny day. There was no guarantee, but he considered himself to be an amateur forecaster that was acquired from considerable outdoors experience.

As he listened to the pine boards crackling, fatigue began to enter his consciousness as he dozed off.

In what seemed to be a short period of time, he awoke to the chirping of birds and the sounds of a forest that seemed to have gained a new lease on life. The morning sun was shining brightly as he had predicted and its rays were penetrating through the tree branches like a giant kaleidoscope. The small fire had consumed the scrap boards completely to leave a tiny mound of grey ashes. His clothes weren't dry but he knew the job would be soon finished in the warming sunlight. He had nothing left to eat but he knew from past experience that the woods would be teeming with small game and it wouldn't take him long to procure a tasty meal.

The psyche of Running Deer was on a high once again because he possessed a strong feeling that his search for the elusive fort would end soon. Soon, he thought, he would be approaching the remains of an era that had long vanished which would help him solve the riddle of the missing colonists. It would take all the knowledge that he had gained thus far about primitive living conditions among strangers in the area and by what method they had used to maintain their progeny and still remain mysteriously lost.

As Running Deer pondered these thoughts, a mid-sized young hare scampered from the nearby brush cover, stopped and stood there, as if to say 'you were looking for me—well here I am'. A quiet shift of movement to one side by him caused the little animal to turn and head back under cover, but he was not quick enough to escape a well placed arrow that guaranteed his hunter a scrumptious morning meal for the skilled hunter. At the bottom of the dense brush, he was able to scrounge an ample supply of dry branches and leaves, so he prepared the tasty meat and devoured another hearty meal.

All was not well, though, because the rushing water had moved his canoe from its moorings and it was nowhere to be seen. Since most of his belongings were left aboard the craft when the storm forced him ashore, he faced the dilemma of losing all of the information that he had gained and which was so meticulously placed in his journal. So, rather than sit and mope, he once again called on the help of Akimko, his feathered friend. He gave the proper signal and waited for a familiar flapping of wings that he could count on in times of trouble.

Akimko seemed to always know the source of his problem, so he waited confidently for a sign of his lost canoe. He had no idea how the huge bird would find it, but he prayed that it had not capsized. In less than a minute, he heard the high-pitched shriek and a flutter of flapping wings. He immediately made his way to the direction of the welcome sound and found that the canoe had floated around a short bend and had snagged itself on protruding cypress roots. His eyes immediately went to the interior where he noticed that everything still looked intact. The sound of Akimko faded into the distance and was gone as quickly as it had appeared.

He took some time out to dry his clothes in the bright morning sun while the tide was beginning to ebb. When they were sufficiently dry enough to wear, he once again loaded his possessions aboard the canoe, struck out to the middle of the channel, and headed upstream. Before long, he was rounding another bend where he faced an entirely different scene. There was no way for him to know that he was spending the night weathering a storm right around the bend from a virtual village. The inhabitants he saw were still a good distance from him but the out-buildings were handsome and plenteous. Both sides of the river was dotted with houses and a waterwheel was continuously rotating beside a sturdy grist mill.

He kept his eyes busy looking for a place to dock his canoe where it would not be too conspicuous for he had a feeling that this was an important trading area and possibly a seat of culture for the mainland. As he continued to move in the middle of the stream, his eyes came upon a strange looking watercraft that was tied up alongside a dock that extended a short distance into the river. Canoes and other small craft were tied up at other places along the dock. He was mystified as to why there was no one milling around the waterfront, but soon it came to him that the day was Sunday. No sooner had this revelation occurred than the sound of a church bell permeated the Sunday morning quietness.

The ringing bell was beckoning the worshipers into their place of worship. Immediately upon hearing the peals coming from the bell, Running Deer was reminded of the times that he followed his parents and grandparents through the woods and across the swamp to a little white church on Sunday morning. It was the only time of week that he saw his friends during the summer school vacation. There was usually not enough time to make up for lost playtime, so he had longed for school to open in the early fall. The small village in which he lived was so sparsely settled that friends his age were very few, so he cherished every opportunity to be with them.

His fondest memories were of 'skinny dipping' in the small river that ran through the little village. The river banks consumed much of his time as he and his best friend, two years his senior, sat there and watched for bass and other fish to pull their corks under. But daydreams are short-lived and pretty soon he was pulling his canoe up to the dock to look for a suitable place to tie up. He purposely sought a location close to the river bank so he would not be in the way of other craft that might be coming in. As he finished the task of tying up, he was interrupted by a high-pitched voice coming from the bank above him. He looked up and saw a little girl of eight or nine peering down at him.

They exchanged greetings and then mutually introduced themselves. Louisa asked him where he was from and where he was going. To be as specific as possible, he replied that he was making his way to the mainland. As for where he came from, he simply said "I came from the other end of this river."

His answer seemed to have interested the little girl, so she said "I like your name—my father was half Indian. What is at the end of this river?" The little girl was much more inquisitive than he had anticipated. He wanted to give her a short answer, but then he thought that she deserved more.

He needed to get some information from her, but he decided that he would accommodate her questions in order to build a friendship, so he began to describe the big water at the mouth of the river and how he had set out on a long journey up the river to shed light on a mystery of long ago. When he said this, her eyes seemed to enlarge, so he knew he wasn't quite through with her yet. After about thirty minutes, Louisa was very excited about what she had heard, whereupon, she offered to take Running Deer to meet her parents. It was only a short walk to her parent's house, so he covered his cargo in the boat and walked with her to the house.

It was a neat little cabin that was nestled at the edge of the woods with impeccable landscaping. The late summer flowers were in bright bloom and were scattered in an organized pattern around the house and yard. Dusk was just an hour away, so activity around the house had come to a halt. There was a plume of smoke arising from the chimney which indicated that supper was at least in the beginning stage.

"Come on in", cried Louisa, "I want you to meet my wonderful parents." The invitation was a dead giveaway as to the love that was an integral part of this household. As he entered, he expected to see a modestly furnished cabin set in a clean and cramped environment, but to his surprise, the furnishings were elaborate and the inside was much larger than it looked in an approach from the outside. Sitting in an area opposite the kitchen and dining area was a man who appeared to be middle-aged. He had just taken a draw from his pipe and was about to expel the smoke from his mouth when he was interrupted by his daughter.

"Papa, I want you to meet a real explorer who has come a long ways to find the answer to a mystery."

"Pleased to make your acquaintance", her father said, "the names Elijah—Elijah Stuart—what's yours?"

Running Deer gave his name and added "according to your daughter, she is quite fond of her parents."

"We are fond of her, too", he said, "she does a lot of reading and is very smart. My wife Hannah—over there in the kitchen—is trying to teach her to cook." When Running Deer looked over at the kitchen, Louisa was busy assisting her mother with the meal.

"You'll have time to meet Hannah but that can wait 'til supper time. In the meantime, sit a spell and let's talk about what you're up to."

Running Deer gave an abbreviated version of his quest before he began to question Elijah about his ancestry. "I'm not much good at history", Elijah said, "but we have an old family Bible that has been handed down from generation to generation. I have never read all of it—due to lack of interest, I suppose—but after you join us in a meal of fried rabbit and slow roasted venison, you are welcome to read all you want."

Running Deer thanked him and said he would certainly love to do that.

He was directed to his seat at the table where he was soon joined by the family. The table was round, so all the diners could reach the food without asking for help. Before anyone reached, though, Elijah offered a prayer of thanks for the guest first, and then for the food. It was evident at the start that this was a very devout family, not only from the prayer that was offered for the bountiful meal, but also from the presence of the huge family Bible that showed its presence to anyone entering the home. Hannah immediately began to help their guest to the different dishes that lined the table and was pleased that Running Deer did not decline any of them.

It was apparent that he was hungry and was very glad that he could partake of a wonderfully prepared meal. While they ate, Elijah began to question Running Deer about his trip and what he expected to gain from it.

"It's a long story," he said, "but I can tell you that I have been on this river for quite a while. There are many stories that I could relate to you, but since you have been living on this river for a long time, my stories would probably be boring to you. I will tell you that my quest and my goal is to locate the old fort that was abandoned by English settlers many years ago. It is my ambition to discover what happened to the colony after the old fort was abandoned. Only one clue was left, so the world knows nothing about their demise. Many theories have been put forth, but none have been proved to be true. I feel that I am nearing my goal so I am confident that I may be successful in my venture."

"I have heard the story", said Elijah, "but I have always considered it to be a legend only. I will tell you that I came from mixed heritage, but other than native American, I am not sure. My Indian heritage came through my mother's side of the family and my father's ancestry was probably English, Scottish, or French. I prefer to think that it was English because of the royal house of Stuart that bears my surname. Whatever the case, I have never been curious enough to research it."

"That's interesting", replied Running Deer, "I am going on the assumption that the missing explorers intermarried with the local natives and began to spread out along the Carolina coast. You said that you had a family Bible. With your permission, I would like to look through it. There's a chance that names listed there may show clues that are vital to my journal."

"You are certainly welcome to look at it and when you become tired of reading, you can retire to the guest bed that my wife has all ready for you. After a good night's rest, we can assemble again at breakfast to resume our conversation. What do you think of that?"

"I thank you very much, and wish to say that it has been a while since I have been treated with such fine hospitality."

"Nothing's too good for a guest", said Elijah, "we are pleased that you happened by."

That said, Running Deer reached for the hefty Bible and followed Louisa to his room. After pointing him to the necessities, she bade him goodnight and left him to enjoy a well deserved night of rest and relaxation.

While perusing the pages of the old Bible, he discovered that there was quite a bit of family lore which was interesting, but of little use to him. He decided to close the old book after several pages and try to grab some shuteye, but just as he began to fold it shut, his eye caught an entry that included the word "English". As he took a closer look, he found that the entry had to do with family genealogy. It seems that in the early 1700s, this person's grandfather had married an Indian maiden. The grandfather's name was Conley and the maiden's name was Lotus Bud. A fitting name for an Indian but no further information was given about her family.

He read through several more pages but failed to find any additional relevant information, so he went ahead and closed the book and carefully laid it beside the bed. He had no trouble falling asleep because the next thing he remembered was the smell of fresh coffee percolating in the kitchen. He didn't dare keep the family waiting for their breakfast because he knew that they probably wouldn't start without him. After donning his clothes and straightening his bed, he joined the others in the dining room. He was treated to a layout of scrumptious fried, cured ham, hominy grits, and scrambled eggs.

As he dug into his favorite breakfast, he couldn't help but remember ham and eggs that his mother and grandmother used to serve at morning meals. He was planning to leave the Stuarts early today but he wanted to enjoy what was to be the last meal with the family. And enjoy, he did, because his stomach was fuller than it had been in a long, long time. After all members of the family expressed their pleasure at having met him, Running Deer thanked his hosts for showing him such great hospitality. He shook hands with the adults and hugged

Louisa and bade her goodbye. He turned then and walked toward the landing only a few yards away.

As he came closer to his canoe, he noticed that the strange craft that he had seen earlier was no longer there. He looked up and down the river but the boat was nowhere to be seen. He guessed that they had left sometime during the night with little or no notice. He would have liked to have known which way they were heading, but now there was no way of knowing. He would continue on his journey and perhaps run into them again somewhere up the river. His anxiety was reinforced, however, when he discovered a deerskin pouch missing from his cargo.

After taking inventory, he found that the old vintage coins were missing from his collection. It didn't take him long to figure out what had happened, so in haste, he departed the landing and moved to the middle of the stream while the tide was ebbing. He was going to have to work harder in the beginning, but in an hour or so, he would be assisted by the incoming tide. He had no way of knowing which direction the thieves were headed but he guessed that they were going in the same direction that he was. He was staking his hopes on the probability that they would meet at some point up the river.

Not knowing how many folks he would have to deal with was not an encouraging thought. He guessed the time to be about ten a.m., so he figured that with nine more hours of daylight, he would be about twenty land miles up the river. Of course, this was just a guess, but he was pinning his hopes on a good day's travel. The next bend was in view, but beyond that, he could only wonder about the landscape. The first hour was very tiring and there was little progress to be made, but then the tide turned and began to help him move along. The first bend was behind him now and the river widened ahead of him going straight for at least another hour.

After negotiating three more bends in the river with no appreciable difference in the scenery, he rubbed his eyes with the back of his hand as he looked straight ahead while he paddled around another short bend. He wanted to make sure that what he was seeing was not just a vision. But sure enough, there in front of him was a small bustling village with several people going about their business and work on this sunny weekday afternoon. Among all of the watercraft that was tied up at the busy wharf was the same craft that he suspected held the thief or thieves that rifled his canoe and lifted his valuable coins.

It looked as if he would be spending some time at this location, so he wanted to take his time to figure out a plan to get aboard the craft and look for his missing property. He selected a spot near the end of the wharf that was hidden from general view. After tying up, he took special precautions to secure his belongings so that they wouldn't be tempting to another thief. He was learning that crime was just as prevalent on the waterfront as it was on the mainland and probably more so.

After looking around for a few minutes, he decided to head in a direction that would take him to the center of town where locals would be congregated. As he drew nearer, he saw that there was some activity around a peddler who was displaying his wares. The huckster was dressed like a river man so Running Deer assumed that he had lucked up on his thief. He wasn't certain, though, until he spotted his coins lying among the assortment of wares. He was not a person who relished a fight, so he began to try to figure a scheme to get his property back without having to buy his own merchandise.

He decided to wait until the thief was in the process of attending to a sales transaction and then he would carefully grab the coins and then disappear from the scene. The plan seemed simple but it didn't quite work out that way. Evidently the man was a seasoned huckster because he seemed to be looking all around as he described his merchandise to the gathering populace. He was standing in the center of a circle of boards on which he displayed the stuff. When a sale was made, he looked all around as if he was expecting someone to steal from him. This was ironic, because he had probably stolen the majority of the stuff traveling up and down the river.

Running Deer was given a lucky break, though, as the crowd continued to gather. It had become more difficult for the man to watch everything as he carried on his business. Although the coins were placed nearer to the inside of the spread, Running Deer deftly swiped them up without anyone seeing except an alert little girl who was tugging at her mother's apron strings while she watched him. At this point, the little girl could stand it no longer, so she yelled to get her mother's attention, but before she could tell her mom what she saw, he had stealthily walked through to the outer perimeter of the crowd and was well on his way to his canoe.

Apparently the thief was unaware of the missing coins because Running Deer was in his canoe and on his way upriver with no one the wiser except the little girl. He was elated to have retrieved the coins because he was sure that they might play an important role in the solution of the missing Englishmen. As he continued his journey up the river, he had a gut feeling that the target of his long quest was just around the bend.

It wasn't long before he had negotiated the bend and was looking at a long straight river channel. The tide was moving at a quickening pace now and he figured that it wouldn't be long before it reached its apex. He was moving at a fairly fast clip and calculated that before high tide, he would reach the end of the moving current straight-away. He was right on target because when he came up on another bend, the current had all but stopped moving and was beginning to reverse its long flow back toward the mouth.

It was a good time to change because the sun was beginning to set and it was time for Running Deer to start searching again for a spot to land and set up camping for the night. Once he had spotted a clearing, he began to look around for possible company. Since his stop at the last village, he was aware that others might be in close proximity. He paddled toward the clearing and within ten minutes, he was approaching a landing that looked like it had been used many times in the past. There was no sign of a shed, however, so he decided to secure the canoe and explore the area. There were signs of previous fires and the lack of undergrowth indicated much activity had gone on there.

There was the remains of a barbecue pit which gave the appearance of a recently used spit for cooking wild animal meat. Well cleaned bones were scattered around the area. Before he made a final decision on the location, he still had enough daylight to survey the area. He did this without removing any of his outer garments for fear of being surprised by unfriendly natives or traveling miscreants. He wanted to be close enough to his canoe to prevent those same types from stealing it. The recent incident with his coins let him know that he was no longer in solitude as he had been further down the river. This indicated to him that he might be nearer to the mainland than he first thought.

The feeling now was that he was nearing the end of his long river journey and he didn't want to take more chances than were necessary at this stage. After walking around for a bit, he discovered an old lean-to that looked like a good possibility for protection from inclement weather or intruding animals. He was not sure about the animals, but the weather looked unpredictable. Even at dusk, the sky appeared to be darker than usual. There had been a shift in the wind and the temperature created a balmy atmosphere. He began to think that his luck was not going to hold out, so his attention turned to shoring up the old lean-to for the eventuality of a storm or heavy rain.

Returning to the location of the shelter, he began to pick up scattered boards and branches on the way. He wasn't back a minute too soon because lightning began to permeate the sky around him. In five and seven second intervals, thunder boomed around him. He made a quick trip to the canoe and began to pull it on shore so that he could fasten it securely to a tree near him. After securing the remaining provisions and cargo, he flipped the boat bottom side up. In a matter of minutes he had taken care of those duties and was headed back to the shelter. Even though pangs of hunger were attacking him, he knew that a few strips of gherkin would have to suffice. At this stage, there was no way to predict when he would be able to cook a more substantial mess.

At first he was able to shelter himself from the downpour, but in a matter of minutes, the rain came down in torrents that was threatening to displace some of his shelter. He worked to replace a few fallen branches, but it seems that he was unable to keep up with the rain's damage, making it hard to keep dry. He prayed for a break in the weather to give him time to fabricate a better shelter 'or better still, he cried, make it stop altogether.' About an hour later, the thunder and lightning subsided, but the rain continued for another half hour. When the rain finally stopped, he began at once to trench the water from underneath his shelter.

The only dry thing around was some pine straw that had been placed inside the shelter for a previous occupant. He scattered some of this on the floor around him, and before long, his lean-to had been converted to a decent place to spend the night. He reached into his storage bundle to retrieve two candles which he had brought with him from the trading post that he had visited earlier. This occasion was the first time that he had need of them. He would not attempt to build a campfire, because to find dry branches would certainly be futile.

He then reached into his storage sack to bring out his journal. He felt that besides from making a few new entries, it would be a good time to review a part of his latest entries. Pausing at the section that covered his stop at the compound where he encountered more people than any other place on the river, he thought maybe he should take some time to analyze his findings there. The people were friendly there, he surmised, especially the ones who befriended him. He bemoaned the fact that he had been unable to stay longer among them. He worried that he had passed up a good chance to have gained many more clues,. but that was in the past now and he was looking entirely into the future.

After going back over his notes from that area, nothing spectacular surfaced, so he put away his journal, doused the candles, and shifted around the area to assure that he would have a dry place to sleep. This task was accomplished in short order and within a few minutes he was back at the task of "sawing logs". During a light slumber, Chief Waccasaw appeared to him in a dream. A conversation ensued that was, for the most part, one sided. Normally, in a dream, very little of its substance is remembered upon waking. In this case, the words of the Chief were very clear and would be permanently etched in his memory. At first, it seemed that the Chief was giving final instructions to Running Deer concerning the final leg of his journey. But, as the dream continued, it became clear that the only instructions he received was to be careful as he proceeded toward the fort site because he might confront unfriendly characters who would create problems for him.

The Chief went on to say that he was indeed on the right path toward his destination, and with a little luck from the weather, he should arrive there at the timing of the next moon. Running Deer had not kept account of the moon changes during his journey, and he could not know exactly when that would be, so he decided to follow the precautions given to him by Waccasaw, trudge on and watch for the next full moon.

The balance of the night was spent in deep refreshing sleep. He arose the next morning facing a cloudless blue sky and a welcoming serenade by multiple species of birds. The first thing he did was to write in his journal. He wanted to recap the dream just as he had experienced it. Then he turned his canoe upright and headed toward the river to begin the most anticipated part of his journey. Each morning seemed to be a new experience for Running Deer, so he proceeded to the center of the river where the current would be the strongest.

The tide had recently changed and had begun its long six hour journey toward its head waters. The surface was as smooth as glass and the bank at both sides produced a reflection of sky and trees that seemed to add another dimension to a natural palette of emerging fall colors. It was times like this that he did his daydreaming and today would be no exception. Since a slight movement of the oar was all it took to keep him centered in the river, he would not be distracted while he moved quietly toward his goal in deep thought.

Even though he had been warned in his dream about possible danger, he would not let those thoughts inhabit his mind as he contemplated success in his quest. He was nearing the first bend now and its direction was discernible. In approximately twenty or thirty minutes, he should be changing directions. This turn was going to take him in a northerly direction which was about what he had expected, since heretofore, he seemed to be headed too far westward. This was only a calculation that was partly conjured in his mind, so there was no way to be certain. After all, the whole trip was based on a "seat-of-the-pants" system and a crude map. Nevertheless, his gut feeling and the beautiful weather gave him a feeling of euphoria as he glided further toward the mainland.

After making the turn, he was in a position to see what was ahead of him. The river took on a look of quietude and magnificence for the only surprise was a narrowing at the far end of his line of sight. As he continued to move with the current, still at a good pace, he couldn't help but feel that the tough part of his trip was over and before much longer he would arrive at his goal. It was a pleasant feeling, but owing to past experience, he remained in an alert mode.

Thirty minutes past and the only way he could tell what progress he had made was to look back to where he had come from since he had left the bend in the river. If there was anything different, it was the increase of the amount of wading birds that strolled along the shore. In addition, sometimes when he struck the side of his canoe with his oar, a startled covey of quail would arise from the forest floor in a flurry of flapping wings. The fishing birds reminded him that there must be an abundance of fish in this section of the river, so he was inspired to look for his next meal at the same place that they were getting theirs. It had been a while since he had tried his hand at spearing fish but he figured that there was no time like the present.

Pretty soon the tide would be changing and there would be ample time for him to head for the shore and spend some time fishing, so he began to look at both sides for his choice of camping space. The river had begun to narrow so it wasn't too difficult to find the choice spot. This time the location was on his left where there appeared to be ample dry branches for starting a fire. At high tide, the river was almost even with the top of the bank, so it was not difficult to step out of the boat and onto the ground. Past experience had taught him to remove everything from the boat, so within minutes he had secured all of his belongings near the campsite, and then allowing enough rope to keep the canoe afloat he secured it to a tree near the water's edge.

Squirrels were scampering along the dry branches and tree tops as if to challenge him, but he was still intent on having fish for supper. But first, he must fabricate a suitable shelter in which to sleep while it was still daylight. He surveyed the sky and determined that there would be no worry about rain, so in a few minutes he had put together an ample lean-to that would protect him from a possible wild animal intrusion.

Having taken care of those chores, he looked around for a tree branch that was capable of being crafted into a suitable spear for fishing. He located a small willow tree close by with sturdy branches suitable for the purpose. He then sharpened one end of the branch and headed for a shallow place on the river from which he could stand and observe the activity under the water. Fortunately, the water was clear, and as if on cue, two rainbow trout swam just underneath the surface searching for available food. It looked too good to be true, so Running Deer aimed the spear at the largest of the two.

This particular target was too smart, though, and darted away from the bank as the second fish had observed the action and led the way out of sight toward the middle of the river. No sweat, he thought, there will be others that will not be so lucky. He was correct because immediately after this thought, an even larger trout swam by and wound up on the end of his spear as the result of quick reaction and excellent marksmanship.

After starting a fire from the previously gathered material, he handily cleaned the fish and cooked it on a fabricated spit. He located a couple of scones that Morning Dove had secretly placed in his pack and proceeded to enjoy a much anticipated barbecued trout. When he had consumed and enjoyed the meal, his thoughts turned to his next chore that was ahead of him. He knew that he had much more river ahead of him, but he could almost envision the scene that would be ahead of him after he negotiated the river bend immediately ahead.

The chief had not divulged this information to him, but he thought that the timing of his appearance was an excellent sign. So after stoking his fire, he began to clear a place to lay out his map, his journal, and other notes in the cleared area in front of him. There was no worry of inclement weather, so he was confident that his work area would be safe. Since he had been so busy making his way toward the head of the great river, he had not taken the time to thoroughly study the map to compare it with his actual moves. After studying the map in greater detail, he discovered that it showed an amazing replica of the route that he had taken.

By now, he was convinced even more that every move he had made was ordained by Chief Waccasaw so that his adventure would be fruitful. He mused, that if this were not the case, he probably would have never met all of the varied and wonderful people that he had come in contact with. Also, a shivering thought entered his mind as he wondered about the danger from wild animals and humans that might have crossed his path. Of course, he was always grateful for his friend, Akimko, that had come to his aid so many times.

He felt elated after having received all of this but was beginning to picture in his mind what might happen in the days immediately ahead of him. He carefully placed all of his stuff in its container, laid it by his side, created a crude pallet on which to sleep, and pretty soon within minutes, he was fast asleep and resting peacefully. The dawn greeted him with the usual sound of birds with their melodious rich tones and inflections. He downed a scone and a cup of fresh percolated coffee for a skimpy breakfast before he cleaned up the area and pushed off from the shore to continue his push around the next bend. Rowing against the tide would last about fifteen minutes but he thought it was necessary to get started so that he wouldn't waste time.

Since it was nearing ebb tide, he would be able to make a little headway and then immediately after the tide turned, he would be able to make real good time. As he approached the narrow bend in the river, his heart began to pick up speed because he truly expected to be able to go ashore and locate the old historic site without a long search. Once he reached the bend, he negotiated a sharp turn to the right and there before his eyes was an open path that seemed to welcome him to the mainland and all that lay beyond. The ruts were clear and wide enough to accommodate more than a foot path. There was no sign of humans anywhere in sight, but he speculated that they were not far away.

As he pulled his canoe up onto the bank, he was careful to hide it in the dense growth along the water so that he would feel safe about temporarily leaving it to explore a ways up the path. After walking and observing around him for about thirty minutes, he came upon a shack that was unlike any that he had seen throughout his journey up the river. The thought occurred to him that he shouldn't be surprised because now he was on the mainland and he should expect to see far different features. The house had a brick and mortar chimney at the rear with multi-paned windows on all four sides of a square structure.

Since the crisp fall air had approached, a wisp of smoke was curling up from the top of the chimney. Not wanting to startle the possible occupants, he slowly and quietly walked around to the front and rapped on the door. At first, there was no response, but after a couple more raps, he heard shuffling of feet making their way to the entrance. Attempting to appear as friendly as a stranger could, Running Deer smiled as he greeted an elderly lady who was holding a written document in her hand indicating that she was probably alone. A further glance into the apparent living room of her humble abode, showed a rocking chair on which she probably had been sitting, rocking and reading.

She replied to his greeting with a "how-do" and then asked what she could do for him.

"I apologize for interrupting, ma'am. My name is Running Deer and I'm just in from a trip up the river and was hoping you could help with directions on finding a place that I have been searching for."

"I don't take to talking with strangers, sir, but since you've told me your name, mine's Fran Smith. Now that we're no longer strangers, what kinda place are you looking for?"

She didn't divulge the fact that she lived alone because she still was not comfortable with talking with a complete stranger. Her husband had died the year before and she had been living the life of a frontier woman since. This sad information was revealed later as they came to know each other better.

"I am told that there is a fort on the mainland that was once occupied by a small colony of English settlers. Can you tell me anything at all about it?"

"I certainly have heard of it, but you'll have to ask someone else how to get there. I heard that they have been trying to keep it from growing up with weeds and trees, but maybe you can tell what it looked like when it was built."

"That sounds very interesting", said Running Deer, "can you tell me about how far it is from here?"

"Well, I've heard that its quite a ways if you travel the path, but a shorter way as the crow flies."

This response excited Running Deer because he knew he was approaching an end to an important leg of his journey. Also he figured that he might be able to emulate part of the crow's flight to save time. His next question was anticipated by the little lady because she yelled toward the rear of the house to summon her teenaged grandson who was playing in the backyard. "Lukey, come here and meet our visitor, he might need your help."

"Aw, Granny, I was making me a goat cart—now I'll never get through with it."

"Shush your mouth, boy", said his grandmother, "you know I've taught you to be nice to people."

"I'm sorry, Granny, what can I do to help?"

"This here's Mr. Running Deer and he wants someone to take him to the old fort. You remember how to get there, don't you?"

She turned to Running Deer and explained that Lukey's daddy died a year ago and he had accompanied his dad to see the fort about two years before he died. It had become her responsibility to raise her grandson because his mother left the two of them to find work farther mainland. Running Deer interrupted to say that he appreciated the thought but maybe he could find the site himself.

"Think nothing of it", she said, "he needs to get out from under my shirttail for a while and the trip would do him good. I'll get some provisions together and you two can leave early in the morning."

After an offer like this, Running Deer couldn't refuse, so he told her that it sounded good to him. After all, maybe the old lady truly wanted Lukey to get out on his own a bit more so that he would be more fit to hunt and become more able to take care of himself. It was a few hours before sunset, so Running Deer asked if it would be alright for him to have a look around the area while the sun was still shining. It was a beautiful day and the hardwood leaves were beginning to turn their yellow, red, and gold palette into a woodsman's paradise. He circled back to his boat to think about how he was going to secure it near the river and get Mrs. Smith's permission to leave it while he and Lukey journeyed inland to locate the fort.

The idea came to him that since the house was built two or three feet off the ground, it might be a great place to store it underneath in case of flooding from the river. There, it wouldn't be a tempting target for a thief. After all, he had been victimized more than he cared to be and he didn't want it to happen again. He carried this idea through with the permission of his hostess and then proceeded to explore further around the premises. Lukey found him walking around the little compound and announced that his grandma had supper ready.

"Come on in", he said, "You just gotta try grandma's chicken bog."

Running Deer had never turned down an invitation like that, so he said "I'm much obliged. That is very kind of your grandma to invite me. Anyway, when you're looking to go on a special trip the next day, its always better to not go to bed on an empty stomach."

Lukey agreed and then invited him to come on in and make himself at home. He had already begun to think about his adventure to accompany Running Deer on his quest to locate the old fort.

Fran Smith's home was very modest inside with just the bare essentials for furniture, but it was neatly arranged and clean as a pin. The victuals were ready and already set at the table. Running Deer was shown a basin and water in which to clean his face and hands and then was given a guest's seat at the wood and peg table. She hadn't said so, but Running Deer assumed that Mr. Smith had passed away. She interrupted his train of thought by saying that Frank, her husband, had crafted the dining table using the few tools that he had and it was always a reminder of his good craftsmanship. She went on to say that she lost her husband to yellow fever years back and that she had barely escaped.

For most of the meal, every one was quiet, but near the end when a fig dessert was served, Running Deer expressed his appreciation to the hostess for such a wonderful meal and especially when offered to a wayfaring stranger like himself. He offered to help clean up, but she refused his offer by explaining that no guest of hers would take part in the cleaning and that she wanted him to relax so that he would be bright-eyed and bushy-tailed for the task ahead of him. She showed him to a divan-like sitting area that was furnished with a candle holder at one end. On this, he could relax or work in comfort. It had been a long time since he had been able to rest his body in this manner so he truly felt pampered.

He reached for his ever present journal and proceeded to enter his latest observations and special notes that pertained to his location. Lukey had gone outside to feed the few livestock that the family had managed to raise this year, including one mule for plowing, and a half dozen hogs that was getting in good shape for slaughtering in the upcoming winter. They had one sow and a litter of five pigs which would probably be ready for the following winter. The mule was used to till the small garden that provided them with fresh vegetables. Also, among the animals was a Holstein cow that provided milk for the family with help from a distant neighbor's bull.

One consolation in his favor was the thought that the trip to the fort would be short because Miz Smith would not want her grandson to be away from home very long. The sun had already set when Lukey touched his arm and woke him from a shallow nap. He was shown to the guest bed where he continued his restful slumber without interruption for the remainder of the night. His wake-up call was preceded by the smell of seasoned country ham and his favorite morning aroma—that of percolating coffee. He sat up in bed and proceeded to stretch his arms as if reaching for a prize that the new day was offering him. The sun was beginning to display its splendor by poking its bright rays through the tree branches that were visible through the single window that stood as a sentinel in his room.

He had no idea why he deserved such a pleasant greeting but he had a feeling that, due to his kinship with nature, there was a message involved that would make itself evident before the day was through. He was pleased to have a companion to accompany him on the last leg of his journey so he was eager to get started. After a hearty breakfast with his hosts, he thanked them for their hospitality and announced that he and Lukey had better get started. He made sure that his canoe was secure and promised that they would return soon after having a look at the old stockade. Having said this, he had no idea of what he would find, whether it would be recognizable, or how difficult it would be to locate. Regardless of the feeling, he was optimistic about the day and what it might have in store for them. All aside, he was looking forward to his meeting with Waccasaw and hoped the feeling would be mutual.

Chapter eleven

F RAN GAVE EACH OF THEM a hug before they stepped boldly ahead to begin their trip. At first, there was small talk between the two until they figured that they were acquainted enough to confide in each other, then Lukey began to relate to Running Deer about his hunting experiences in the area and how he had always wanted to explore a little farther from home. There had been very little contact with folks from further inland, so as a result, his education was very limited. There had been very little for him to read and no one, including his mother, who was able to teach him. Fran Smith had come from a very poor family and the man she had married by common law had only managed to reach the fourth grade in a church sponsored school that was near his family's home farther up the river.

Running Deer listened intently to his story and revealed to Lukey that his own story was very similar, but he was fortunate to have had older siblings who shared their reading knowledge and the family was fortunate also to have had teachers who were proficient in the three "R"s. Lukey wanted to know what that meant so he explained that the three "R"s stood for "reading, riting, and rithmetic." His answer satisfied Lukey, so he turned to another subject by asking Running Deer where he had acquired his love for adventure. That answer was easy for Running Deer, so he proceeded to relate stories about hunting and fishing with his pa and grandpa.

The weather remained pleasant throughout the remainder of the day and the trip was uneventful except for the appearance of a few small furry animals that scampered about on the forest floor and a bobcat that was perched on a branch of a huge chestnut tree. The cat must have been content because it did not growl or attempt to move from its reclining position. And, of course, the travelers weren't going to do anything to disturb it. For most of the time, an old pathway was accessible to them, so they were able to make more progress moving toward their target. They emerged into an area in which Lukey was familiar which included a pond that seemed to be fed from an underground stream. The water was clear enough that you could see the bottom and it appeared to be shallow, but upon further testing, it proved to be deeper. Lukey revealed that the spot marked the approximate halfway point of the trip, that they were now moving farther inland, and that the terrain would change drastically.

This sounded like good news to Running Deer but he wanted to know what he meant by "drastically".

"Its simple", Lukey told him, "we are out of the tangled underbrush and the unknown surroundings. From here on, there will be a clear path and we will be able to make much better time. If the weather stays with us, we will reach our goal about noon tomorrow."

This news of course, was welcomed by Running Deer and his only response was—"Great—I can hardly wait."

The bright sun was moving toward the western horizon where it created a panorama of red, orange, and yellow hues against the clear fall sky since now—for the first time—their visibility was expanding. The setting was a perfect backdrop for establishing a campsite for the night. They shed their backpacks in a clear flat area near the pond and decided to use the remaining hour of the day to relax and get more acquainted with each other.

Lukey confessed that even though he had made the trip before, it had been a long time and that his only interest at the time was learning to hunt deer with his father. Running Deer was pleased to hear of his love for hunting because it reminded him so much of himself at an earlier age. Time had come to set up a shelter and he found that his partner was adept at that too. When they were satisfied that their accommodations were sufficient for the night, they unrolled a package of dried beef that Fran had provided for their trip. They helped themselves to the tasty meat but were careful to save enough for the remainder of the trip. Dusk finally arrived and it was time to think about preparing a comfortable place to relax and rest for the night. They easily found a sufficient number of small dry branches and leaves that did the job well. So well, in fact, that both of them slept throughout the entire night without waking a single time. Sleeping in the woods was getting to be "old hat" for Running Deer but Lukey admitted that it would take some "getting used to" for him.

A slight turn in the weather greeted them at dawn but it didn't seem foreboding. The sky was a bit grey in the east which allowed an occasional "peep-through" by the morning sun. They could only hope that the cloud would dissipate soon and leave them with another fair day for travelling. It is too close now, thought Running Deer to have an obstacle like the weather in the way. On second thought, he mused, there is nothing I can do about the weather, so I shouldn't be overly alarmed about it.

After about two hours into the new day, his worst fear materialized. The cloud became darker and within a few minutes had completely covered the sky bringing with it a deluge of rain and lightning too close for comfort. There was not a shelter in sight and it was not a good idea to be under a tree with lightning all around them. As frightening as it was, it was equaled by the joy expressed by both of them when the rain suddenly stopped to reveal a bright sun shining through the tree tops. An instant before the black cloud disappeared to reveal the bright sun, Running Deer could have sworn that he saw an image of Chief Waccasaw at the edge of it.

The image vanished as quickly as it had appeared and he wasn't about to mention the phenomenon to Lukey. He was convinced, however, that the chief was instrumental in turning the storm off. Drying off was the big problem now but they both guessed that the bright sun would do the job in an hour or two. While their apparel was drying, they had a chance to go over their plans for the remainder of their journey.

Running Deer was overcome with excitement generated by the prospect of reaching his goal within hours now and not days. He reminisced within himself and shared some of the experiences that he had encountered on his way there. Lukey, of course, was unable to share the enthusiasm because he was not capable of understanding the real reason for Running Deer's quest. In that regard, however, he was no different from any of the many friends that Running Deer had encountered on his long trip up the river.

An hour before midday, their clothes had dried sufficiently to wear and they were on their way again. A beautiful day followed and although they were still deep in the forest, they thought that they could hear voices in the distance. The idea was soon discarded and was charged to the quietness of the surroundings and their imagination. An old path was chanced upon and they were able to make considerable headway throughout the balance of the day. As luck would have it, they walked up upon an abandoned shack that was still upright and in fairly decent condition. They looked at each other and suddenly realized that this would be a good time to stop and rest for the evening.

Both of them were ready to relax after a long day of walking. They rarely had to use their knives to clear underbrush, but the constant walking had been tiring for them. After securing a place to sleep in the old shack, they still had some daylight left, so they decided to explore around the perimeter while they still had light. In less than five minutes, they ran across a wider path that showed the markings of old ruts. This was an interesting discovery because Lukey recognized the old roadway and revealed to Running Deer that they were not far from the site of the old fort now and it would take less than a day's journey to arrive there.

Running Deer received this news with great excitement and motioned for Lukey to follow him back to the campsite. Upon arriving back at the shelter, he asked Lukey to help him gather material for a fire so they could brew some coffee and discuss their plans for the following day. He also made entries in his journal before they turned in for the night. A dim light from the embers was still glowing after both of them had entered into a deep slumber and rested well without interruption.

They arose thoroughly renewed at early dawn. The thought that entered Running Deer's mind was an old saying that was taught to him by his grandmother. "Early to bed and early to rise makes a person healthy, wealthy, and wise". He wasn't as interested in the wealthy part, but the healthy and wise part made sense to him. And when his pa had chores to be done, he would tell him to go to bed early and rise in the morning "bright-eyed and bushy-tailed" so he would be fit for the job. The weather was cooperating for the day and there was a general feeling of an upgrade in their enthusiasm. To put it mildly, they were experiencing a calm after the storm and felt that nothing would stand in their way of reaching their goal before sundown.

When the clean-up was through, they stepped out into the direction that was pointed out by Lukey and they were on their way again. The temperature was slightly less than the day before because of the onset of fall weather, which was much appreciated because it allowed them to walk at a faster pace without tiring. When the midday sun was overhead, they decided to take a short break to remind their stomach that it had not been forgotten. Mrs. Smith had made sure that they would have plenty to snack on as they travelled. The scones and dried beef, along with fresh water found at a spring near their campsite, was sufficient for them.

Approximately a forty five minute break was enough to provide them energy for the rest of the day. As they continued on their journey, it was apparent that the wildness of the forest was slowly fading away. As a matter of fact, it had been hours now since they had seen a rabbit or a squirrel. The lack of small animals to hunt did not concern Running Deer because he knew that once they reached their goal, some type of food would be available.

"I believe we are getting closer now", said Lukey, "I thought I heard the sound of a barking dog."

"If that is true", replied Running Deer, "we should be arriving at our destination in about thirty minutes".

Of course, they didn't know what to expect, but Running Deer was inspired by the possibility of some kind of activity around the old fort. Since, according to Chief Waccasaw, the fort was the last known place of habitation of the colonists, it might also be the location where he would discover the solution to the mystery. At any rate, he was becoming overly excited and didn't want to show this to Lukey, his travelling partner. He made a vow to himself to keep calm and contain his emotions even at the moment of meeting the chief.

As they trudged ahead, it was evident that Lukey was correct in his assumption of hearing the dogs in the distance. It was now becoming apparent that the presence of the two strangers approaching from the woods had alerted the keen senses of two busy bloodhounds. They were apparently penned because all they could do was bark. Nonetheless, they were a little unsettling to the two travelers. As they moved closer to the barking dogs, it was apparent that the increased sound had alerted their owner because they first spotted a short figure peering around an outbuilding in their direction. He didn't call the dogs down at first sight of the two visitors. Instead, he waited until Running Deer had convinced him that they were friendly travelers and that they would like to stop a while and chat with him.

"Down", he called, and the two dogs stopped barking and headed towards a shelter in a corner of their pen. "Come on 'round front", the little man said, "I got benches where you can sit a spell and take a load off your feet."

Nothing else was said until they were shown to a bench that was attached to a table. They rid themselves of their backpacks and hunting equipment before they settled down to get better acquainted with the man. "I am Running Deer and this here's my travelling partner, Lukey Smith", he said.

Before he could continue, the man said "my name is Grey Beaver. I live alone out here in the edge of the woods and that's why I keep Streaker and Wally over there in the pen. 'Sides, they're great hunters. You never know when some of these hunters will break in on you and take what you got. I keep my old muzzle loader in the house there and everyone hereabouts knows that I'm not afraid to use it."

After an introduction like that, Running Deer and Lukey knew that he meant business and that he might be their connection to the area, so Running Deer began to question him. "We are looking for an old fort site that is supposedly nearby, so perhaps you can help us locate it. Lukey, here, has visited the site before, but it has been many years since he visited with his pa."

Lukey broke in to say "I was just a young lad, but I remember that it was near here because I see familiar landmarks."

"You're right, son, the fort is only minutes away—it will take about half an hour for you to reach it. I don't understand what is so important about that old growed up palisade since a stranger could walk right through there and never recognize it. A lot of folks have visited there over the years saying that it had something to do with a lost colony, but none of them have ever found anything interesting—at least, I have never heard of any results from their visit."

Not wanting to reveal his relationship with Chief Waccasaw, Running Deer acknowledged Grey Beaver's concern and thanked him for his information. During their conversation, the time slipped away while the sun had quietly gone through its descent to the horizon. Grey Beaver was feeling comfortable around the two strangers following their exchange, so he invited them to spend the night and share some "pot-luck" vittles. They weren't about to refuse him, so both of them nodded in appreciation.

The chance meeting was exactly what Running Deer was hoping for. He needed time to go over his notes and journal before his encounter with Chief Waccasaw. He wanted to be prepared so he could have a more intelligent discourse about his journey. As soon as he and Lukey were shown to a comfortable sleeping arrangement, he motioned for them to join him in his kitchen.

"I've got salted mullets and smoked ham that I've been waiting to share with friends. I believe you two fall into that category. So, looks like you are the lucky ones. I'm gonna go out back and cut some fresh greens to boil up for a vegetable. It won't take long, so make yourselves comfortable in my little living room. Its not much, but you can stretch out and make yourself at home."

Both thanked him for his hospitality, and after offering their help which was refused, entered the small living area and made their self as comfortable as possible with the meager furnishings. There was room on the floor to spread his map and a lamp table large enough on which to spread out his notes and journal. Since Lukey had no interest in his display, he distanced himself from it while he made his way to a vacant corner to stretch out on the floor.

Way sooner than expected, the host called for his guests to come to the kitchen and see what he had put together for them. It was a feast that Running Deer had not seen since his stopover at the Lanes. His hunger pangs really acted up when he spotted the baked ham and stewed mullets that Grey Beaver had prepared and spread on the dining table. Whatever this man lacked, he sure made up for it in his ability to cook. The meal was enjoyed by all while very few words were spoken as they stuffed themselves. After the meal, the guests again were refused their request to help with the cleaning chores. Grey Beaver practically ran them from the kitchen and ordered them to make themselves comfortable again to let their food settle so they would sleep better.

When they returned to the living area, Lukey said "if its alright with you, I'm gonna go ahead and turn in. I'm sorta tired from a busy day."

"Go ahead", Running Deer responded, "I'll follow you shortly after I have a chance to look over my notes". So after Lukey left the room, he went over his entries for a few days preceding his stop at Fran Smith's to make sure that he had followed his plans correctly and again to coordinate with his map. After reassuring himself that he had taken the correct route, he packed his stuff away and joined Lukey in the adjoining room.

It was difficult for Running Deer to fall asleep because of the excitement at the possibility of meeting the chief the next day. It was a meeting that he had been looking forward to for a long time. He tried to imagine their conversation as they discussed the details of his journey. These thoughts tired him, so eventually he fell into a deep slumber and awoke the next morning feeling thoroughly refreshed. Lukey had slept an hour or so longer than he had, so he was already up and walking around when he found him on the outside. Grey Beaver had arisen earlier than either and was busy with chores around the place such as gathering eggs from the nests and feeding assorted livestock that he kept around the place. The sun had barely arisen when he called to Running Deer and Lukey to join him in the kitchen.

This meal was going to be a simple one but hearty enough to last them for the day. He guessed that they would not have sufficient supplies on hand to keep them fed properly on this last leg of their journey, so he packed enough extra to take with them. Both thanked him and told him how much they appreciated his thoughtfulness. They wished him the very best and then resumed their trek toward the day's goal. Before they were out of sight and hearing, Beaver yelled and wished them well. It was as if he had enjoyed having visitors and perhaps there was a little envy in watching them walk off. The pathway was much clearer and they were able to travel with ease as they neared the area where the fort should be located.

Since the forest was less dense, the bright blue sky and bright sun were able to show off their beauty. It was as if the two wayfarers had emerged from a tunnel and was making their way to a brightly lit panorama of beauty. Running Deer turned to Lukey and said "well, what do you think—are we nearing the last gathering place of a lost people?"

"If my memory serves me correctly", responded Lukey, "we can walk toward that tall tree yonder and when we get there, take a long look about ninety degrees to the left, we will spot the old stakes that supported the wall of the fort."

Running Deer was elated. He wanted to jump for joy, but then he thought better of it because Lukey could be wrong. After all, it had been quite a while since he had been here. Nevertheless, it was time to find out. They proceeded toward the tree and when they walked up beside it, they were met with another discovery when they looked just above their head height on the tree and saw the letters C-R-O etched into its trunk. The letters were amazingly preserved because of the turpentine that had oozed out of the trunk and filled the etched surface. There was no question in his mind now that he had arrived at his goal. The next step would be to proceed to the fort itself and confront Chief Waccasaw as planned.

Chapter Twelve

THE TRICK NOW WOULD BE to figure out how to separate himself from Lukey while he had a private consultation with the chief. He didn't want to hurt his feelings, so here was the plan. He asked Lukey to search around the area for food since they would likely be spending the night. While Lukey was busy doing this, Running Deer could summon the chief as he was instructed to do at the beginning of his journey. After Running Deer convinced Lukey that he would be perfectly alright while he explored the fort alone, the two separated and proceeded to walk in opposite directions. Neither knew what they might find. The inland setting was immensely different from the place which Lukey had seen before, and Running Deer, with a unique agenda, far different than any he had ever experienced. Nonetheless, with help from beautiful weather, each felt that their day would turn out to be a winner.

It didn't take long for Running Deer to reach the area along the perimeter of the fort where the entrance had been. The opening was amazingly preserved, so he stepped inside hoping to find an area that was not covered with woods growth. He was able to walk through the growth that had occurred over the years and was able to find the outline of the interior walls. He was surprised at its small size, but amazed at how well the little compound had been fortified.

When he turned to walk back toward the entrance, he spotted a clearing near the center that immediately brought to mind his reason for being there. That spot could very well be the location, he thought, that Chief Waccasaw had especially provided in which to hold their powwow. With that in mind, he proceeded to the clearing, and upon arriving there, found two crude yet comfortable chairs that looked as if they were purposely placed there.

While divesting himself of his equipment, his eyes were miraculously directed toward the amulet that hung from his neck. At the same instant, the instructions given him by the chief came to mind. He settled in one of the chairs and reached to touch the amulet, but suddenly withdrew his hand to go over some things in his mind so that he could be fairly certain that he was ready to confront the chief. He was feeling a surreal sense of awe at being in the same space in which the earliest European settlers had occupied over two centuries before.

As he sat down in anticipation of having Chief Waccasaw soon join him, a feeling came over him that transcended anything in his past. He was about to become a participant in solving one of the most famous mysteries known to man. After glancing at his journal, which he had kept in meticulous order, he sat in the clear open area of the fort and looked up into the sky as if he was confirming that it was the day that he had been anticipating. His mind was racing as if in a whirlwind as he tried to conjure up answers to possible questions that would be posed to him by the chief. Nothing seemed to materialize, though, so he managed to calm down just before he reached for the amulet.

His hand moved toward his neck again and gently rubbed his fingers across the face of the amulet hanging there. A light glow emanated therefrom and he was joined instantly by the chief who occupied the second seat. As if to calm his fears, the chief spoke to Running Deer and said—"thank you for your outstanding help, my friend. Without it, I would have been unable to convey to the world the solution to a great mystery. When I reveal the answer to you, then you may take it to your people. Never again will this brave group of people be known as a lost colony."

The chief continued—"all of the clues that you have gathered and placed among your written notes are very important and might have led to a solution. The intermarriage of Englishmen and natives, the European coins, the burial site, the carving left by the settlers—indeed all of those and more would have led to the answer, but the only true and authentic answer will come from me. Only the Chief Waccasaw holds the secret. Listen very carefully, Running Deer—it is very important that you pay close attention to what I am going to tell you."

Before Waccasaw uttered another word, Aaron heard his ma calling him to supper. He shook his head and gazed all around. The first sight he saw was Lucy, the mule, standing off to the side of the plow munching on grass. It took a few seconds to realize that he had been daydreaming again. Part of the dream had begun to fade, but he remembered that in this dream, he was once upon a river and on the trail of a solution to something about a lost colony of Englishmen. And also the last part where the expectant voice of an Indian Chief was about to reveal the answer but then trailed off and he never heard what he was going to say. Now, he thought, the actual solution will always remain a mystery.